DEATH OF FAITH
A GABRIEL DE SADE THRILLER

ERIC MEYER

First published in the United Kingdom in 2012
by Swordworks Books.

ISBN 978-1-909149-17-5

Typeset by Swordworks Books
Printed and bound in the UK & US
A catalogue record of this book is available
from the British Library

Cover design by Swordworks Books
www.swordworks.co.uk

DEATH OF FAITH
A GABRIEL DE SADE THRILLER

ERIC MEYER

CHAPTER ONE

Teresa Santos hurried to the elevator. She was perspiring slightly, fired up by the need to get home in time to shower and change for her night out. Already, the building was darker as the departing workers switched off the lights. The modern office block, concrete and glass, gleaming chrome and thick carpets, bustling with the constant hum and flow of humanity through the day, had gone silent. No phones rang; no footsteps muttered along the corridors, no muted conversations took place in quiet corners, there was nothing. Just a dark building, already starting to cool down and the automated heating system started to reduce the temperature for the overnight hibernation. She'd stayed to finish off the Stuyvesant report. Her line manager made it clear that although she'd wait for it, she wouldn't wait too long. It was best to finish it and get home with a clear conscience and a clear desk. Just as she reached the control panel, she dropped her purse and the contents scattered all over the floor. She knelt down to pick them up, keys, cellphone, cosmetics. Damn, the lid had come off her foundation cream. Thank god none of it had poured out on the carpet. As she stood up, she saw the light on the panel wink off. Damn! It meant that they'd turned off the elevators, so she'd have to take the stairs. Fourteen floors, at least it was all downhill. She checked her watch, yeah, it was past eight o'clock, and she should have kept an eye on the time. She walked over to the door to the staircase, and saw the echoing hallway looming in front of her. Dark. That was strange, why were the lights off in the stairway?

It meant she had a long, long descent with no way to see where she was going. Not even a flashlight. And she was wearing heels, of all the damned days. She checked her watch again. She was due to meet her best friend, Louise, at eight thirty. She'd have to hurry, and hope to hell she didn't lose a heel on the way down. She sighed, fourteen floors. Well, she'd better get moving. She started down, clinging onto the rail to keep her balance. One floor, then the next, and the next. Only eleven to go, she smiled to herself. She needed to keep moving, otherwise she'd be late. She walked carefully down two more flights of stairs. She was getting the hang of it now, only nine to go, she was nearly halfway down. The she froze. What was that, was someone there? It had been just a tiny sound, like the scrape of a foot on a concrete stair. She wasn't sure, was there someone lurking down there. Was it a rat, oh my god, surely not.

"Hello, is anyone there?" Her voice echoed around the stairwell, disappearing into the black depths and then there was nothing. She smiled to herself. It must have been her imagination. Nothing more.

She started on down again, this time she had her purse

gripped in her hand ready to strike out if it was a rat. Or something else, something maybe even worse. Her purse was pretty heavy, a solid level Coach, filled with her personal possessions. If she hit anything with it, a rat or an attacker, they'd sure feel it. Her progress was a little slower, more careful. She didn't want to stumble, or run into anything unexpectedly. Rats, ugh! The skin of her legs crawled as she thought of the nasty creature creeping up, clinging to her pantyhose. Yuk! She'd brain the little bastard if he tried it. She increased speed, yeah, that might be best, she'd have to chance tripping in the hopes that moving faster would keep her safe from any rats. She heard it again! A soft scrape, what the fuck was it? Like the rubber sole of a shoe, sliding a few inches on the concrete again. Could there be anyone there. Right, if there was, she'd stun him with her heavy purse and run for it. How could she run in heels? Well, there was an answer for that. She stopped, bent down and slipped off her pumps. If her pantyhose were ruined, it was too bad. At least she could run and keep herself safe. She started on down again and realized that she was moving almost silently now. Good, maybe she'd be a lot safer now, whatever it was in the stairwell, if she was silent she could slip down the stairs unnoticed. It was well worth buying new pantyhose to be safe.

Three more flights, she was well past the halfway mark now. She reckoned she was safe, all she had to do was keep going for a few more flights and she was home and dry. She wondered if she'd be in time to meet Louise in the bar. God, she could sure use a drink. She wanted to check her watch, but with one hand on the rail and the other clutching her purse, her weapon, she couldn't look at her wrist. Besides, it was too dark, so she wouldn't see the dial in any case. She mentally shrugged, she'd be out of here in a few more minutes, and she'd have all the time in the world and plenty of light to see her wristwatch. She went down another flight of stairs. There it was! That odd scrape again. It hadn't caused her any trouble, so it probably wasn't a rat or a potential attacker. It must be part of the building, something to do with pipes or air conditioning. Still, she'd keep her shoes off, she was moving silently. That was best, safest. Shit, she was fucking Wonderwoman, swift and silent, any bastard gets in my way and I crack his skull with my purse. Yeah, stay out of my way, buster, whoever you are. She was fucking incredible, smiling every step of the way now. God, she was good! Then again, why the hell had she been so frightened? She wasn't a kid, no way! She was twenty-three years old, fit and strong. Damn, she needed that drink. Five more flights to go. Then a hand clamped over her face.

She struggled, tried to strike out, but her attacker had one hand over her face, the other holding her arms to her body. He was terrifyingly strong. He picked her up and almost threw her to the floor, following her down with his hand still clamped over her mouth. The voice chilled her even more.

"You move and you're dead, bitch. I've got a knife, next to your throat, feel it."

It must have been a switchblade, for she heard a click and the cold steel was pressed against her flesh.

"Can you feel that?"

She nodded, as best she could. She couldn't speak, the hand blocked her mouth.

"Good. Just remember, one sound, one false move and I'll cut you. The knife is sharp, very sharp, so don't even think about doing anything stupid. Clear?"

She nodded again. She could feel his breath, his face was close to hers, he stank of garlic, booze, tobacco, and something else. His body, it was rank. A stale, sour smell. Then his hand reached under her skirt and with one powerful heave he ripped away her pantyhose and briefs. Jesus Christ, fifty dollars worth of underwear, the bastard. She had to be still, she'd read enough material about these situations. Don't fight, don't argue, let him do it and gather as much information as possible so that she could identify the rapist to the cops afterwards. If she tried to fight he might kill her, there was no one to hear her screams, and all she'd achieve would be to panic him. She did her best to start remembering everything, the smell of him, and his voice, anything that may be of use to find him afterwards.

His hands reached greedily between her legs and with despair she felt his fingers slide inside her, roughly, savagely, it hurt, oh god it hurt. Then he lifted his body over here and she felt him guiding his prick into her, it was huge and hard. He started pumping her and she felt overwhelmed with grief. How could this be happening to her? She felt so powerless, she wasn't Wonderwoman at all. She was just Teresa Santos, an office worker who wanted to go home.

"Please," she whispered. "Please stop. Please."

She could feel him going harder, his body went rigid, she knew he was about to come. Maybe it would end. She smelled his body again, that sour, rancid smell. It was, almost corpse-like, a nasty, dank smell. The smell of death, she understood, at the same moment as he reached his hand up, touched a switch and suddenly the stairwell was flooded with light. She saw his face! As he slashed the razor sharp blade across her throat, it occurred to her that she knew him, she was sure she knew him. She didn't feel the pain, not at first, but she could feel the wet blood trickling down her neck. She was dying, how absurd was that, in a stairwell in the office block where she worked. She looked at her attacker for the last time, filled her nostrils once more with his stink, then it all went black.

He stared in to her eyes, looked at the pretty face, pale, terrified. They always were. She knew she was dying, he could see the resignation filling her expression. Then they eyes started to glaze over and he judged the moment with precision, with the skill that only comes from much experience. As the light finally left her eyes he heaved and came, ramming into her with as much force as he had. He was omnipotent, the feeling of raw power was like nothing on earth, again and again he rammed into her body as it transitioned through that dark tunnel between life and death. Then she was gone. He removed his penis, now he knew he had to be very careful not to leave any forensic traces. They'd say he was insane, and he probably was. He didn't care. All he knew was that this moment was the only one worth living for. He removed the condom and slipped it into a baggie he had ready. The only part of him that had touched her was his hands, and even those were covered with latex surgical gloves. His clothes would be burned, and he had installed a gas powered furnace for the purpose. If the cops wanted to try and gather evidence afterwards, they could try as much as they liked. They'd be out of luck. When he left his latest lover, there'd be nothing to connect him to her. He always called them his lovers. That's what they were, weren't they? They fulfilled his urge for human love. There were two more things before he left. They were most important. When they saw them, they'd know it was him. Then they really would be frightened. He started to cut.

* * *

When Gabriel de Sade entered the restaurant, he looked around and saw his friends already seated. It was a small Italian place close to Washington Square Park, in the day you could even see the arch if your seat faced out of the window. There were only twenty tables, all of them full. The reputation of the small eatery was popular to those people who had found the bland, slightly shabby street entrance and chanced going in, to find a tasteful, quiet environment, attentive waiters and first class food. Jonas and Galina were already there, the two people were his best friends, the people he trusted and loved most in this world. Apart from the girl who sat with them, that was. She would have turned a few heads when she walked in. She was petite, barely above five feet tall. Slim and classically beautiful, with an elfin face, she wore her usual pageboy haircut over warm, dark brown eyes. The girl had smooth, creamy skin underneath glossy, dark hair. As usual, her face wore a serious expression, that belied her full lips, made for kissing, or at least, he thought they were. It was as well she was his partner. Her name was Faith Ward, and she was a former FBI agent that he had met on a former assignment. He'd almost lost her, not to another man, but to something he couldn't fight – religion. But she'd chosen him over the austere life of a nun, and he thanked   his lucky stars every day of his life that he'd found her. She was everything a man could want, beautiful, clever and a total fireball in bed. What a waste she'd have been as a nun.

"What are you thinking?"

She was grinning at him.

"Oh, nothing, just a heavy case load we've got down at the precinct."

He meant the Ninth Precinct, the building where he worked as a detective with New York's finest, the NYPD. It was true, for the caseload right now was heavier than ever, after too many financial cuts and increasing crime levels. He should have remembered she was no fool.

"De Sade, I know that look. When it's plastered on your face, there's one thing on your mind."

He felt himself redden. Jonas and Galina were grinning at him.

"I reckon she made you there, buddy," Jonas muttered. "Bang to rights."

Galina, his Russian girlfriend, raised her eyebrows and smiled even wider, but Faith came to his rescue.

"I could have been wrong, Jonas. He could have been thinking about his work."

De Sade nodded, until she came to the punch line. "Always assuming he'd transferred to the vice squad, of course."

They roared with laughter, all except Gabriel. He protested, "Hey, give it a break. I've had a bad day."

He meant it, and Jonas picked up the tired voice at once. The two men been together on and off since they served in an elite unit in Afghanistan. Team Bravo, a Delta Force Squadron that had seen action in some of the worst hellholes in the country. Several times since those dark and bloody days, he'd called on Jonas Savage to support him during some of the operations he'd been involved in. And

Jonas never failed to deliver. He'd been nicknamed 'The Tank' in the Deltas, because he was virtually unstoppable. Yet as hard and tough as he was, he was very perceptive.

"Things are pretty bad down there, buddy?"

De Sade nodded. "Yeah, we've had a couple of nasty ones."

He leaned forward, the others leaned nearer and he pitched his voice low. "We have a serial killer on the loose in the New York City. It's not been made public yet, the Mayor doesn't want to frighten our good citizens. But the pressure's on to find him fast, before he kills too many more."

"It's not been on the news. Don't the people have a right to know if a maniac is on the loose?" Galina asked. There was more than a hint of anger there. She'd come from Russia, where people were routinely kept out of the loop. She believed in America, the land of the free, where theoretically everyone had a right to know. Theoretically.

"Not if the Mayor says they don't, no."

He made an effort to clear his mind of the gruesome trail of corpses he'd been forced to look at over the past fortnight, there'd been four so far, the killer was murdering at a rate of one every three days. The guy had turned into a one man murder spree, and the Mayor wasn't entirely unfair to his citizens. A city that was panicked and terrorized would be no safer for its citizens and could be a lot less safe. Everyone remembered similar episodes in the past when innocent people had been gunned down by trigger happy vigilantes. He changed the subject.

"How's everything going with this new venture you're working on?" he asked Galina.

"Our antiques gallery is good, very good. Did you know

that Faith is joining me, a fifty-fifty partnership?"

He looked at his partner. "You didn't tell me."

Faith shrugged. "I thought I'd get it finalized first and then surprise you. We've taken over the lease of a small showroom in Brooklyn, a former art gallery. Galina had already arranged for the first container of religious antiques from Russia. With any luck we'll be able to open our doors in the next fortnight and start trading."

De Sade glanced at the Russian girl. "Your contacts with the Orthodox Church must have helped?"

"Of course. I worked for them for many years, they owe me a favor or two, so when I asked them to let me know where we could source some religious antiques for export to the West, they were glad to help."

"Worked for them? You were a nun. Is that what they call it, I thought it was more of a vocation? Although Jonas told me they nicknamed you a 'nun with a gun'."

She chuckled. "I didn't have much time for praying, as you know. I seemed to spend most of my time troubleshooting."

"Suitable employment for a former Spetsnaz trooper, I would have thought."

Her smile faded, she was doubtless thinking of her more violent activities. The Orthodox Church had enemies, and not all were able to be persuaded with sincere words. Her job was to find other means to resolve them. Violent means.

"Yes. It was suitable employment for a former Spetsnaz soldier."

They were all quiet for a few moments. Apart from a mutual love and respect, all four share something in common. They had all killed other people in the course of their working lives. The difference was that while Jonas and Gabriel were comfortable with the necessity of taking down the bad guys, Faith and Galina had at one time both belonged to a convent. Nuns didn't kill people, not usually. But both these women had not had a choice, when it came down to kill or be killed. That was the nature of what had faced them at extreme moments in their lives. Gabriel again tried to change the direction of the conversation.

"So where will you source these antiques, it can't be that easy? I know that high-end dealers have enough trouble finding good stuff to sell, the religious market is surely much more rarified."

"You're right," Galina nodded. "What we're offering is much more than just an antique shop, though. We're providing research, restoration, authentication, you name it. If a Jewish family wishes to track precious relics stolen from a synagogue during the Nazi occupation of Europe, we have many ways of doing that. There are also a great number of religious relics floating around South America. Some of the goods we've come across from there date back to the days of Hernán Cortés, and even before then, to the time of the Aztecs."

"Who?" Jonas looked puzzled.

She smiled at her lover. "Cortés had only six hundred men, and he achieved one of the most audacious feats in history. The conquest of the Aztec Empire, no less. At that time the Aztecs had hundreds of thousands of warriors. After landing with his men, he made his way to Tenochtitlan, capital of the Aztec Empire. That's modern day Mexico, of course. Along the way, he defeated their vassal states, and added their strength to his. He reached the capital Tenochtitlan in 1519 and was able to occupy it without a fight."

"Quite a guy," Jonas murmured. "We could have done with someone like that in Afghanistan."

"Yes, he was quite a guy," she agreed.

Faith leaned forward. "As a matter of interest, we've got first refusal on a consignment of religious artifacts in a church in Mexico. All Christian things, some even came over from Spain hundreds of years ago."

"Why do they sell these things?" Jonas asked her. "I thought the churches were particular about not letting their precious relics into the wrong hands."

She shook her head. "They're always selling things off, land, buildings, statues, all kinds of artifacts, even complete churches. It's finance, they need to raise money, and they look around to see what they have to sell. I understand that this particular collection was partly donated by a number of churches to help build a new cathedral in Northern Mexico, but it never got started. All it's done ever since is rot in a basement storeroom."

"Was it corruption that stopped the cathedral going ahead?" Gabriel was a policeman, so he knew there were few motivations for people breaking the law. Money was 'numero uno'.

She nodded. "Corruption, that's what we heard killed it off. Someone siphoned off a lot of the money, but the result is they're left with these relics and they want to turn them into cash. Maybe they'll do something good with the money in the end."

"So this stuff is in Mexico City?"

She shook her head. "The goods are stored in a locked room in a church just south of the border, a town called Nogales."

He exchanged a look with Jonas.

"Nogales Mexico?

"Yes, that's right. Nogales. Why, what's wrong?"

"You're not thinking of going there, are you?"

The two women both wore puzzled expressions. "Of course we're going there," Galina replied. "How else could we put a valuation on the goods and arrange to transport them back to the US?"

"You can't go to Nogales," Jonas almost shouted, betraying his concern. "It's a toilet."

A passing waiter gave him a startled glance, maybe thinking his was talking about the restaurant.

They both laughed at Jonas. "Of course we're going."

"Faith, Galina, listen to me." They both turned to Gabriel. "NYPD sometimes has dealings with the Nogales Police as well as the Federales. Nogales has suffered a huge increase in violent, drug related crime in the past twelve months. It's become one of the most violent cities in Mexico. Street crime, armed robberies, assaults, car thefts, burglaries, and murder. They're at an all time high. And then there are the big shot drug dealers, they're happy to slaughter their rivals by the score. And U.S. and foreign visitors are more vulnerable to crime as they are often seen as wealthier than the local folks, likely to be carrying large amounts of cash and other valuables. Sometimes it's just a matter of being in the wrong place at the wrong time. It's a hellhole, believe me."

They were all silent after his outburst. Galina looked at Faith, and she glanced back at Gabriel and Jonas. Finally, she replied, "Whatever it is, you know we can take care of ourselves. We go where the business takes us, and that means Nogales. I'm sorry, but we can't have you telling us where we can and can't go."

"So you're going down there?"

Faith glared at Gabriel. "We're going down there. We'll do the deal and we'll come right back. That's it."

They were silent again. Abruptly, Gabriel's cellphone rang. He looked at them in apology, then answered the call

"De Sade."

"We've got another one."

It was Carlo Estevez, his new partner. De Sade smiled as he pictured him attempting to control the crime scene. Carlo made detective a few months ago and was already making his name at the precinct. He wasn't imposing to look at, of medium height and build and darkly Hispanic in appearance. With his pencil thin moustache and loud suits he had the look of a seedy night club owner. It was an image he cultivated, and more than one suspect had underrated his detective's skills. Before he became a cop Carlo was a law graduate and veteran of five years in uniform. Pounding the bricks gave him valuable knowledge of their beat. When they'd told Gabriel of his new partner, he was pleasantly surprised not to be saddled with another complete rookie like his last partner. Martin Belton, the preppy kid who liked to take short cuts to get ahead. The short cuts had only shortened his career. He was currently serving eight years in Rikers for corruption and accessory to homicide.

"Where are you?"

"East 7th Street, near the park. Tompkins Square Park."

"Yeah, I know where East 7th Street is. What number?"

"It's the tower block offices, I'm in the stairwell."

"You need me right away? I was having dinner with some friends."

18

"Nah, it's not me. It's Captain Kruger who needs you, so take up your dinner arrangements with him."

"Yeah. I'll be there in ten."

He clicked off.

"I have to go."

Faith looked angry. "Surely someone else can handle it? It's not as if you have much time off."

"The Captain wants me there."

She nodded wearily. "Ok, then. I'll see you later."

He said his goodbyes and called a cab and after cutting through the evening traffic he arrived at the building, a modern office block. New concrete, glass and chrome, a scattering of cruisers and unmarked cars parked randomly across the street. Blue and red lights flashing, yellow tape, and a pair or harassed uniforms trying to move the inevitable rubberneckers along. He walked inside and nodded to the cop who guarded the entrance, then badged his way through the cops crowded around the entrance to the stairwell. They directed him up the stairs, on the tiny landing between the fourth and fifth floor lay the body of a young woman. Her arms ended in stumps, the killer had cut off her hands. Both severed limbs lay nearby, like two parts of a modernist sculpture. A tribute to the excesses of man's cruelty and inhumanity, perhaps. What was in this sicko's mind?

He nodded to Carlo. "Any leads?"

"Not really." He pointed to the dead woman's bare breasts. Nestling between them was a chess piece, a pawn. "Just like the others, it's the same guy. The M.O. said she was raped, but the guy used a condom, like the others."

A fingerprint team was dusting around for prints, but they all knew that there wouldn't be any. This killer had struck before, and his victims always bore the same M.O. No forensic residue and a chess piece, always positioned on the victim's body, between the breasts.

"What about the building CCTV? Have you checked it all out?"

"I've got a guy looking through it, but the super said that it looks as if someone disconnected the video feed. It was almost certainly the perp, so we're not expecting any miracles there. This guy is real careful."

De Sade noticed a uniform frowning at Carlo, for taking command of the crime scene. Like so many others, he underestimated the detective, mistaking his street Latino appearance for second rate abilities. He ignored him, the guy would learn soon enough, age and experience wasn't everything, and neither was appearance. He bent down to look at the body. She'd been an attractive young woman. In death, her face had relaxed, and someone had closed her eyes, probably the perp. She looked calm, composed, in a deep sleep. Except for ghastly pallor of her skin and the red cut on her neck, with a pool of blood underneath. He looked around the bare concrete of the stairwell; it was little more than an emergency exit.

"Did anyone hear anything?"

Carlos shook his head. "Not a thing, at least, no one has come forward. We're not sure why she chose to exit the building down the stairs, but I'd guess that the perp switched off the elevators and she had no choice."

There was a commotion on the next floor down. A guy came up the stairs, powerfully built, elegantly dressed, his hair carefully coiffed in the kind of style that Wall Street bankers use when they want the world to know what bigshots they are. In this case the hair was unnecessary.

Everyone knew who this guy was. Congressman Richard Bryant was a politician and a millionaire, the money earned from his numerous financial holdings, although they were now held in a myriad of trust funds. Gabriel stood up and nodded a greeting.

"Congressman, what are you doing here?"

The Representative looked down at the body, his face white, the expression was strange. Not quite shock, more fascination. Gabriel supposed it was horror at the scene of violent death. The man looked up. "She worked for me, in my offices on the fourteenth floor. I only just heard that she was dead, so I came straight here. Her name is Teresa Santos." His voice was controlled, steady, but laced with shock. "How did she die?"

De Sade pointed wordlessly to the blood pooled under neck and the stumps of the arms. "Throat cut. Raped as well. Hands cut off too, pretty unpleasant. Do you know what she was doing using the stairs?"

He shrugged. "No idea, we all use the elevators, the stairs are only for emergencies, like in a fire. I've never used them myself."

Carlo gave him a surprised glance. "Not even in a fire drill?"

Bryant stared back at him. "With deference to my age and Congressional rank, they let me know in advance, and I go down in the elevator before the drill starts."

Carlo grunted and raised his eyebrows at de Sade. The rules were different for the rich. He turned away to examine the floor area around the body.

Bryant stared intently at de Sade. "Do we have a serial killer running around the streets, Detective?"

"Why would you think that, Congressman?"

"Don't be stupid! We've had a number of unexplained killings in the city, they all seem to feature a young woman raped and murdered like this one. I do read the papers, Detective. As do most New Yorkers. They're entitled to know if they're in danger."

Gabriel thought for a few moments, but there was nothing he could say without making it a lie.

"I can't confirm it, Sir. Perhaps you should speak to my Captain, that's Kruger. He's in charge of things around here."

Bryant's stare didn't waver. "I'll do that, Detective. I trust that you're working hard to find the killer and get them off the street. Teresa was a very well liked and valued member of my staff."

"All of the victims were valued by someone, Sir."

The Congressman's eyes narrowed. "What exactly are you doing to get this character behind bars?"

"We're doing everything we can, Sir. If you need more information, Captain Kruger will be pleased to talk to you, he'll be outside shortly. Now I need to get on with solving this crime, if you could wait outside the yellow tape. This is a crime scene, Sir."

Bryant gave him another long, hard look. Then he turned away and went down the staircase without another word. Carlo came over to him.

"Interesting character, Congressman Bryant. Rich, too, although I guess they all are."

"You didn't seem too impressed with him."

He looked thoughtful. "I don't know. Something about him, I can't put my finger on it."

"He's a politician, maybe that's the bit that you don't like."

Carlo grinned back at Gabriel. "Yeah, probably you're right."

His thoughts went to his time in Afghanistan. They'd been assigned a mission to escort a high ranking Afghan minister and his aide on a journey from Kabul to Jalalabad. The man was one of Hamid Karzai's most trusted ministers, and it had been impressed upon them how vital it was to keep him safe from Taliban attack. The minister declined a helicopter. At the time they'd assumed it was because of fear of flying, or maybe it was a religious objection. The aide arranged for him to travel in the second vehicle from the rear of the column, a black civilian Toyota Land Cruiser, with two Team Bravo guys in the car with him for close protection. The aide traveled at the front in their armored Humvee. They'd been offered a larger force, but elected to take Team Bravo in fast and light. They reached Jalalabad without a hitch and their small convoy drove into the center of the city. The sudden rocket attack sliced into the minister's vehicle and the rest of them hurtled for cover. The minister was killed outright when the missile hit, as were the two Team Bravo soldiers who were with him. Two men dragged the aide into a nearby building, the rest of them fanned out to look for the shooters. They found two boys on a rooftop, using Soviet built RPG's. Both reached for their AK47s, the ubiquitous weapon of choice for most Taliban. One of the boys was killed outright, cut down by one of the Team's assault rifles, the other was wounded. Gabriel had tried to talk to the boy, but he was silent, either because of the shock of his wounds, or because he refused to speak to the infidel soldiers. Jonas brought up the minister's aide to talk to the man, hoping the familiar dialect would be better received. The boy's eyes opened wide when he saw the aide, then he looked away, as if he felt guilty for recognizing the man. In that moment it all became clear to them. The aide was next in line for the minister's post. They arrested him and returned to Kabul with the man in handcuffs, but regardless of their report, the aide became the new Minister for Environmental Affairs. That meant a huge pot of UN and American money to play with. The next time they were in Kabul, Jonas went out one night for a walk, leaving no word of his destination. The new Minister was found dead in his bed the next morning, sprawled in his fortified bungalow in a defended compound on the outskirts of Kabul. Jonas never said a word to the Team, but a message was quietly circulated to the Kabul government. If you want to assassinate each other, go ahead. But don't involve any of the ISAF units, not if you want to live to see the benefits of your murderous exploits.

CHAPTER TWO

It was three o'clock in the morning before he got back to his apartment block. The building was one of the older ones in the city, dark brownstone with large enough windows to give a good view across the city, for the upper floors. He walked into the brightly lit minimart next door, over spilling with goods. The owner Lee Fat was behind the cash register as usual. Did the guy never sleep? Every available space was jammed with groceries, cleaning materials and a host of unidentified packets. Some were printed in Chinese, for the area had a fair sized Chinese population that Lee served.

"Hi Lee, you got any Schneider Kristall for me?"

The Chinese storekeeper always kept a small stock of the premium beer, just for him. He'd acquired a taste for it in Afghanistan. They'd rescued a beleaguered German 'Medecin Sans Frontiere' medical team, and his squad had been invited to share a case of Schneider Kristall. Since then, he'd never drunk anything else if he could obtain the German beer, perhaps because it reminded him of the shared camaraderie of tough, highly trained professionals sharing both good and bad times under the most adverse conditions in the world. Maybe it was because he liked the taste.

"Too right, I have beer. You want six pack?"

"Yeah, that'll be great. Thanks Lee."

"You welcome, Detective. Your lady, she come back hours ago. She in apartment now."

"Right, thanks."

Lee regarded it as his personal mission in life to keep the NYPD detective up to date with whoever was in his apartment. On at least one occasion, it had saved him from a world of grief when a shooter tried to ambush him. He paid for the beer and went up in the elevator to the home he shared with Faith Ward. He felt both angry and worried about her planned trip to Nogales. She was asleep when he went into the bedroom, so he undressed quietly and climbed into bed.

"How was it?"

He should have known she'd wake when he came in.

"Pretty bad. We've got a serial killer on the loose."

"What's his M.O.?"

As a former FBI agent, she would naturally be interested in the killer's Modus Operandi.

"He cuts their throats, rapes them and leaves a chess piece on the body."

She flinched. "It's a horrible way to die." She shrugged. "I guess there isn't a nice way to die, though. Do you have any leads?"

He shook his head. "Nothing so far, this guy seems to know how not to leave any forensic residue. This is the fifth body to turn up with a similar M.O., and there may be more we haven't discovered yet."

"There'll be a panic on the streets when people find out."

"That's up to the Mayor. So far, he wants it kept quiet."

She grimaced. "People have a right to know. Anyway, it may not be his choice. The media will soon be on to it, it's impossible to hide a story like this."

Her words were prophetic; he got up at seven, feeling almost as dead as the corpse from the crime scene. He showered and poured himself some juice. Faith was already dressed, browsing the internet on her laptop. He turned on the TV, and there was the office building in East 7th Street, stark in the early dawn, with the park in the background. A female news reporter smiled at the camera with a mouthful of expensive teeth.

"The shocking murder of Teresa Santos has left this part of the city in a state of terror. Where will the killer strike next? The Chess Killer has the NYPD totally unable to find either the killer or the motive. Not only does this maniac slaughter his victims, he cuts off their hands and leaves a chess piece on the body. It seems that to the murderer, he sees his victims as just a part of his games. Miss Santos was Congressman Richard Bryant's administrative assistant. People are saying that if the police cannot even protect the local congressman's staffers, they have a serious problem. In other news..."

He turned it off. Faith was staring at him.

"Yeah, go ahead. Tell me you told me they'd be onto the story like flies on a corpse."

She grimaced. "An apt simile. But I wouldn't do that, I was just thinking about the other thing, that business in Nogales. I have an email from Galina, she heard back from the church. The arrangements have been put forward by twenty four hours, and we're flying down this evening."

"To Nogales?" He was startled. The subject had clean slipped his mind after the events of the previous evening.

"To Nogales, of course. We're flying down to Phoenix and renting a car, it's the most convenient way. We'll drive to Nogales, Arizona and cross the border."

"I wish you weren't going, it's a dangerous place. More dangerous than you can imagine."

"Really! And New York City is safe for young women, is that what you're trying to tell me?"

He flinched. "Ok, we've got a problem," he conceded. "But it's different. Killing is a way of life down there."

"We'll be ok. It's important that we go there. After all, this deal could make or break our new antiques gallery. Some of the relics sound very exciting, amazing, in fact."

In spite of his worry, he was curious. "Relics like what?"

"They've got all the usual stuff. Crucifixes, nails and pieces of wood from the true cross. The sponge that was soaked in vinegar to give Jesus a drink. I know it's all rubbish, but there are on ore two pieces that may be genuine. There are a number of paintings, wood carvings and statuettes. A piece of a gospel that they say was examined and rejected at the Council of Nicaea in AD 325. It could even be true. And there is also a burial cloth, you know, like the Turin Shroud."

He laughed. "That was shown to be from the thirteenth century, wasn't it?"

"Yes, something like that. But this one looks much older, a burial shroud that appears to date from an earlier period. Of course, we'll need to look into it further, but who knows?"

There was something in her eyes that Gabriel recognized, he'd seen it before. This relic, the shroud, meant something to her. It was driving her along, even though there was only an outside possibility that it could be from, well, the first century AD. Surely that was crazy?

"You don't honestly believe it could be THE shroud, do you?" he asked her. He didn't want to name the name. Jesus Christ.

She shrugged. "Who knows? I doubt it. But whatever it is, it would have come over to South America on one of the early Spanish expeditions, when the monks were keen to convert the South American Indians. The Aztecs, Mayans and other tribes. No doubt they thought it would be a powerful talisman, something to work a magic on the primitive savages and persuade them to believe in Christ."

"Well it obviously worked, aren't they're all pretty much Christians these days."

"Yes, that's true," she murmured, lost in thought. "I wonder..."

"Faith, I was only joking. You surely don't believe in these things?"

Her eyes stared at him, intent and piercing. "Yes, of course I do. You know I do."

He sighed. "Even if there was any kind of magical power attached to these old relics, there's no way of knowing what this one is or where it came from. The Turin Shroud had the Catholic church fooled for centuries."

"You're right. But Galina and I have uncovered accounts of strange things that have happened in the presence of this cloth. Miraculous healings, that kind of thing. Divine revelation, too. It all happened a long time ago, before the shroud was lost. We do need to check it all out further, and find out if it's the same cloth and of course, whether we can authenticate it beyond doubt."

He shook his head in frustration. "I can hardly believe what I'm hearing. A weird piece of cloth found in an old Nogales church. It's rubbish, Faith, and you shouldn't be taken in by it. And you shouldn't go down there, not alone anyway. I told you. Nogales is one of the murder capitals of the world."

"We'll be safe, don't worry. Safer than here in New York City. You catch that serial killer, and maybe we can all breathe more easily."

He knew he couldn't persuade her to change her mind. Faith Ward was the most stubborn and determined person he'd ever known, perhaps that's why he'd fallen for her. He held her close and kissed her passionately.

"Just one thing, if you run into any problems, promise me you'll call."

She smiled. "I will, don't worry. And I'll bet that Jonas is saying the same thing to Galina. We'll be fine."

He left the apartment filled with misgivings, but knowing that she would do it her way. He walked into the large, gray building that housed the Ninth Precinct. Rebuilt in the year two thousand, the building had been clad using the original stone facade. It gave the place a classy, retro look, but inside it was different. Like many modern buildings, it had its drawbacks. Heating that didn't work in the winter, air conditioning that broke down in the summer. And the smells and sounds of police departments the world over. Disinfectants, vomit, stale tobacco, and of course, fear. Phones forever ringing, the vicious shouts and snarls of the clients. Often angry and frightened while they were processed through a system that was as stubborn and unstoppable as a train. When a person was booked in here, they became just another code in a computerized filing system. A set of binary numbers. There was no way out, until their guilt or innocence was proved either way. The unlucky ones found themselves in Rikers, the island prison in the Hudson that served New York City. It held thousands of inmates, and de Sade knew that not all were guilty. Except they were guilty of being picked up and processed by the system. That was enough. He nodded to the desk sergeant, and raced up the stairs to the detective's room on the second floor. Halfway along, almost buried beneath the noise and bustle of forty detectives working their cases, he spied Carlo Estevez at the desk they shared. He waved to some of his acquaintances as he made his way through the room. Carlo looked up, he wasn't smiling.

"I've got a bad feeling about this one. Every time that fucking phone rings I think it's going to be the next corpse."

"No leads, no forensics?"

"You got that right, buddy. No leads, no forensics, we're right at square one."

"I hear you. Look, I know some chess guys that play down in Washington Square Park. I'm going to walk on down there and see if they've got any ideas."

Carlo looked up. "You think one of them may be our guy?"

Gabriel shook his head. "No, I don't, we're not going to get a break that easily. But I think there's something we're missing about this chess thing."

"I don't think we're missing anything. He puts a chess piece on the victim that relates to the kind of person he kills. That girl, the Congressman's clerk, she warranted a pawn. Then there was that banker, he got a castle. The only question is whether the guy is going for as many kills as it takes to use every piece on the board."

"They've all been white pieces. Had you noticed that?" Gabriel pointed out.

"No, that's interesting. Any ideas?"

"Not yet, but I'm going to chat with my contacts in the park, see if they can throw any light on it."

Carlo grunted. "I can't see where you're going with it. The guy's a psycho, not some kickass chess player."

"He could be both," Gabriel pointed out. "They may have some ideas, someone they know who fits the profile."

"Good for them. But playing chess isn't illegal, so I think you're wasting your time. I'll stay here and concentrate on the other part. Homicide is illegal, last time I checked. So is cutting off someone's hands, I'll see what I can find out."

"Yeah, well maybe this chess thing'll help, maybe not. I'll see you later."

It was a fine winter's morning in Manhattan. The sun shone, and the sky was cloudless. All of which made it bitterly cold, too, but Gabriel knew that he'd find the die-hards playing chess in the park, they were there all year round. The streets were as crowded as usual as he shouldered his way through. Tonight it would be different as word of the serial killer swept the city. Many of the women on New York would stay at home, at least while this case was high up on the news agenda. As soon as the furor died down, they'd be back out again. Until the next victim, of course. Christ, they had to get this guy! He entered the park and walked under the famous, iconic arch. Samuel Aaronssen was sitting in his usual place, waiting for an opponent. He was slapping his hands against his body to ward off the cold, and he looked up eagerly as Gabriel arrived.

"I guess you're looking for a murderer, Gabriel? You've come to the right place, sit down and I'll see how long it takes me to hang, draw and quarter you."

Gabriel smiled. "Hi, Samuel. I've come for a chat, you've heard about this killer."

"The Chess Killer? Of course, we all have. You don't think it's one of us?"

"You can relax," he smiled. I don't think it's one of you. The guy we're looking for is very, very strong. Most of you chess players are not in his league, not physically, anyway."

"I don't know whether to take that as an insult or not," Samuel murmured to himself. "Anyway, while you're here, play a game and we'll talk."

Gabriel sat down, drew black and began to play the Sicilian defense, much to Samuel's amusement. "You can do better, Gabriel, that strategy is as full of holes as a Swiss cheese."

"Bobby Fischer played it," he objected.

"Bobby Fischer, he was a schmuck."

"He was world champion."

"He was a schmuck, I tell you. Look at the life he led."

"Tell me about chess, Samuel."

The older man closed his eyes and sighed. "Chess developed over 1500 years, it started in India.

When the Arabs conquered Persia, the Muslim world took up chess and it spread to Southern Europe. In Europe, chess evolved into its current form in the 15th century. In the second half of the 19th century, modern chess tournament play began, and the first world Chess

Championship was held in 1886. The early form of chess was known as chaturanga, which translates as four divisions. These divisions were military. The infantry, cavalry, elephantry, and chariots. They were represented by the pieces that would evolve into the modern pawn, knight, bishop, and castle, or rook. In Persia around 600 AD chess was known as chatrang. They called out Shah Mat, the king is helpless, for checkmate, when the king was attacked and could not escape."

He opened his eyes. "That's all I know of chess. Apart from how to play to a modest standard, of course. You're in check, by the way."

Gabriel looked down. In the space of half a dozen moves Samuel had demolished him. He tipped over his king, the signal that he resigned and acknowledged he was beaten. "I think you've got me, my friend. Maybe next time I'll do better."

"Maybe." Samuel looked dubious. "I'm afraid I haven't been much help with your investigation. Except that..." He looked around the park, Gabriel waited. There was something he was trying to bring to mind. "Yes, there was a man who came through here, about four weeks ago. Hamid, come over here."

A swarthy old guy got up slowly came walked over. "You want a game, Samuel?"

"Not now, Hamid. You know Detective de Sade?"

The guy nodded a greeting. He was obviously an Arab, and by the look of him, a Moslem. Gabriel wondered about their conversations, how long it took for them to turn into argument. Or maybe chess was a uniting factor.

"Gabriel's looking for this serial killer, the one that's causing trouble in the city. He has some sort of a chess connection, do you remember that guy that came around here, asking about us. He asked did we see chess as a true game of life or death."

Hamid smiled. "You told him no, it was much more important than that."

Samuel looked irritated. "Well of course it is. But there was something about him, I remember you mentioned it."

"Yes, that's right. I was just going to Friday prayers, I taken a shower and was wearing clean clothes. He stank, real bad."

"Stank of what?" de Sade asked.

"Death."

"Death? What does that smell like?"

"I suppose I mean the stench of dead bodies, corpses. We Moslems bury out dead straight away, in the hot climates we come from it is the only way. Yes, this man stank of death. As if he'd been around either bodies or body parts and hadn't washed."

Gabriel thought about the missing hands. None had ever been found.

"What did he look like, this guy?"

Hamid shrugged. "It must have been a month ago. He was big, really big, like a nightclub bouncer, but he looked real wealthy, wore an expensive suit, two thousand dollars it if was a cent. That smell, it was strange on a guy that like that one."

"What about his face? Was he white, black, Hispanic?"

"White, I guess. But I honestly can't remember, it was a month ago, I was in the middle of an important game at the time. You remember, Samuel, the fall tournament when I played the Ruy Lopez defense?" He chuckled. "I tied that guy in knots. Mate in fourteen. What a match."

Samuel dragged him back to the present. "Hamid, this guy, he could be our killer. Do you remember what he looked like?"

He shrugged. "Sorry, I didn't really look hard at his face."

Gabriel gave up and handed them both one of his cards and asked them to call if they remembered anything more. A big, wealthy, white man in an expensive suit. It was something, more than he had to go on before he talked to them.

He returned to the precinct entered the detective's room. Straight into the arms of Captain Kruger, who was waiting for him. He generally got on well with the Captain, despite the fact that he was a by-the-book cop with a strong nose for the winds of politics. His appearance never changed, his head was bald, and he was dressed in a dark-gray off the peg suit. It was all he ever wore; he had five identical ones in his closet. Together with his crisp, white shirt and dark-blue tie, with the heavy, black, cop shoes polished to a mirror shine, he was the very image of shining efficiency. Which he was. Although he ruled the Precinct with a will of iron, he stood up for his men and was well-liked. But he expected his men to keep to the same high standards as he set himself.

"De Sade, how's this serial killer investigation going? What have you got?"

"Yeah, Captain. It could be better." He went on to bring him up to date on Hamid's description of the guy in the park. "It may be something, on the other hand, maybe not. I'll get a sketch artist to have a chat with them down there, see if he can come up with anything."

"That may have to wait. I've got some problems here.

The first is that the FBI has talking with the Mayor, they want to stick their snouts into our investigation."

"Christ, Captain, they've got nothing! They'd be starting from scratch."

"Maybe, maybe not. We're not bursting with leads either. Those chess players in the park, it's a bit of a stretch. But that's not the only thing we're concerned with. The brass has received a high level request from a politician in Arizona, he's anxious to get to grips with the local crime figures. He asked for one of our detectives to go down there and talk to his people in the Phoenix PD about the way we do things in the city. I understand their figures are way down on ours. I want you to go down there and talk to them."

De Sade groaned. "Captain, we're shorthanded enough around here as it is. That's a crazy idea. I've got my work cut out with this current case."

"Yeah, well, you can tell that to the Commissioner and the Mayor. If you can't change their minds, you're booked out tomorrow morning. Pass over your caseload to Frank Willard, he's a good detective. When you're done with Frank, get yourself over to Federal Plaza and help our FBI friends to get up to date with the case. If you're gentle with them, you can arrange for a shared investigation, just swapping information as and when it comes in. If you're heavy handed, they'll want it all and we'll be out of the loop. It should take you most of the day to deal with all of the admin and get yourself ready to go. When you get to Phoenix, your contact is Police Chief Oliver Simpson. The actual request came from Congressman Max Carson. He's a firebrand on law and order, apparently. Spend a few days down there, tell them everything they need to know about the way we do things and get back here."

De Sade shook his head in exasperation. "You know the Feds won't pull in this serial killer? The chances are we could have more corpses by then. It's the kind of case that needs local knowledge to work it."

"Yeah, I'm sure you're right. That's why your partner Carlo will continue working the case and Frank will give him any help he needs. You're going, de Sade, so you'd better get used to it. Dismissed."

He nodded and left Kruger's office. He went over to Frank Willard to talk about the handover. As usual, Frank looked worn down, looking forward to his retirement in four years time. Wearing his usual rumpled, polyester suit, as rumpled as the skin on his careworn face, he looked every inch the TV notion of a veteran detective. Which he was, Frank could be relied to chase down every lead to close a case. At this moment he had a sullen black youth slumped in a chair opposite his desk, de Sade ignored him.

"You heard from the Captain?"

He looked up. "Yeah, I heard. What have you got for me? This Chess guy?"

The black youth perked up. "The Chess Killer? Jeez, you ain't caught that motherfucker yet?"

"Shuddup!" Frank snarled at him.

"Yeah, I've got a couple of interesting leads to run down. I'll pass it all over to you before I leave."

"Hey, that's gonna be some whitey, ain't no brother doing that kind of shit. I'm tellin' you..."

Frank looked at de Sade in mute appeal. Gabriel nodded and leaned down and rammed a fist into the guy's belly. He screamed and hunched over, favoring the pain in his stomach.

"You motherfucker, I'm gonna get my lawyer to sue you for that, it's police brutality. Fucking Five-oh."

"Button it, unless you want another one," Frank murmured quietly.

"Yeah, but it's an assault."

"I never saw a thing. If you shut up, you won't get hit again." He looked up again. "So you're off to Arizona. The weather'll be better than it is here. I could do with some sunshine myself. Maybe when I retire, I'll be able to do some of the things I want."

Yeah, but first he'd need to get out from under the crushing weight of a whining wife, four scrapping kids and a Manhattan apartment that was twice the rent he could afford. Then he could think about taking it a bit easy, going down south and enjoying some sunshine. Frank had a lot of millstones around neck, most of the detectives were astonished that he managed to keep going.

"You sure will, Frank. I'll hand over the files to you later.

Frank waved an acknowledgment and turned his attention to the noisy youth. De Sade returned to his desk, where Carlo was writing up the murder book from last night.

"So you're leaving us, heading for the sunshine. Lucky for some."

He smiled at his partner." Yeah, the luck never ends. Drug dealers, human traffickers, snakes, Arizona is a real haven of peace and tranquility."

"You speak any Spanish?"

De Sade shook his head. "Nada. Just American and Russian."

"Not too many Russians down there."

"No. Can you get a sketch artist over to the chess players in Washington Square Park? There could be something there, it might help us."

"Yeah, I'll get that done today. Anything else?"

"No, Frank is taking over some of my cases, so the main one is the Chess guy. You know about the Feds?"

"Yeah, Kruger told me. I'm not optimistic. They'll run around making lots of noise and blowing smoke. I expect we'll have the Behavioral Analysis people telling us it's a white guy between twenty five and forty with a bad upbringing. Then it'll be up to us to find the guy from about two million men that are a good fit."

Gabriel smiled. "That's the way it goes. Anyway, good luck with it, I'll be back in a few days."

"Don't get sunburn." Carlo chuckled. "Just remember us poor bastards freezing our balls off back here."

The thought of freezing cold took him back to Afghanistan, where the winters could be as cruel as the Taliban. The unit sniper Al Gray, and his back up man, were dropped by helicopter into the mountains near Tora Bora. The slopes were covered in thick snow and the soldiers wore white camouflage suits. The following day, the rest of Team Bravo made their way into the bandit country. At the time it was rumored to be the hiding place of Osama Bin Laden and Mullah Omar. The expected ambush came mid-morning, a heavy force of Taliban were dug in fifty yards from the road. Al was dug in five hundred yards away. When the Afghans opened fire, they revealed their positions and Al went to work. Hidden in the snow, his white camouflage suit making him invisible to the fighters, he fired repeatedly using his standard, bolt-action sniper rifle with a telescopic sight. There were fifty rebels, and Al killed more than half of them in less than two minutes, making every shot count. Discouraged and starting to panic, the survivors began to melt away. Moving through the snow, they left tracks that were easy to track and the helicopter gunships were ready and waiting to make short work of the survivors. But it was cold, the coldest they'd ever know it. A few of the Taliban survivors were wounded, but the intense cold bled the life out of them as mercilessly as their gunshot wounds. Two of Team Bravo suffered minor injuries, but they were swiftly medevacked to Kabul. The Taliban did not have the luxury of warm clothing and advanced medical facilities, so they died for what they fought for. A primitive and savage society with little or no thought spared for those who fell by the wayside. Gabriel wondered what they would have made of sunny Arizona, those fighters who'd fought and perished in the bitter, snowy wastes. He decided they wouldn't be impressed. They seemed to fight and thrive on suffering and misery.

CHAPTER THREE

They watched the former soldier as he strolled along the sidewalk. There was something of the big cat about the way he walked, as if he possessed huge reserves of both strength and an almost supernatural agility. A dangerous man.

"It is him, the one they call Savage? Jonas Savage?"

"Yes, there can be no doubt."

"Is everything ready?"

"It is. Rashid is waiting with the truck and he says he has the motor running. As soon as we call he will drive forward and knock down this Savage as he crosses the road. He will start the detonator in the truck as soon as he is clear. He will pretend to run to get help. When he is clear the truck explodes, the man will be dead and many other infidels at the same time. God be praised."

"Praise to his name, yes. That particular infidel deserves to die a slow, lingering death. A pity we could not organize it for him."

"He is very resourceful, Malik. Better this way, to know

that our mission cannot fail and he will be punished."

"Perhaps you're right. I thank God that my brother Zafar will at last be avenged. Listen, I have decided on a change of plan. I do not trust Rashid to do this properly, I want to make certain of the explosion. As soon as the truck hits this Jonas Savage, set off the bomb. You have the cellphone that will remotely detonate it?"

"I do, yes."

"But that is my brother in that truck," he thought. "It is right for Malik to take revenge for the death of his brother, of course, but why does he have to kill MY brother to do it?"

"Good. You know what to do. I must leave now, for I have other matters to attend to. My face is known to the police, so I cannot be seen near here when the bomb goes off. Good luck, my friend. God is great."

"God is great," he agreed. The cell leader walked away and he made the call to his brother Rashid.

"Change of plan, my brother. Do not arm the bomb."

"Why is that?"

"Our great leader was planning a double cross. He wanted to see you in paradise before your time. Never mind, the target is approaching now. He is wearing blue jeans, black leather boots, a brown leather aviator's jacket and Rayban Aviator sunglasses. You cannot miss him. Knock him down, if Allah wills it he will die then. If not, well, perhaps another time. Then get out of there."

"But how will you explain the bomb not detonating?"

"A misfire. They happen all the time. But make sure you hit him."

"As Allah wills it."

Jonas looked up as the white delivery truck jumped a red light. Goddamn New York truckers, they were a law unto themselves. As pretty girl in a tight fitting skirt walking precariously on bright red high-heeled shoes distracted him, it took him two valuable seconds to come to his senses and for his brain to register what his eyes told him. The truck driver was an Arab. Arabs and Delta Force didn't mix. But he was too late. He felt a terrible shock and searing pain as the fender smashed into him, then his head struck the curbside and everything went black.

* * *

De Sade walked across town, enjoying the winter bustle of the city. There was no snow yet, but people were wrapped up in woolen coats and colorful scarves. It was a cheerful scene, a familiar scene. Yellow cabs scuttling in and out of the traffic, New Yorkers walking with that purposeful stride, careful not to meet any of the eye's that came towards them, always in a hurry. Brightly decorated retail outlets, the occasional surviving Mom and Pop store, Chinese and Italian in many cases. The sights, the smells. Some said it was an over populated hell. Others that it was paradise. For him, it was home. The last thing he wanted was to leave the city and fly down to the arid, desert state of Arizona, sunshine notwithstanding. Except that he'd be nearer to Faith and Galina, of course. That made all the difference. Nogales, both US and Mexican, was only a hundred and sixty miles south of Phoenix, so he'd be on hand if they hit problems. He smiled to himself, it sure was a dangerous place, but he should be more confident in their abilities. They were a pair of tough, capable women. He walked off the street and into the gray, institutional interior of One Federal Plaza. The concrete bastion that sheltered the legions of FBI Special Agents behind it's carefully controlled faced. A painting of J Edgar Hoover was on the wall behind the reception counter. At least he was in a suit, not the dress that many said he wore in his more private moments. The guy on reception called up to advise them that he had arrived, and within minutes the elevator opened and a familiar figure walked out. He had the skin and looks of an Arab, betraying his Middle-Eastern heritage, but the smart suit, white shirt and tie were all-American FBI. Joe Hafiz, the agent he'd got involved with during a violent episode in Jerusalem. Joe was a Moslem American, and one of the best agents he'd come across. Totally loyal and totally reliable. Maybe this wouldn't be so difficult. They shook hands.

"Joe, it's good to see you.

"You too, buddy. But you may not be when this meeting is over."

"What's the deal?"

"They want to take over, the hunt for the serial killer, all of it. The brass wants it all."

"Yeah, I heard the bureau wanted in, but it's not a good idea to shut us out. This one needs local involvement too."

"I know that, I tried to persuade them to keep your people in the loop, but they were adamant. I guess they want the glory for themselves."

"If they catch the perp," de Sade grunted. "Otherwise there won't be any glory. Are you the lead agent on the investigation?"

Joe nodded and grinned. "I'm the fall guy, yeah. Reporting to the Assistant Director, he's the guy you're about to meet."

He pressed the button and the elevator shot up to

the eleventh floor. They emerged into an altogether different world. Thick carpets, sound proofing, heating and ventilation what worked well. Joe noticed him looking around.

"Yeah, we mere mortals don't get up here too often. I guess we play too rough for these people."

He was still smiling as he knocked on an office door and went in. The guy behind the desk was Mr. Corporate America. Everything about him and his surroundings spelled success. Expensive suit, hand stitched shoes, immaculate haircut and a gym-toned physique. Office furniture in real wood, as well as two watercolors on the wall. They were not prints, either. He nodded at the two men.

"Joe, thanks for coming. So this is Detective de Sade."

Gabriel nodded a greeting. "That's me."

"I'm Assistant Director Bradley Moore, I've been charged with apprehending this serial killer, the Chess Murderer, I believe the media have named him. What can you tell me, Detective?"

"Nothing."

"Nothing!" He glared at the detective. "So after all these man hours of NYPD time, you've not come up with anything. It's no wonder we've been asked to take it over. What the hell do you people do down at the Precinct?"

Gabriel ignored him. This was a guy who got off on bullying subordinates. Not that he was subordinate to an FBI chair polisher.

"We're sending a sketch artist, some people in Washington Square Park saw a guy that may have been the perp. With any luck we'll have something to circulate later today."

"You don't circulate anything, Detective. Anything you get, it comes to us, savvy?"

De Sade shrugged. "You got it. Was there anything else?"

"You in a hurry to go somewhere, Detective?

"Yes, I am."

"Something more important than this investigation?"

"Congressman Carson and Police Chief Oliver Simpson, they'll be waiting for me down in Arizona. They've asked me to go down there. I can stay longer, but you'll need to explain it to them."

Moore had made a career out of playing office politics, so he knew when de Sade had trumped his ace.

"I guess it'll be ok, if you've found nothing there's no point in wasting any more time. If there is anything you think of that can help us, you can let Joe here know."

"I'll do that."

He turned on his heel and walked out, and Joe followed. After the door had closed, the FBI agent smiled.

"That was the shortest meeting on record. He was hoping you'd be more cooperative, and maybe give him a pile of info. Enough to run down the unsub singlehanded, he smiled. It looks like I'm going to have my work cut out."

Gabriel shrugged. "I wasn't hedging in there. We really don't have much to go on. I'll pass your details on to my partner, Carlo. If anything comes in, I'll make sure he lets you know."

They shook hands at the door.

"Good luck down in Arizona. From what I hear you may need it."

De Sade wanted to press him to ask what he'd heard, the

prospect of having Faith and Galina south of the border worried him still. But he left it alone. He had problems enough without involving the FBI.

He got back to his apartment block in the late afternoon. Faith would already be on her way to Mexico, somehow he didn't want to go back to an empty apartment for an evening on his own, so he was tempted to call Jonas. But that would result in them endlessly talking about the two girls, and speculating on the trouble they could be stepping into. Instead, he decided to stock up on Schneider Kristall and watch some football on the tube, to take his mind off the many threads he was involved in that could unravel at any time. He walked into Lee Fat's minimart.

"Hi, Lee. How's the stock of my favorite beer?"

"Is good."

What was wrong with Lee? He was normally so cheerful. Maybe he had something on his mind, didn't everyone? Maybe his partner was going somewhere damned dangerous too. He decided to be tactful and ignore it, he was certain that Chinese were sensitive about that sort of thing.

"Right. Give me a six pack."

He realized that Lee was staring at him, directly into his eyes. His face was expressionless, but the eyes weren't. What was up? He glanced at the reflection in the store window behind the countertop. Lee's store was empty of customers, no, wait. There was someone, a guy, right behind the rack of canned vegetables. A problem? He kept his voice level, chatting to Lee.

"How's trade these days, Lee?"

He stared back so that the elderly Chinese knew he had understood the message. Then he caught another reflection, yeah, a guy in a ski mask. So it was a stick up. He eased his Glock, out of the holster fixed to his waistband.

"You got any more of that under the counter, Lee?"

The man looked perplexed. "No, not under counter."

"Sure it is, you put it under there yesterday, take a look."

He moved his eyes downwards, and Lee at last got the message and ducked down behind the counter. Gabriel made a last visual check, but the store was empty of customers. Well, regular customers. He deliberately swiped a stack of bottles of the countertop, special offer, only ninety-nine cents. They fell to the floor with a smash of broken glass.

"Damn, I'm a mutt. I'll pick them up for you."

He bent down and went into action. As soon as he was out of sight of the perp, he rolled behind a nearby display stand and crept along a stack of washing powders until he estimated he was behind the guy in the ski mask. He was worried, he couldn't see him at first, but then he saw that the guy had crouched down himself, he stood up abruptly and started to walk towards the counter, armed with a sawn off shotgun. When he got there, he started muttering.

"Where the fuck is everybody? Hey you, the guy that knocked over the bottles, where the hell are you?"

Gabriel worked his way right behind him. "Hold it, armed police. Drop it, you don't stand a chance."

It appeared to happen in slow motion. The guy swung around and loosed off a shot, but already de Sade's Glock had spoken. Two shots cracked out, and by the time the finger tightened on the trigger of the shotgun, he was already falling, dying. The pellets went wide, boring rows of tiny holes in the ceiling. De Sade crouched down, pulled away the shotgun and checked the pulse, but he was dead.

"You can stand up now, Lee. You'd better call 911."

The Chinese storekeeper stood up slowly. "Did you kill him?"

"Yeah, he won't bother you anymore."

"I am in your debt, Detective."

"Nah, that's what I get paid for, Lee. Just make the 911 call. I'll wait here until the uniforms turn up."

By the time he'd finished dealing with the formalities, it was getting late. He said goodnight to a pathetically grateful Lee Fat, then went up to his apartment. He felt depressed, he was on his own, it was late, he was tired, Faith was on her way to one of the most dangerous spots on earth, and he'd just killed man. Today would go down as one of the worse days he's had recently.

* * *

"My name is Father Juan. Welcome to our church, and welcome to Nogales. Did you have a good journey?"

Both of them were already perspiring, they'd transferred from the air conditioned environment of Phoenix International to an air conditioned Chevrolet, but the short walk to the hot, humid church was enervating. They were standing in the Church of the Blessed Virgin, in Nogales. It was ornately decorated, filled with gilded woodwork, spun tapestries and painted statuettes. A little garish for North American tastes, but both Faith and Galina owed allegiance to the Eastern Orthodox Church, which was no stranger to the ornate and overblown decor. Sunlight shone through the stained glass windows, picking out the dust motes that rose as they walked. Faith and Galina shook hands with the priest, who's English, thankfully, was very good. He was quite short and stocky, like many Mexicans, and his face looked almost pure Aztec. His hair was almost jet black and cut in a peasant fringe. But his smile was pleasant enough, and his dark brown eyes were warm and welcoming.

"We did, thank you Father. It is a beautiful church, really lovely."

"I'm glad you like it. I'm afraid the town is not so beautiful, I'm sure you're aware of the problems we have here?" He stared at them intently. "You know of course not to venture out of your hotel after dark?" They both nodded. "Good, it is not safe. When would you like to see the storeroom? I imagine it will take you some time to inventory and value the items there?"

"Yes, it probably will," Galina replied. "But we do try to work fast, so we won't be in your way for too long. Could we see it straight away?"

"Of course. Our only requirement is to raise the money as soon as possible, so the sooner the better for us. I don't know if you noticed, but the roof of our church is beginning to sag, it needs replacing. We also have a problem with woodworm infestation. Some people say that it is only the woodworm holding hands that keeps the structure in place." He smiled. "We are hoping to raise enough money to do both things."

"We will give you a fair price for the articles we buy, of that we can assure you."

"I appreciate that. You are of the Catholic faith?"

"Kind of," Galina smiled. "Eastern Orthodox."

"A church with a history as old as ours," he nodded.

"Some would say older," Faith interjected. "But we're

not counting."

Father Juan looked uncertain. "Let me show you the storeroom."

He led them through the back of the church to the left side of the altar. There were three stone steps, and a heavy, oak door. He unlocked it and they went through a long passageway. At the end was a further oak door, with heavy iron fittings. The priest unlocked the door and switched on the overhead light. They were faced with what looked like a junk store, but this one was filled with a glorious and muddled selection of religious artifacts. The effect was stunning. Crucifixes, statuettes, candlesticks by the score, paintings, robes and altar cloths. Most of it was junk, worn, threadbare and faded. And yet, there were sure to be some pieces of value. Father Juan looked anxious.

"What do you think? I was so certain it was worth a lot of money, but seeing it now, I'm not so sure."

Galina tried to re-assure him. "You're quite correct. No doubt much of it will prove to be almost valueless. But usually we find there are a few pieces that are worth much more, and so until we can make a full inventory and valuation we'll have to reserve judgment. Don't worry, Father, we've all seen much worse."

"The shroud is here."

They both looked at Faith. She was standing motionless, staring towards the corner of the storeroom.

"Yes, I believe there is an old burial shroud." He laughed. "But I'm afraid there's no provenance for it, it's without doubt an old fake."

He hadn't understood that strange note in her voice, but Galina had. It wasn't a question. When she said 'the shroud is here', that's what she'd meant, a statement. And she didn't mean a fake.

"Faith, we can start doing the inventory tomorrow, there's a lot to do."

"Yes. We should pray before we leave this room."

"Pray?" The priest was surprised.

"It is a church, Father. Surely Catholic churches say prayers," Galina said, a little more tartly than she'd intended.

"Oh, yes, of course. I'm sorry. I have been too long in this town and seen too many ungodly acts. I'm not used to my visitors wanting to pray." He put his hands together and closed his eyes.

"God of mercy, you know the secrets of all human hearts, for you know who is just and you forgive the repentant sinner. Hear my prayer in the midst of destruction; give me patience and hope."

Both of them recognized the prayer. It was the prayer for hope in the midst of destruction.

"Are things truly that bad here in Nogales, Father?" Galina asked when he'd finished.

He looked at her, obviously surprised at her question. "Are they that bad? No, I wouldn't say that. They're worse, a hundred times worse, a thousand times worse." He sighed. "But we will overcome. If we survive."

"May I join you?"

The two girls whirled to look at the door. A man was standing there, or more specifically, a monk. As they stared at him, he removed his woolen cowl, his head came into view. His face was leathery and lined, with deep wrinkles that suggested a hard and austere lifestyle. No doubt a monk in Nogales would find life to be pretty tough. He was very thin and tall, well over six feet. His gray hair was tonsured and he stared at them from a pair of twinkling blue eyes. He looked old, seventy years or more, but they afterwards found out he was sixty four. Father Juan hastened to introduce him.

"This is Brother Sebastian, Sebastian von Braun. He is attached to this church and helps out with much of our outreach work. Brother Sebastian, this is Faith Ward and Galina Polotsova, they are here to inventory and hopefully purchase the contents of the storeroom."

He didn't reply at first, he was staring intently at Faith, as if he'd seen her before. She looked embarrassed and he averted his gaze.

"I'm sorry, it's just that I thought I recognized you," he apologized.

"I don't think we've met before," Faith replied in a puzzled tone.

"No, we haven't. That isn't what I meant. How long will you be here for?"

"As long as it takes, a few days, I guess."

His accent was curious, he spoke perfect English but with an accent that was a mix of German and American.

"Von Braun," Galina said, looking at him with interest. "So you're German?"

He smiled. "I was born in Germany, but I have spent most of my life outside of my home country. For the past thirty years I have been here in Mexico. And by the way, I don't use the 'von' part of my name. I keep telling Father Juan, but I think he believes it lends the church a touch of class to have a Junker name on the staff. Just call me Sebastian."

It was strange, he looked more like a former soldier than a monk, but they let it go. "Very well, Sebastian it is.

What did you mean, you thought you recognized me?"

"Perhaps I meant a kindred spirit, someone with an interest in religious artifacts. It is a personal hobby of mine to study religious art and relics." He looked away as he spoke, he couldn't meet her eyes. It was clear he meant something else. "Perhaps I could be of some assistance, I would be more than happy to assist with your inventory. It is a labor I would enjoy."

"Do you know much about these particular items?" Galina asked him. "Someone with some local knowledge of the history of this stuff would be very helpful."

He hesitated for a moment. Then he replied, "Only some of it. Not all."

They arranged to start work the following morning. Father Juan gave them the keys so that they could have access when they needed it without referring to him for entrance. They said goodbye to the two men and left the church, got into their car and drove to the Hotel Plaza, which Father Juan had recommended to them as the best in Nogales. It was not impressive. They walked up a filthy stairway to their floor as there was no elevator. Outside the double room they'd been given there was water leaking through the ceiling onto the carpet, where there seemed to be some variety of local fungus growing. When they checked the two single beds, the top sheet on one of them had a huge hole in it. The other bed's bottom sheet was so thin they could see the mattress through the thin material. They exchanged glances. It was going to be an interesting stay. The bathroom was bearable, although grimy and dilapidated. Both women unpacked, and decided to explore as there was still some daylight left. They went outside and found that the grounds had trash everywhere, and the pool was extremely dirty.

"We won't be doing any swimming," Galina commented wryly. "I don't think I'm up to date with my shots."

"Maybe it's just as well. From the look of that storeroom we're not going to have much spare time. And even if we did, I don't think we'd spend it here."

"You mean in the hotel?"

"I guess I meant Mexico," Faith smiled.

They decided to take a stroll around the town before it got dark. They asked the desk clerk for directions.

"You're sure?" He asked doubtfully. "There is not much to see."

"We just want to take a look around. We're not after anything specific."

"But it is not safe for two American women to walk alone in the town, not even in the day."

"I'm not American, I'm Russian," Galina corrected him.

"Russian! We do not get many Russians here in Nogales."

"I wonder why that is," she said with a deadpan delivery. "We'll be fine, no worries."

He directed them to the nearby town center. They were already on the main street. All they had to do was walk along the Alvaro Obregon, the main street, until they came to the shopping area. There were no malls, it was mainly low rise, low rent, with a few dusty stores, most of them boarded up. The streets were crowded with battered old cars, and a few more modern American trucks.

"Ladies, you must be new in town. Would you wish for a guide to show you the sights? Allow me to introduce myself, I am Javier Garcia, I can offer a range of services to help foreign visitors."

A Mexican man of about twenty five, lean and dark. He wore jeans and a T-shirt that was designed to show off his muscular body. Doubtless the local girls would be impressed. His thin, pencil moustache was laughable, in New York City he would have been called a Spic. Though maybe not to his face, he looked tough enough. He also looked like trouble.

"No, we're fine, thank you," Galina replied with a smile.

"It's no trouble." He fell in and walked beside them. "For example, if you're looking for jewelry, genuine Mexican Indian pieces, I can show you where to go. I know the best bars and restaurants. I can even get you a good discount."

"No thanks." Galina gave him a hard look, and they increased their pace. He kept up.

"What's the matter? Am I not good enough for you? You don't like Mexican men?"

"We're fine on our own, thanks."

He grabbed Galina's arm. "I can help you, believe me, it would be best for you to let me show you around. You shouldn't disrespect me, believe me, it could be dangerous for you."

His face had changed. It had become darker, and where it had been pseudo-politeness it was now threatening. "Really, I'm only trying to help, if you…"

The girls stopped. "Let go of my arm, now!" Galina snapped at him. "I won't tell you again."

He kept hold of her. "If you want me to go you must pay me compensation for lost trade. Fifty dollars, that's all. Is cheap."

She swung around on her heel, took hold of his arm

and twisted. The Mexican spun around and crashed to the ground. She put her foot on his neck and applied pressure.

"I warned you, buster. Are you going to leave us alone or do I have to really hurt you?"

"No, no, I leave you alone. Let me go!"

She removed her foot. "Just stay away from us, next time I'll hit you where it really hurts."

He nodded, his face dark with anger, and they walked on. Faith grimaced, "I don't think he enjoyed that. He's likely to cause trouble if we run into him again. He may even go and round up some of his friends to help him next time."

"In that case, we'd better make sure we're ready for it, or anything else that we run into in this crappy place. We need guns."

"Guns! Where would we get those in Nogales?"

"There."

She was pointing at a bar. If there was a building that could be called a dive, this was it. Outside, half a dozen Mexican youths were horsing around with a couple of girls who looked more than willing. Inside, it was dark and dusty. The barman looked startled at the sight of two American women in his place.

"What do you want, ladies?" he muttered.

"Two glasses of cold orange juice," Galina replied. She fixed him with her eyes and indicated that she wanted to speak quietly. "And two small automatic pistols. There's three hundred dollars if you can fix it up before we drink our juice."

He looked doubtful. "What are you, cops?"

"Nuns," she replied. "Do you want our money or not?"

He sneered. "Nuns." He looked around the bar and

saw what he wanted. "Alright. The guns will cost you a thousand dollars for the two."

"Five hundred, that's our price. And they'll both need to have full clips. That's it buddy, take it or leave it. We can always go on to the next bar."

He nodded. "Ok, ok. Wait there."

He put their juice on the dirty countertop and walked to a table in the dim corner of the bar. He spoke to a man who sat in the shadows. They saw his head nod once, a youth stood up and walked out the back door. Five minutes later he was back clutching a plastic shopper. He gave it to the barman, who returned to them.

"I have two Beretta Bobcats. Full clips, they're good guns. Seven hundred for the two, not a cent less. They're valuable guns. Take it or leave it."

"Show me."

Galina peeked into the bag. The two small pistols looked ideal, easy to conceal and packing a good enough punch with their .25 rounds.

"We'll take them."

She handed over the cash, a thousand dollars with his finder's fee. The pistols fitted into her purse and they got up and started to leave.

"Hey, you didn't pay for the juice," the barman shouted.

"I reckon we're a few drinks in credit," Galina called to him. "I wouldn't push it buddy."

Outside, the light was beginning to fade. They headed back to the hotel, careful to avoid the gangs that were starting to assemble on the street corners as daylight faded and the dark cloak of night came to Nogales to hide the mean, filthy streets and the even meaner and filthier people who occupied them. In the hotel, they both slept poorly, for the deadbolt on the door didn't work. They put a chair against the door and kept their pistols under the pillow. Doors opened and closed all night, it was obvious that the hotel was in use for the oldest profession in the world. In the morning they rose early. The shower didn't work, so they made the best of the water taps in the basin. Then they left to head for the Church of the Blessed Virgin, but Brother Sebastian was waiting for them in the street outside the hotel. He stared at Faith with an intensity that was almost startling.

"I thought I'd walk you to the church, it's such a beautiful morning. Unless you plan to drive."

"Thank you, Brother, a walk would be good. It's very kind of you to accompany us."

"Believe me, it's a treat for me. It's rare that two young women as pretty as you two visit the church." He stared again at Faith. "You know what's in that storeroom, don't you?"

She hesitated. Then said," Yes, I believe I do."

They began walking along the street, the Alvaro Obregon. At this early hour it was already busy, laborers on their way to work on the farms and in the few factories that still operated in the town. The monk was partly right, for it was almost a beautiful morning.

CHAPTER FOUR

De Sade checked through the arrivals procedure at Phoenix International Airport. An older guy stood waiting for him, carrying a card with his name on it. The guy looked to be a Native American, with walnut skin, and black hair in a ponytail. He was of medium height and wiry, fir looking. He wore faded jeans and a tartan shirt, with a bead necklace showing above the open collar. A gofer, presumably, Gabriel assumed he handled the manual work in the police headquarters. He held out his hand.

"I'm Gabriel de Sade."

The other guy took it. "David Whitehorse, Phoenix PD. They sent me to pick you up."

He had an unmarked cruiser parked in a prohibited zone. He took hold of de Sade's overnighter and stowed it in the trunk. Gabriel got in the front, not wanting the guy to sit him in the back. He hated that kind of master servant crap. Whitehorse started the engine and drove away without uttering another word. When they were on the highway that led into the city center, de Sade decided to try and make conversation. The landscape was desert, flat and uninspiring, and he needed something to break the monotony.

"So what do you do for the Phoenix PD, Mr. Whitehorse?"

"I'm a detective, same as you, and the name's David."

So much for his powers of deduction, he grinned to himself.

"Right. What are the main crime problems around here?"

The man was silent for almost a minute, so long that Gabriel thought he wasn't going to answer. Was this the silent Indian treatment?

Then he spoke. "What you'd expect. Human trafficking across the border, drugs, illegal weapons, that kind of thing. I gather you're here to show us how it's done in New York."

Was that a hint of criticism? He couldn't blame the guy. They'd have felt the same in New York if an out of town cop was drafted in to show them how to improve the clear up rates.

"It's nothing formal, and it sure isn't my choice. Some bigshot politician wanted a view from the other side, so to speak."

"Politicians." Whitehorse almost spat out the word.

"Yep, politicians. Like death and taxes, they're a fixture."

He kept driving, and Gabriel thought he'd gone silent again. Then his head turned slightly.

"What's happening in New York right now? What's the big story?"

Gabriel told him about the hunt for the Chess Killer. He didn't feel particularly proud when Whitehorse asked him about leads.

"Nothing, zip, nada. This guy is real clever; he's going to take a lot of catching. You got anything like that around here?"

"We get 'em from time to time, yeah. We had the Baseline Killer not too long ago. He worked the Phoenix metro area up to 2006. Perp committed nine counts of first degree murder in addition to fifteen sexual assaults on women and young girls, kidnapping, armed robbery, you name it."

"You collared him?"

"We did, yep. Guy called Goudeau. He was convicted on all counts. He's on Death Row right now, waiting for the big injection."

He drove on, and went silent again. "What's on your mind, Detective?"

Gabriel came to with a start. He'd been dozing; the endless desert had that kind of hypnotic effect on people who passed through it. "It's Gabriel. What do you mean, what's on my mind?"

"Something's worrying you, you've got the look."

He grinned. "Is that some kind of Indian thing, reading minds?"

Whitehorse chuckled. "It's a detective thing, is all. And yeah, I'm Indian, Navajo. I'm only a part time mind-reader.

He'd been thinking about Faith and Galina. They were so near, and yet stuck down in Nogales far enough away that he couldn't keep an eye out for them.

"What's Nogales like?"

"Nogales? It's right down south, on the Mexican border. It's ok. Why?"

"I meant Mexican Nogales."

Whitehorse visibly shuddered. "Mexican Nogales, now that's a different ball game. You want it straight?"

Gabriel nodded. "Call it as it is."

"Ok. It's a shithouse. Crime, drugs, prostitution, human trafficking and murder. That's Nogales."

"Yeah, that's what I'd heard. So it's not so good?"

"The only good part is the view in your rearview mirror as you drive away from the place. You got a case down there?"

"No, my girlfriend is down there, on a business trip."

He told David about Faith and Galina's trip to Nogales. The detective frowned.

"They may be ok, but I wouldn't want any woman of mine down there."

"They can take care of themselves. They're pretty good, ex-military and ex-FBI."

"They need to be, there's a lot of cops and Feebies have bitten the dust down in Mexican Nogales."

Gabriel made a decision, there and then. He took out his cell and called Jonas, it was time to get the girls some backup. The number rang half a dozen times and went to voicemail. He left a message for Jonas to contact him and hung up.

"You're looking for someone to go down there?" Whitehorse asked him.

"Yeah, something like that."

"He'd better take a small army with him if he goes."

"Jonas is a small army."

Phoenix PD was a huge, modern slab of concrete. Bland and featureless, it was a metaphor for the state itself. Whitehorse took him past reception and in the elevator up to the Chief's office. He knocked and a voice shouted at them to enter. When they walked in, there were two men in the office. A man behind the desk in Police Chief's uniform, and a civilian in a designer Italian suit, the effect ruined by the garish handmade snakeskin boots. Whitehorse made the introductions.

"Chief, this is Detective de Sade. Detective, this is Chief Simpson and Representative Carson, one of our Arizonan Congressmen."

The politician spoke first. "Glad you could come, Detective. I'm Max Carson, the guy that dragged you away from New York. And this is our Chief, Oliver Simpson. He's the guy I don't envy, trying to keep the scum off the streets of our city."

Gabriel nodded a greeting. The chief was paunchy, too many years sat behind a desk, moving up the ladder until he got to the top. On the way, there would have been too many doughnuts to fill the empty feeling in the guts brought on by stress. Congressman Carson, by contrast, obviously kept himself in trim, he was tall and tanned. The boots would have cost him anything from five hundred to a thousand dollars, maybe he fancied himself as a cowboy, probably he spent a lot of time outdoors working on his image to please the voters. Carson checked his watch.

"I only stayed to say hi, I'll call in later in the week and see how you're getting on." He fixed Gabriel with a piercing gaze. "And I want to see the Chief's jail bursting with captured felons, you hear?"

He slapped Gabriel on the back, waved to the Chief and left the office. David Whitehorse was totally ignored. Maybe Carson didn't pursue the Indian vote.

"Maybe you can take a look around the town, see some of our guys in action, so to speak," the Chief growled.

"And then give us a heads up on the way you do things up in the big city. Not that I think it'll make a coyote's fart of a difference. My department here is tight, runs like a Swiss watch. But we've got to keep the politicians happy. Now, I've got a shit load of work to get on with, so don't let me detain you good folks."

They took the hint and left. Gabriel had caught the distinctive smell of Bourbon on the Chief's breath. Interesting. David showed him to a desk.

"This is where I work. Where do you want to start?"

"Phoenix International departures?"

Whitehorse smiled. "Yeah, I'm with you there. I gather you worked out what kind of shitload of work the Chief has going on?"

"About a forty degrees proof caseload?"

"That's about it. He likes to knock back the sauce, I'll say that."

"Does it harm his work?" Gabriel asked.

Whitehorse chuckled. "What work?"

"I get it. Look, David, I've no idea what I'm doing here. Suppose we take that unmarked car and you show me the city, give me a better idea of what you're up against. Then I can send in a report and get back to where I belong."

"Sure thing. It's still signed out to me, we may as well go."

They went down to the car park and climbed into the cruiser and drove away. Gabriel took out his cell and tried Jonas, but again he was directed to voicemail. It wasn't like him to be out of touch, or to fail to answer a message. He decided to try later. David sensed his concern.

"I gather you're really worried about your girlfriend?"

Gabriel nodded. "Yeah, I didn't realize it was as bad as

you say. They could be in over their heads."

"It's not far away, if anything comes up you can always drive down there in a couple of hours."

"I hear you, but I'm hoping that nothing does come up. I'll give them a call."

This time the call was answered.

"Gabriel, how's things in New York City?"

He told her where he was.

"Phoenix? It sounds like you're following us south."

"No, it's an official thing. I'm here to liaise with the local cops here in Phoenix."

"Right." He heard the humor in her voice. "Like showing them how to beat a confession out of them without showing any marks?"

"I don't think they need any lessons in extracting confessions down here. The problems they have here are pretty bad. It's not a place for bleeding heart liberal policing methods. But tell me, how are things in Nogales?"

"Wonderful!" He heard the enthusiasm in her voice and was pleased. "We've got a roomful of beautiful things to look at, and one or two that are really special."

"Special? Like what?"

"You wouldn't believe it if I told you. This is strictly for believers."

"Try me."

"No, not yet, not until we're surer. There's a lot of work to do yet."

"I tried to get in touch with Jonas, has Galina heard from him?"

"No, I don't think so. What did you want with Jonas?"

"Nothing really, just a chat," he replied, but he knew as he said it that she knew exactly what he'd wanted.

"We're fine, Gabriel. We don't need Jonas. We can take care of ourselves. Look, I have to go, we're about to examine the prize exhibit."

"Yeah, what's that?"

She hesitated for a moment. When she spoke again, her voice was different. Serious, even awestruck. "It's a shroud."

"A what?"

"A burial cloth."

"Ok, yeah." He tried and failed to put some enthusiasm into his voice.

"It truly is, Gabriel, if it is what we think it is."

"You mean like the Turin Shroud?"

"Not the same, but something like that, yes. I have to go, love you."

She hung up, and he was left to think about what she'd said.

"Trouble?"

He looked across at David. The Indian detective looked concerned.

"No, I don't think so. I'd be happier if I could get hold of my partner, Jonas. He's a handy man to have around if things go wrong."

"Is he another cop?"

"Jonas?" He smiled. "No, we served together in Afghanistan. He's a freelance right now."

"So what were you, Green Berets?"

"Delta Force."

"Right. So you saw some action, I guess."

"Yeah, I've fired a few shots." He looked at the street they were driving along. "Which part of the city are we driving through now? It looks interesting."

David chuckled. "Interesting, yeah, I like that word. We're in South Phoenix. It can get pretty hairy around here, especially at night. Maryvale, Tolleson, parts of Mesa and Sunnyslope, that's in the center. We've got a huge Mexican immigrant population, and many of them are transient, passing through after jumping the border on their way to find work in the Northern states."

"So they're bad, the Mexicans?"

"Not at all. There are as many good ones as in any other culture or race. And as many scumbags. We've got 'em all here, it's a kind of melting pot. Throw in the huge profits to be made from drugs, trafficking people and guns, and you've got something more explosive than C4. Those Mexican drug gangs, they're armed to the teeth. If they come over the border, we have to call out the military on occasion, the governor lets us use the National Guard when it's too much for us to handle. It's strictly unofficial, of course. Have you been over to Mexico lately?"

Gabriel shook his head. "Not for a long time, no, and then it was in the South of Mexico."

His thoughts drifted back to the operation they'd conducted just after they got back from a tour in Afghanistan. A group of gun runners were based in Campeche, bringing shipments of arms in from Cuba and selling them on to some of the worst of the drug cartels that operated in Mexico and the US. These weren't ordinary arms, like assault rifles and pistols. The cartels had decided they needed heavier weaponry to take on the police and the army. Contacts in Cuba sold them Soviet equipment, anti-aircraft guns, land mines and even shoulder launched missiles. They'd been transported C-130 to an area three miles inland and made a HALO drop, landing as close to their objective as they dared. HALO was 'High Altitude, Low Opening,' a method of clandestine insertion they'd used many times before. The landing went like clockwork. There were ten of them in the team. They made their way to the coastal hacienda of the kingpin, the Mexican who ran the whole operation. He had an underground warehouse close to his mansion, where the weapons were stored. Local police and Federales were heavily bribed to stay away, and so the only way was the direct way. Jonas had picked the lock of the warehouse and set explosive charges. But that was only half of the mission. The guy had a family, and they'd timed the mission to coincide with a visit to cousins in Mexico City. Their intercepts had told them that the wife and children would be away, only the head honcho would be in residence, together with some of his soldiers. It was one of those times when everything went right. The timer set of the explosives and the men came running out to find out what was happening. They had four sniper rifles trained on the house, and they picked off the men one by one, until only the leader was left. He ran out, with his arms held high. He knew exactly what they'd done, and he shouted to them.

"Please, I'll give you what you want. I have a wife and children, do not do this. Tell me what make this right, I'll give you anything."

The final outrage that had impelled their leaders to plan this mission was a raid on a bank in Tucson. The bank robbers planned to use a missile to open a stubborn vault door. During the raid, two children were killed. They were with their mother, holding her hand. She watched in disbelief as her children were both hit by stray bullets from a MAC-10. Gabriel stood up and walked towards the

Mexican. The man saw the soldier approaching, covered in weapons and armor. He knew that he faced death, but he still tried.

"Please," he screamed. "Tell me what can fix this."

Gabriel emptied his M4-A1 assault rifle into the man's body. Then he walked up to check that he was really dead, his orders were to get confirmation. He took a picture with his cellphone and sent it back to Washington. Then he leaned over the body and spoke a two word epitaph. "It's fixed."

He realized that David was speaking. "What was that?"

"I was pointing out one of our seriously bad guys. Over there, Ricardo Valdez."

Gabriel looked to where the detective was pointing. A Mexican guy, aged about in his late twenties. He leaned nonchalantly against the hood of a chromed, bright yellow Hummer H1. The guy was looking back at them, a confident sneer on his face; he'd made them before they even got near. He was surrounded by other Hispanic males, perhaps twenty of them in all. By the way they stood and carried themselves, it was obvious they all possessed concealed weapons.

"He's a drug dealer, I imagine?"

David shrugged. "Drugs, people trafficking, murder, and he's got Phoenix sewn up with prostitution. Guns, I guess as well, although we've never pulled any of his people for illegal weapons sales. He's one mean mother, if you get my drift."

"American citizen?"

"Oh yeah, he bought his Green Card, no problems. His people are all legitimate too, he offers them a Green Card to come over here."

"Really? That's generous of him."

"Not really. When he needs to have someone killed, he recruits a Mexican to cross the border. If they pull it off ok, they get their papers."

"So they're all killers, his people?"

"Every last one of them, yeah. If you ever tackle that gang, you need more than a peashooter, that's for sure. A unit of Air Cavalry maybe would be a good idea."

They drove on and David finished his brief introduction to the movers and shakers in the criminal community of Phoenix. When they were heading back to police HQ, he looked across at Gabriel.

"You're really worried, aren't you? About those girls down in Nogales."

He nodded. "Yeah, I guess I am. Should I be?"

"As I said, I would be," the Indian replied. "It's easy to get into trouble down there and hard to get out of it. I'd try hard to get this partner of yours to check up on them. Are you going back to your hotel now? I can drop you back there."

"Yes. I'll unpack and take a shower. It's been a long day. Can you pick me up in the morning?"

"Sure, I'll be there at eight."

He climbed out of the cruiser outside the hotel, took his bag out of the trunk and registered into the hotel. The Phoenix PD had booked him into a Holiday Inn, about two miles from the city center. When he got to his room he found it to be clean and comfortable, with a high pressure shower that was fierce enough to bring a corpse back to life. He dressed with a clean shirt and called Jonas again. Nothing. Where the hell was he? Missing one or two calls was odd, missing more than two suggested that something was seriously wrong. Christ, what a situation! Faith and Galina in one of the world's shitholes across the Mexican border, and the one man he'd always been able to rely on was missing. Unless Jonas was on a clandestine mission, of course. He relaxed a little. It was the most likely explanation. There was only one other reason for him not answering his cellphone, and that didn't need to be considered. If something had happened to Jonas, something bad, they all had problems.

He needed to take his mind off things before they drove him crazy. There were only three outlets to remove that kind of pressure, and two of them, booze and sex, weren't in the running. He called down to reception.

"Do you have a gym here in the hotel?"

"On the first floor, Sir. Call down to reception and we'll show you the way."

"I'll need to borrow some sweats, I came down here light."

"No trouble, you can borrow everything you need."

He spent the next hour and a half working up a sweat and venting his frustration. The fitness room was bright, smart and modern, with every modern fitness appliance known to man and television screens to take your mind off of aching muscles. He showered for the second time and went back to his room. He knew what he should do. He needed to get reception to hire him a car so that he could drive down to Nogales, cross the border and keep an eye on Faith and Galina if things looked like they were cutting up rough. Yet he was here professionally, at the behest of a Congressman, no less. If he took off after the first day, the shit would really hit the fan. Besides, Faith would go crazy if he demonstrated such a lack of trust in their ability to look after themselves. He checked his Glock, and made sure that the clip was full and the spare was also full and easily accessible in his pocket. Then he thought, 'What the hell!' He could at least hire the car, if there was a need to get down there in a hurry, he'd be ready to take off. He ran down the stairs to reception, feeling the blood pulsing around his body, he was still on a high after the session in the gym. The clerk eyed him curiously. Gabriel realized he must have looked slightly manic, covered in sweat, his hair awry, and a fixed gleam in his eye.

"I need a car."

"Of course. You have a license, Sir?"

He wanted to rip the guy's head off. What kind of a question was that?

"Yeah, I've got a license."

"Name, Sir?"

"Detective Gabriel de Sade."

The man looked up. "Oh, yes, the New York cop. I didn't recognize you. What would you like to hire?"

"The fastest car you have."

"It'll be expensive, a fast car. Our compacts are much cheaper, and we have a special this week…"

"I want it to be fast. The best."

"Right, Sir. I'll give them a call and see what they have."

He talked on the phone for a few minutes, and then looked up. "They say they have a Cadillac CTS-V, that's the fastest vehicle available at present."

"A Cadillac? Jesus Christ, I wanted a fast mover, not a motorized armchair. It doesn't sound like the kind of car that'll fit the bill at all."

"One moment, Sir, I'll speak to them again."

He spoke for another minute, and then turned back to him. "Yes, that's the one you want. They say it's faster than most of the Porsches and Ferraris."

"Ok, then, that sounds like what I need, I'll take it. Would you ask them to bring it around here?"

"Certainly. Do we put it on your bill?"

He thought about the bill. Technically, it was being paid by Phoenix PD. They'd have a coronary when they saw the bill for a rental like that, but it was too bad. If he was needed in a hurry, he had to have the wheels. Besides, he was doing Phoenix PD a favor. He didn't want to be here in the first place. At worst, they'd tell him not to come back. That suited him. He went back up to his room and tried Jonas again. Nothing. Then he tried Faith. This time there was no answer.

CHAPTER FIVE

She was beautiful, dusky, smooth skin and huge, moist brown eyes. Her dark hair shone in the light of the table lamp next to the bed, and he felt himself getting excited. It was a pity about the cheap motel room. He'd have liked something better for what he had in mind. He ignored the cheap furnishings, the stained bedspread, he could smell her now, and his arousal took over his mind. That unmistakable musk that young women exuded when they were in a warm environment. Or when they were sexually aroused, not that he had any illusions about that. This was a strictly pay to play job. He knew she was an illegal. The stupid kid couldn't even speak any English. Fucking wetbacks, they all wanted to cross the border but they were too ignorant to learn the language. He also knew she was a virgin. It had been the price of her ticket, a free crossing in return for some easy work for the traffickers who had brought her through the tunnel. What could be easier than lying on your back and having sex with a good looking guy like him? Hell, she ought to be paying him!

He took opened the top drawer in the bedside cabinet and found the baggie of coke, just where they'd said it would be. He snorted it up both nostrils and felt his strength and power growing, as it always did.

"Here you, take some."

"No!" she shouted. "I don't do drugs."

"I couldn't give a shit what you do. Just take it."

He forced her to inhale from each nostril by holding his hand over her mouth so that she had to sucking through her nose. Her eyes widened as she felt the power of the drug course through her. Then he put his hand on her breast and felt her flinch.

"Take your top off, honey. I won't bite." Not fucking much I won't.

"Please, Señor, I am afraid. I do not want to do this."

"Sure you don't honey, but you know you gotta pay your way across the border. Either that or they'll take you back to Mexico."

"I cannot go back. My father is sick, and I have to earn money to pay the doctor."

"So get on with it. You'll earn great money working for Ricardo. He's a good guy, dear. He'll make sure you earn lots of dough to send back to your folks."

"He will?"

"Sure, I know he will."

"But I wanted to save myself for my husband."

"That's fine, if it's worth killing your father for."

"No!" Her cry of anguish was sharp and full of desperation. He loved it, yeah! He was getting harder and harder. The sheer feeling of power, literally of life and death, yeah, it was unbeatable.

"Then get your top off, darlin', and let's see what you've

got."

She started to undress. It was artless, yet the sheer naivety of her movements was thrilling. He found himself intensely aroused at the sight of her breasts, the smooth, olive skin. It was firm, warm, oh so warm. He felt giddy with the intensity of the moment.

"How old are you, darlin'?"

"I am fourteen, Señor. Is not a problem?"

He chuckled. "No problem at all, you're just the way I like 'em."

He fondled the two, beautiful, firm tits, smiling at the way she flinched and closed her eyes with embarrassment. Then he slid his hand down under the waistband of her panties. She automatically started to pull away.

"Hey, you know you want this as much as I do. Just relax, let's have some fun."

He slid two fingers inside her, and felt the tight vagina, then stopped when he reached her hymen.

"You sure are a virgin, aren't you? You're in for a lot of fun with me. Just relax and let it all happen. Lay yourself down on the bed. That's fine, close your eyes and we'll see some action here."

He lay down on top of her. Her eyes flew open when she heard the 'click' of the switchblade.

"What is that knife for? I do not want you to cut me."

"It's a little something to add to the fun, darlin'. Yeah, keep your eyes open, I want you to watch everything."

He put on a condom and guided himself inside her, felt the obstruction as he reached her hymen, saw her eyes fill with tears of pain, then he pushed past and he was inside, pumping, thrusting, oh Jesus it was good. She was crying softly, understanding the price she had to pay to keep him happy, to pay for her father's medical bills. He felt himself becoming more and more aroused. Nearly there.

"Keep those eyes open, I want you to see everything."

He was almost there. He put the blade hard against her neck.

"Please, do not hurt me."

"I'm sorry, darlin', but I have to. You see, you're gonna die. I'm gonna cut your throat with this knife. How about that?"

She went to scream, but he was ready for her and he put his hand over her mouth. He was almost there, it was time.

"Watch me, keep those eyes open!"

Then he cut, a long, red line opened up underneath her chin. He came straight away, and as ever it was astonishing, the sheer power of the moment, he felt like a god. No, he was a god. The look in her eyes, terror, realization, and then that moment when the spark left them and she was dead. It surely was the greatest thing in the world. He climbed off her and carefully began to finish the ritual. The condom was tied in a knot and he put it in a baggie to dispose of later. Then the hands, it was hard cutting through them, but he finally finished and carelessly abandoned them on the floor. He had a change of clothes in his briefcase, jeans, a windcheater and t-shirt. The clothes he'd worn here would be destroyed. There was no sense in leaving any evidence. The only things he'd kept to wear away from here were his boots. He'd made sure that they were well away from the body, so they didn't catch any stray splashes of blood. He stuffed his clothes in the briefcase and took a shower. Then he dressed in his clean stuff, made a final check of the room and pulled on his boots. No way would he lose a five hundred dollar pair of handmade snakeskin boots. He almost laughed out loud, he'd just experienced more in the past fifteen minutes than most ordinary people enjoyed in a lifetime. God, how he hated them, ordinary people. They were so small-minded. They'd never understand. There was just the one final touch and he could leave. He put a chess piece on the body, between the breasts of the rapidly cooling corpse. It was a pawn, for he judged the girl rated no more than that. The motel room was at the back of the building, he pocketed the remains of the coke, no need to waste it, and he went out through the rear exit and headed for his car, parked two blocks away. His brain, his whole body, they were on fire. It was a high like nothing else. As he walked away he was wondering what it would be like with two girls at once. Now that would be something.

* * *

They'd worked all day, dragging out dusty relics and keying in their details to a laptop. They left the small, iron trunk that lay in the corner, hidden underneath a pile of old vestments. Galina had been curious about it.

"That trunk, we should take a look before we go any further, there could be something valuable in there, something that'll make this trip worthwhile. There are a few good pieces here, but a lot of junk. We could do with a real find."

"There is something valuable in there, the shroud, but I'd like to leave it until tomorrow."

She looked at Faith, puzzled at the answer. "What do you know that I don't? You think it's authentic?"

Faith shrugged. "It's just a feeling, nothing more."

"Have you been talking to that monk? Does he know what's in the trunk?"

"I believe he does, yes."

Galina started to feel uneasy. There was something not right here. But she couldn't yet work out if it was bad or otherwise. The trunk, Brother Sebastian, and Faith's obvious unease.

"So what do we do next?"

"We've all but finished for the day. I'd like to say a prayer before we leave here."

"Wouldn't it be better praying in the church?"

"But the shroud is here, not in the church."

Faith's expression had become intense again. It was as if she was going through some kind of religious ecstasy. In a dusty old storeroom? Galina felt a surge of irritation.

"Look, you've no way of knowing that what's in the trunk is authentic. Ok, you've had a feeling about it, I understand that. But until we open that trunk and check it out we've no way of knowing even what century it came from. For all we know it could be the bed sheet from a Spanish nobleman who came over here two centuries ago."

Faith nodded. "Of course, you're right. But I would like to pray, here."

"If you wish."

She looked up. Brother Sebastian had come back silently and was watching them from the doorway. He nodded a greeting.

"Did you have a productive day?"

Galina gave him a brief smile. "It went fine, thank you. We were about to leave."

"With a prayer, I see. May I join you?"

"Of course." She turned to Faith. "Perhaps you would say the prayer."

Faith closed her eyes. "Remember, O Lord, those who have departed from this life, and those who have served Thee, and the blessed founders of the Church, and grant them rest with the Saints in Thy eternal dwellings."

Sebastian looked up sharply as she finished. "That is not a Catholic prayer."

"No, it is Orthodox Christian."

"A prayer for the dead, I gather. To whom did you dedicate it?" He looked to the back of the storeroom, to the corner where the trunk lay, still undisturbed beneath the pile of old vestments. "To one of the blessed founders of the church?"

"Yes."

They left the church and began walking back to the hotel. The streets were busier than ever, teeming with people of every age and social class. Laundrywomen, cleaners, farm laborers, store clerks, as well as the underclass of Mexican society. The drug dealers, the prostitutes and the pimps. And the scam artists. They saw him watching them, Javier Garcia. He was leaning against a beat-up truck, surrounded by four young men of similar age.

"Hey, 'putas', you come here for nice fuck fuck from handsome Mexican boys?"

The tried to walk past, but Javier and his friends blocked their way. He stared at them. The malevolence that oozed out of him was thick and tangible.

"You tricked me, but it isn't going to work now. I have my friends to make sure we play fair. Now, you owe me money for my work."

"What work would that be?" Galina asked. Her voice was calm. But icy. Faith recognized the tone, the Mexican would do well do take note of it.

"My work as a guide, showing you around Nogales. You cancelled the contract, that's your right, but you must still pay me. The price is now a thousand dollars. I'll bet you've got more than that in your pretty purses, ladies. I want cash." He looked around at his friends. "We don't take American Express down here, do we muchachos?"

The laughed, and Galina smiled with them. Javier's face went bleak.

"What's it going to be, do you pay what you owe me or do we take our payment another way?" He was raking his eyes up and down their bodies, and his buddies laughed again. "Are you gonna pay or do we do it the hard way?"

Galina smiled. "Javier, let's not make this unfriendly. I want you and your friends to just leave us alone and we won't hurt you."

His jaw dropped. "Hurt us? You fucking bitch, I'll show you who does the hurting. Get them!"

Javier's friends surged forward. Their arms reached up to get a hold on them and drag them down. Faith, a former FBI Special Agent, twisted to one side and took the leading man's arm and twisted. He screamed and went down, his shoulder dislocated. The man's partner followed, she swiveled and kicked him in the groin and he dropped to the ground to join his companion. Galina took the other two. One received an elbow strike in the solar plexus that left him gasping for breath. The other guy took a high kick that smacked into his throat. He stumbled away, massaging his neck, choking and gasping. Javier watched in astonishment, then stepped back, his hand swept inside his jacket and he brought out a pistol. It looked familiar, and Galina recognized it as a Colt 1911 automatic, a weapon that was in common use the world over. He started to raise his gun. She had no choice, one moment her hand was empty, the next it had swept under her skirt and re-appeared clutching the small, .25 Beretta Bobcat she'd bought the day before. He looked uncertain.

"Don't even try it, my friend. I can put two rounds into your balls before you even pull the trigger. Give me the gun, there's a good boy. You can always live to fight another day."

Both girls could see him trembling with indecision. It was the second time his macho, Hispanic pride had been wounded. It was a hard and bitter pill to swallow. But he was not a total fool, for he lowered the gun and handed it over to her. She expertly pulled out the clip, ejected the shells, dropped them into a nearby sewer grating and gave him the gun back.

"You'd better get your friends to the clinic. They look as if they could do with some treatment."

"Who are you?" His face was a mixture of hate and astonishment. How could two mere females overcome five tough, macho hombres?

"Someone you'd do best to avoid, unless you want to add to your nightmares. Find someone else to hassle, Javier. The next time we see you we won't be so easy on you."

The Mexican hoodlum helped his comrades limp away, but a few yards up the street he turned and stared back at them. The look was purest venom. Then he walked away.

"He'll be back," Faith murmured.

"I know."

Dinner at the hotel was not a happy affair. The cuisine was some kind of a variant on the Mexican staple, rice and beans, with a little stringy chicken thrown in. They were the only diners. For most of the hotel's clients eating was the last thing on their mind. The dining room featured peeling, yellow paintwork and furniture that owed much to the wonders of handyman repairs. They had to prop their own table up with coasters to stop it swaying like a lantern in a storm.

"I could even grow to like MacDonald's if I lived in a place like this," Galina smiled.

"I've tasted better," Faith replied, pulling a face. "It's a pity you had to draw a gun on that character. Now they know you're armed. They'll assume I'm carrying too, it would have been better in this town to keep it as a surprise."

"It wasn't my choice to show the gun, he was about to take the shot."

"Whatever, we'll need to be more careful. It may be harder next time."

"Yes," Galina replied thoughtfully. "I'm wondering if it would have been better to ask Jonas to come down here with us."

"Call him, it's not too late. Besides, I know you're missing him already."

"Missed his body, anyway," Galina chuckled. She took out her cellphone and called, but the call went to voicemail. She left a message and hung up. "He'll call back when he gets the message, and I'll talk to him about coming on down here."

They ordered coffee and sat in silence for a few moments. Faith could see that her friend had something on her mind.

"What's up, Galina? You look troubled."

"Yes, I am. We're in one of the most violent towns in Mexico, which in itself is quite a feat. We've already had problems with some of the local lowlifes, and I can't get through to Jonas. He wanted to come down here with us, we should have accepted. This place is not like anywhere I've ever seen before."

"Try him again now."

She dug out her cellphone and called, but it went to voicemail again. She shrugged and put the phone back in her purse. "Maybe he'll call back later, he's obviously busy somewhere."

"Yes, of course. Is anything else worrying you?" Faith asked.

"Isn't just being in this place enough?" Galina grinned. Then she looked serious again. "Yeah, there is something else troubling me. You."

"Me? What have I done?"

"It's what is in that storeroom, something that troubles you, in the trunk. You know something more than you've told me."

"It's an old burial shroud, that's all."

"Just an old burial shroud! Yeah, I know that. But whose shroud? You can't take your eyes off the trunk, and neither can Brother Sebastian. He worries me too."

"Brother Sebastian? He seems harmless enough," Faith countered.

"Maybe, maybe not. But what's he doing here? A monk, obviously a very clever and well-educated man, attached to this church? It doesn't ring true. I mean, if this was some important chapel or cathedral, that would be understandable. But why here, in this flyspeck of a town?

It must be that trunk, or rather the shroud that's inside it. I assume there is a shroud in there, we haven't even opened it yet."

"Oh, it's there," Faith replied swiftly. "There's no doubt about that."

Galina hesitated again. Then she lowered her voice. "You don't think that this is the real thing, do you? Like the Shroud of Turin, but genuine. The shroud that Jesus was wrapped in for burial?"

"No, of course not. I know it's not that shroud."

"How could you possibly know that, when you haven't even seen it? More of your weird intuitions?"

Faith shrugged. "Intuition is not really a word I would use. It's more like messages that come to me. I just know they're true."

"Well, ok, I'll accept that for now. But how do you know it's not the burial shroud of Jesus Christ?"

"Because I know whose shroud it really is."

"Señoras!" A waiter had run up to their table. "There is a Brother Sebastian wants to speak to you."

"Invite him in," Galina smiled.

"He said it is a private matter, he wanted you to come outside to speak to him."

They exchanged glances. "This could be trouble," Faith muttered. "Remember, we're in Nogales. I don't like this."

"Maybe. Do you have your piece?"

Faith nodded at her bulging purse. "And yours?"

"Yes, I have it. Let's see what the good monk requires of us."

It was obvious why he hadn't wanted to come into the hotel restaurant. He'd been beaten, his monk's habit was torn and bloody and his face bore the cuts and bruises of a vicious attack. He limped towards them.

"Brother Sebastian! What happened?"

"Some thugs, they attacked me, there were eight of them. I came here to warn you to be careful."

"You should go to a hospital. At the very least you need to be checked over."

"No, no, I'll be fine."

"You should also contact the police. Were you robbed?"

"The police? In Nogales? I don't think that is a good idea. No, I wasn't robbed."

"So why did they do it?"

"They want me to tell them what is in the storeroom. I told them I didn't know and they wouldn't believe me."

"But, it's just a load of old religious junk," Galina objected. "There's nothing of any value to them, if they want it and they're prepared to use violence to get it, why not just let them go ahead. We don't want it if it's going to cause you a lot of trouble."

Sebastian glanced at Faith. "It's not that simple, is it? The business of the shroud?"

"It isn't the burial shroud of Jesus, if that's what you're thinking," Galina told him.

"Really?" He looked up sharply. "How do you know that?"

She was about to reply when Faith interrupted. "Because the Turin shroud has been proven to be a fake, and there's no suggestion that what's in that trunk is any more authentic. Probably a lot less so. It's not worth wasting our time on. One thing we all know, it's not the burial shroud of our Lord."

He looked at them both. "Haven't either of you felt something, a kind of an entity when you enter that room.

As if there is some kind of supernatural force. I know there's a relic in there that has a power that is beyond our understanding and I assume it's the shroud in that trunk. I guess those men have heard about it and want it for themselves."

Galina fixed him with a look of scorn. "Now I've heard everything. A religious relic that cheap hoods want to steal! No, that's nonsense. I don't believe it. Did you tell them anything about the shroud?"

He looked indignant. "Of course not. If they knew that it had any kind of value attached to it they'd break down the door and steal it."

"But it has no value! What possible value could an old, unidentified piece of burial cloth have?"

He sighed. "I'm not sure that's the whole truth. Long ago, during the time when the church was much busier than it is now, there were stories of miraculous healings. People would bring their sick relatives to pray at the Chapel of the Virgin, the railed off Lady Chapel at the side of the altar. Some said that many got better. Then, the building was damaged during a small earthquake and builders were called in to repair the chapel. They removed many of the fittings and furnishings and put them in the storeroom. Afterwards, the healings ceased. People came, but none were healed."

"When did this happen?"

"According to the records, it was in 1906, the year of the San Francisco earthquake. There were many tremors at that time."

"And you think that the burial shroud was moved out of the chapel, causing the healings to stop?"

"We know that the trunk contains an ancient burial

shroud. And we know that it was moved during the rebuilding work. If we could only authenticate it, of course, we may have a better understanding of what we have in the church."

"But Faith, you said that you…"

"That I wasn't sure what was in the trunk, yes, that's right. The source of these miraculous healings could have been anything. Or nothing, just coincidence."

Sebastian looked disappointed. "I was certain that you sensed something in that storeroom. You looked like," he searched for the words. "Like someone who had been hunting for something for a long time, and thought they had found it."

She shook her head. "I'm sorry, you must have misunderstood. We're only here to purchase a load of old relics and church furnishings. Did we find something mystical, some lost relic with supernatural powers?" She smiled broadly. "I'm afraid not, Sebastian. But if we do find anything like that, you'll be the first to know. Perhaps what you're looking for is elsewhere in the church. I assure you it's not in that old trunk."

He looked disappointed. "Very well, I must have misunderstood. Please, let me know if you do find anything that is important. It would mean a lot to me."

"We'll do that. Can we drive you to the hospital, we have a car here?"

"No, no, I'll be fine. Thank you for your kindness."

He walked away. Galina fixed Faith with a curious gaze.

"What was that all about? You were about to tell me about that shroud."

"Tell you, yes, not him."

"Father Sebastian, don't you trust him?"

"When we came out of the hotel, he had a limp. When he left, he walked normally. Would you trust him?"

"I guess not."

They went back into the restaurant. Their coffee had gone cold, and they ordered some more. It was only after the waiter had left that Galina remembered what she had been asking Faith.

"So whose shroud do you think it is?"

"I don't think anything. I know whose it is. It is the shroud of James the Just. He was the brother of Jesus, of course, and the man who was supposed to lead the Christian church after Jesus' death."

"You're sure of that?"

"Yes. That is what I've been told."

Galina hesitated to ask the obvious question. Faith was at times prone to puzzling revelations.

"So you think Sebastian is trying to identify this relic for his own purposes?"

"I'm sure of it. If he knew what it was, he'd have taken it. I'm sure he's waiting for us to authenticate it. I guess he wants confirmation of what exactly it is. I have no idea what's behind it, but I don't trust him."

"Hmm, I smell something," Galina murmured.

Faith looked around. "What? I can only smell the coffee."

"This is an altogether different odor. It's called The Vatican."

CHAPTER SIX

"There's been another one."

David Whitehorse had offered to pick him at the hotel, but he elected to drive himself. They both arrived in the Phoenix PD Car Park at the same time. The Indian detective glanced at the Cadillac sports car, but made no comment, not even a raised eyebrow. Gabriel guessed that Indians were like that. Anyway, it was their reputation. They entered the building and detected the buzz almost immediately. The desk sergeant studied them as he spoke.

"Another what?" Whitehorse looked puzzled.

"The serial killer, you know, like that last one, where he left the chess piece on the body."

The sergeant seemed satisfied with jolt his words gave them. De Sade felt icy cold. He was here, in Phoenix, Arizona? The same guy that had killed in New York? How could it be possible? They went on up to the detective's room. Plain clothes cops were milling around. The Chief came in, red faced and angry. "What the fuck is everybody doing about this killing? The locals are going nuts!"

Gabriel walked up to him. "Chief, this could well be the same guy who's doing the New York killings. We need to work together on this one."

Chief Simpson fixed him with a sneer. "Son, I thought the Feds had taken your investigation off you. Maybe they thought you weren't up to it. We aim to solve this one ourselves. Look, no outside agency is taking charge of this one. We want that 'sumbitch' nailed to the wall, not lost in some Federal bureaucracy. Now you get on with what you're supposed to be doing and we'll locate this Chess Killer for you. And when we do find him I'll stick a chessboard up his fucking asshole. And those little pieces can go up there as well!"

The Chief turned away to talk to his men and David hustled Gabriel away to his desk space.

"Ignore the Chief. He's just blowing hot air as usual. My assignment is still to work with you to look at our procedures, so let's just keep our heads down and get it done. When it's done, type out a report and go home."

"It's all bullshit, David," Gabriel growled. "There's a killer on the loose between here and my city and they're playing fucking games. The Feds in New York and the Chief here."

"Yeah, I know it seems crazy," David commiserated. "Forget it, let's get on with this job and then you can get out of here. What do you want to look at this morning?"

Gabriel spoke quietly. "Where was this woman murdered?"

Whitehorse shook his head. "Oh no, the Chief won't like you going out there."

"I don't give a damn. Besides, don't they want me to look at procedures? Ok, let's start with this particular crime scene procedure."

David thought for a moment. Then he nodded. "Yeah, ok, I guess it's no big deal. But keep it quiet, will you?"

"Sure."

Out in the car park the Indian went to climb into his unmarked car, but Gabriel stopped him.

"We'll take mine, it'll speed things up and I want to see how well it goes."

The other detective smiled. Suits me, I never thought I'd get a ride in one of these things."

De Sade started the engine and the 556 brake horse power engine purred into life. When he eased out onto the freeway the needle went straight up to a hundred, and he dropped it back to seventy.

"I'd watch out for the State Troopers, if I were you," David warned. "They're using every gadget known to science to catch speeding motorists."

"They won't give another cop a break?"

"In one of these? I doubt it. They way they see it, anyone who drives one of these can afford to pay the fines."

They pulled up outside a motel on the outskirts of town. Literally on the outskirts, the buildings ended. There was the motel, and then the endless Arizona desert. The motel had a sign outside, 'Oasis Motel – Rooms'. Some of the letters were loose and hung askew. The sign had the appearance of being built by an amateur build it yourselfer. It was a fair analogy for the motel itself.

"Pretty isolated, this place. Ideal for a murder."

David nodded. "Yeah, it is. It's not the first murder we've had here either. But nothing like this one."

They went past the yellow tape and into the room where the murder had taken place. Crime scene people were still there, on their knees searching for forensic evidence with ultra violet lamps. The body lay on the bed, and Gabriel looked at the face. She was very young and had once been very pretty too.

"She was about fourteen. A virgin, almost certainly, before she was raped and murdered. The killer cut off her hands afterwards. The bastard."

It was as if it was the ultimate indignity, almost outweighing the horror of the rape and murder. An older man faced them, tall, very thin with sparse pale blonde hair and a thin moustache. He held out his hand.

"I'm Doc Richards, the ME."

David Whitehorse made the introductions.

"Her eyes" Gabriel asked him. "I'll bet they're open. If they are, maybe the killer wanted her to see him as he climaxed. That's my guess, anyway."

"You've seen this before?"

"New York city, yeah, it looks like the same guy."

But Gabriel was puzzled. It was a long way to commute, and why would he do it? All the way from New York City to Phoenix to commit a murder? There was no reason. Then an idea occurred to him. It could be two killers. Two men who knew each other, who used the same M.O. It wasn't the most likely theory, but it was possible. It had been done before, but it posed a huge number of questions and problems for law enforcement. Finding one killer was difficult enough, but when murders were committed by more than one killer, the permutations became endless.

"I don't think it's the same guy as we have in New York City. I think you may have a copycat here in Phoenix."

David stared at de Sade. "That seems a bit of a jump. How could the guy here know which methods the other one uses and copy them? Unless they're in touch with each other."

"Or are involved with the investigations, or both."

"You think he's a cop?"

"Not he, they. It could be a cop," Gabriel explained, "But equally it could be anyone who has an inside track on the investigation. In which case you should run the cases jointly with the NYPD."

"Isn't the FBI handling the New York side?" David asked him. "You heard the Chief. He won't let them take over here, no way."

"In that case, I'm going to have to handle it myself," Gabriel fired back. "There's no way this bastard is going to run around for much longer."

The watched the ME working, taking the temperature of the body and examining it for signs of evidence. David asked him, as he was wrapping it up, "Did you get anything that may help us?"

Gabriel looked up sharply at the word 'us'. The ME shook his head. "I told the two lead detectives, they left just before you got here. This guy knows what he's doing. He doesn't leave anything lying around. No hairs, no fibers, no semen or other bodily fluids. He's one very careful hombre. Coke user, probably, certainly either him, or her or both of them, there's evidence of coke on the victim."

"Thanks, Doc. I guess we'll have to do this the hard way."

They called at the reception desk, a guy sat behind the counter in a stained wife beater t-shirt. He looked up from the television quiz show he was watching. David showed him his shield.

"What I want are the CCTV tapes from last night."

The man smirked. "That system ain't worked for the past fourteen months. I keep telling the owner but he don't give a shit."

"Right. I also need to look at your guest list from last night."

"Knock yourself out."

The guy turned the pad around so that they could see the names. It was handwritten, for it was obvious computerized management hadn't yet reached this part of the US hospitality industry. The room where the murder had occurred was registered to John Wayne.

"What did he look like?" David asked him.

"Who?"

"John Wayne."

The man shrugged. "Big guy, he rode a horse. Carried a six shooter." He smirked.

De Sade snatched at his lapels and dragged him over the counter.

"The man asked you a question, asshole."

"Hey, you can't do that, it's police brutality."

He punched him in the kidneys and the man screamed in agony. "No, that's police brutality. Now what did he look like?"

"Ok, ok, I'll tell you. Let me go."

Gabriel released him and the man dusted himself off and straightened his grubby t-shirt.

"He was about twenty, Hispanic, probably Mexican. Came here yesterday, about midday. Paid for the room, went inside and then left about ten minutes later."

"Did you see which car he drove?"

"No. He must have parked behind the building. No,

wait, I saw him coming in, that's right, he drove an old Dodge, one of those muscle cars."

"A Dodge Charger."

"Yeah, that's the one. It was red, I think, with a black roof."

"Anything else you noticed?"

"No." But he looked doubtful, and they waited. "Well, it's just an impression. You know, guys like that, they don't book rooms here to bring whores to. It's normally the older guys do that. Kids like that use the back seat of their cars. I reckon he was booking the room for someone else, that's all."

They nodded and thanked him. Driving away, David glanced across at de Sade.

"What do you want to look at now?"

"Some of the bars where these Mexican kids hang out. See if we can see a red Dodge Charger with a black roof."

"We could try looking at the mall, Metro Center, that's a hangout they use."

"That'll do to start with. Which way?"

They pulled into the Metro Center parking lot. At first Gabriel couldn't see it as a gang hangout, until David directed him to a far corner near a greasy looking bar. Several motor cycles were parked outside, together with a few trucks and beat up cars, held together by rust. A half dozen Mexicans were sat outside, smoking and drinking. They glanced at the Cadillac enviously. David Whitehorse went up to them and showed him his badge.

"Anyone touches the car, and I'm holding you all responsible. If any of you want a holiday in Maricopa, go ahead and let somebody touch it."

The Mexicans stared at them without expression, but

de Sade could see that the message had got home. They walked into the bar.

"What's the business with Maricopa?" Gabriel asked. "They didn't look too impressed."

David smiled. "I'm not surprised. Joe Arpaio, the local sheriff, brought back the chain gangs a few years ago. It's a pretty hard regime out there at Maricopa. He set up a Tent City when they ran short of space. He calls it a concentration camp, which I guess isn't too far from the truth. It gets real hot in those tents, especially when the temperature in Phoenix hits 118 degrees. They measured the temperature inside Tent City at 145 degrees, and there isn't much air con under that canvas. Some of the inmates complained that the fans weren't working, and even their shoes were melting from the heat. Joe Arpaio told them it's 120 degrees in Iraq and the soldiers are living in tents over there. They even have to wear full body armor, and they didn't commit any crimes. So the inmates could shut up about it."

"Doesn't the city have problems with lawsuits?"

"Sure, there are some. But it keeps the re-offending rate down. That means no-one complains. Except for the inmates, of course."

Gabriel peered through the gloom. A bunch of bikers were playing pool. A girl was serving behind the bar, and two tables were occupied by Latinos, typical gang banger types. They all looked up as the two detectives entered. They were unwelcome. The cops were left in no doubt that they had just invaded their space. The bar stank of stale beer, smoke and urine.

"I want your attention!" David shouted.

There were a few grumbles, and Gabriel heard, 'fucking

cops', and "shouldn't allow Indians in here,' but that was all. They all looked at the two detectives blankly, hating them, willing them to leave. They tried the Latinos first, for they were looking for a Latino.

"Who owns a red Dodge Charger with a black roof?" Whitehorse asked them.

They stared back at him.

"Ok, guys, we'll do it the hard way. This is a bust, turn out your pockets, if anyone is carrying anything illegal, you'll be taking a trip to Maricopa. Drugs, weapons, anything. I find a Kleenex and you're going down. Unless I get a name."

"It's Manuel Duarte you want," one of them shouted.

The others rounded on him. "Shut up, Manuel will fucking kill you."

"Where will we find this Manuel Duarte?"

The guy kept quiet, he'd already said too much. But both cops had seen the look on the face of the younger guy stood next to him. He knew. David beckoned to him. "You, you're under arrest."

"Me?" The kid looked astonished. "What did I do?"

"I haven't decided yet, I'll tell you later." He put the cuffs on him and they led him out of the door. They pushed him onto the back seat of Gabriel's Cadillac.

"Hombre, this is some cop wheels," he blurted out, awestruck. "Where you taking me?"

"Maricopa, hombre. They've got a nice, warm tent waiting for you."

"What the fuck? I ain't going there. Is there any way I can get out of this shit?"

"Yeah. I want to know where we can find this Manuel Duarte. Where is he?"

"Man, he'll kill me. You don't know him, he has big connections."

"So have we. Do you tell us where to go or do we book you and pack you off to Maricopa?"

"Ok, ok. He lives in Maryvale. I do not know the address, but I can show you the house. You will not tell him?"

"My lips are sealed. I'm an honest Injun," David quipped.

The house where Duarte lived was a detached, wooden bungalow on the edge of Maryvale. As expected, groups of youths hung around the corners and storefronts. The area had the taint of serious decay about it, one of the victims of the economic downturn. Many of the houses and bungalows had foreclosure signs on them, and a good number were boarded up already. The place looked tense, and they could both feel many eyes on them. Sullen, resentful. Waiting. These were the disenfranchised, the poor and dispossessed, many of them undocumented illegals. Many of them also undoubtedly armed. Automatically, Gabriel checked that his Glock was ready for use. David smiled.

"Yeah, that's the way it is around here. The place makes you feel nervous."

"The natives are hostile?" Gabriel asked, with a straight face.

David chuckled. "Too right, like a tribe of renegade Apache on the rampage."

"But not Navajo."

"Oh no. My people are known for the friendly greeting they give to the white man that comes to steal their land."

"So I've heard. That means you give you a warning

before you start shooting."

"Right. Not like the folks around here, we need to watch our backs. You've got places like this in New York City?"

"Yeah, some. The place is not so bad now, Giuliani cleaned it up when he was Mayor, but we have our problem areas. They're slowly being gentrified, but slow is the word. Too slow."

"I hear you. You see what I see?"

He was looking at a vacant lot at the side of Duarte's place. There were several cars parked there, two were junkers. One was a red Dodge Charger. With a black roof.

"I see it. How are you going to play this?"

"I'll let them think it's a routine enquiry about some burglaries they've been having in the area. When we get our friend Manuel on his own we can turn on the charm." He smiled. "With a name like yours, de Sade, I gather you're good at piling on the pain?"

"I like to keep up with the family tradition," Gabriel replied. He turned to the young Hispanic on the back seat. "If I were you I'd duck down low and make sure that no one sees you."

The man nodded and crouched down on the floor.

David knocked on the door. After almost a minute it opened, and a young Hispanic girl stood there. She was about fifteen years old, very curvy, wearing a top that left little to the imagination.

"What do you want?"

"Just enquiring around the area, Ma'am, it's about the burglaries. Have you seen anyone or anything suspicious?"

"No, nothing."

"Is there anyone else at home we could ask?"

She opened her mouth, she was about to say 'no', but

there was a noise in the house, the flush of a cistern. She saw them look.

"It is my brother, but he saw nothing."

"We do need to ask him, Ma'am. Could we come inside for a moment?"

Without waiting for a reply, they eased inside the house. She turned around to call her brother. "Manuel, two cops are here, they want to ask about the burglaries."

The door to the living room opened and Manuel Duarte came in. He was a mean-looking youth, of medium height and powerfully built. We wore a silky windcheater jacket with a bulge that betrayed a pistol tucked into his waistband. He glared at his sister.

"What the fuck did you let them in for? They're cops. Didn't you tell them they need a warrant to come in here?"

She gave him a frightened, pleading expression. "Manuel, if happened so fast, there was no chance."

"Yeah, I'll talk to you later." He turned to the two detectives. "You want to know about some burglary? I don't know nothing, so you can get the fuck out of here."

"What we want to ask you about is the Oasis Motel, Manuel. You booked a room there, yesterday morning."

"Who the fuck says I did? That's a pile of horseshit. Anyway, even if I did, what business is it of yours?"

"A woman was murdered in that room, last night. That makes it our business. Did you murder her, Manuel?"

He was shocked. "Murdered? Jesus Christ, I didn't kill her."

"Maybe not, Manuel. But we need to know about that motel room. Who did you book it for?"

"I don't know." He looked around, wildly, as if for inspiration. Or a way to escape. He was fast, he swerved to his left and made for the back door, but Gabriel was faster. As Manuel reached the door and put his hand on it, pulling it half open, de Sade kicked it shut, trapping his hand in it. He screamed and bent over, favoring his injured hand.

"Motherfucker, you broke my hand."

"Yeah, sure. The detective was asking you about that motel room. Who did you rent it for? Either give us a name or you're going down for murder, Manuel."

The Mexican stared at de Sade, a mixture of hate and fear filled his face. "I swear I don't know. It was some guy, he asked me to do him a favor. I never saw him before."

David Whitehorse got out his handcuffs. "Manuel Duarte, I'm arresting you for murder."

He read the guy his rights, all the time Duarte was shouting and screaming that he didn't know anything and his sister screamed hysterically that they were hurting her brother.

"Last chance, Manuel, before you go to Maricopa. Who asked you to book that room?"

It was the mention of that name, Maricopa, which did it. Who wanted to be booked into that hellhole, dressed in pink prison garb, locked into a chain gang and forced to endure the murderous extremes of heat and cold? Not Manuel Duarte. He finally told them everything he knew. Ricardo Valdez had ordered him to book the room under an assumed name, and leave a baggie of coke in the cabinet.

"That was it, I swear. I did what he said and left."

David and Gabriel exchanged glances. Why would Valdez, a bigshot drug dealer, take so much trouble and get a third party to book a room? It didn't add up. Valdez wouldn't give a shit about his anonymity.

"Why did he want the room?"

He only hesitated for a few seconds. But Manuel had started to pour out information, and there was no holding back now. The magic word was 'Maricopa'.

"It was for a friend of his, an acquaintance who wanted to entertain a girl somewhere quiet."

It still didn't sound right.

"Why a motel? Ricardo must have plenty of places of his own."

"He has, but this guy needed somewhere where he wouldn't be seen by anyone. He's well known, a local bigshot, so he can't go to one of Ricardo's places. It had to be a quiet motel. The Oasis is the quietest place in the city."

"Who is this client, what's his name?"

Duarte grimaced. "I do not know. If I did know and I told you, he would kill me. But I swear I do not know."

"Did you see the guy ever?"

Duarte hesitated, it was enough.

"Manuel, we know you saw him. What did he look like?"

"It was dark, his car stopped next to Ricardo one night, to talk to him I guess."

"What kind of a car?"

He shrugged. "I dunno. Black, big, it could have been anything."

"A limousine?" David persisted.

"Maybe. Maybe not. This guy, he put his foot outside on the ground while he was talking to Ricardo."

"His foot? How does that help us identify him?"

"The boot. It was snakeskin. Expensive. That is all I

know."

They had to let it go at that. If Valdez found out that Manuel Duarte had dropped the dime on him, he'd be killed, without a doubt. Ricardo Valdez was a wealthy and ruthless drug dealer in Phoenix. He hadn't got to a position of such power by behaving leniently towards subordinates who ratted him out to the cops. The question was who had the room been for? Obviously one of the dealer's clients or contacts, but getting him to name names would be impossible. It was doubtful he'd own up to his own name. But at least they had a start, a black car, snakeskin boots. They climbed back into the Cadillac and sped away from Maryvale. After they'd let the young Mexican out of the car Gabriel looked at David.

"What do you know about this Valdez? Is he likely to have any contact with any public figures? Possibly someone with a connection to New York?"

Whitehorse shook his head. "If he's got any high profile contacts here in Phoenix he'd keep them well hidden. I don't know of anyone."

"So which high profile figure in Phoenix wears expensive snakeskin boots?"

David thought hard. "Only guy I can think of is Congressman Max Carson."

"The guy who asked me to come down here to look at Phoenix police procedures? It doesn't seem likely, does it? Carson seems like a guy who's tough on crime."

Whitehorse shook his head. "It's not likely at all. I'll keep looking."

* * *

Back in the Duarte house, Manuel was on the phone to his boss.

"Ricardo, I had a couple of cops here, asking me about the motel room. Did you know she was killed?"

"What did you tell them?"

The voice was cold. Manuel shuddered.

"Tell them? What could I tell them, I didn't know anything. I said I booked the room for a friend of mine who was coming to town."

"Which friend? What name did you give them?"

Manuel was squirming, and he felt a drop of perspiration ran down his back. "Hey, they didn't ask, so I didn't tell them."

There was a silence on the line. Then Valdez spoke again. "Ok, come over here tonight, I've got some work for you. I've got some people coming in from across the border. I want you to take care of them. Good money."

Manuel breathed a sigh of relief. Valdez believed him, thank the Lord Jesus. Besides, he really hadn't said anything to help those two cops.

"I'll see you later, Ricardo."

But the dealer had already hung up.

CHAPTER SEVEN

Even though winter had arrived in Mexico, Faith and Galina relaxed in the garden in front of their hotel. It was still a balmy evening and they were enjoying a couple of martinis to wash away the dust of yet another day working in the storeroom, cataloguing and trying to estimate the value of what they found. The last thing they'd done that day was to open the trunk. It had been locked, but Galina was expert at opening locks with improvised picks and she managed to do it without damaging the trunk. Inside, as expected, there was a piece of cloth, a burial shroud. It was linen and probably very, very old. A hundred years, two thousand? It was hard to tell, but not impossible to estimate.

"The pattern of the weave will give us an idea, there were very different styles that emerged over the centuries," Galina explained. She leaned down to look closely at the weave, using a powerful magnifying glass that she carried during the cataloging process.

She frowned. "This is weird. The pattern is unlike

anything I've seen before. It could be a hundred years old, a thousand or five thousand."

"I'm certain of what it is."

Galina sighed. "I understand what you're saying, Faith. But the revelations you get are not shared by the rest of us. You could be wrong, you know."

"You mean deluded?" Faith pressed her.

"Deluded? Not at all. But who knows if an idea you get in your head comes from within or without. I'm not certain either way, that's all. Just allow for the fact that anything is possible." She smiled, to take the sting out of her words. "Especially where religion is concerned."

Faith was about to answer, but there was a sudden movement at the gate and a priest rushed in to the hotel garden. Father Juan.

"I'm glad I found you here, there's something of an emergency. Do either of you know anything about first aid, medical things? I mean, you told me you were both nuns at one time."

They exchanged glances. "Galina was a nun, I was only a novice," Faith replied. "Why do you ask?"

"There's been an accident, people have been hurt. We need help, it is desperate."

"But surely there is a hospital in Nogales?" Galina countered.

He shook his head. "We cannot use the hospital. The people who have been hurt were engaged in something illegal. If the police or the Federales find out, well, Mexican prisons are not nice places."

"So we understand. What kind of an accident?"

"They were in a tunnel when the roof collapsed. There were almost fifty people in all, some of them women and children. Some are still missing, but we managed to pull thirty two people out. They have cuts, bruises and in some cases more serious injuries, broken limbs and two with fractured skulls. Can you help us?"

They both nodded. "Of course," Faith said firmly. "We'll come at once, do you have medical supplies, dressings and so on. Any drugs?"

He flinched. "A few dressings. Drugs are very plentiful here, but they may not be the kind of drugs you need. We have a little cocaine."

"If that's all you have, it'll have to do. Let's go," Faith replied. She snatched up her jacket and they followed him out of the hotel.

Father Juan led them to an old hardware store, now closed and shuttered. It was on the northern edge of town, close to the border. A man was watching for any signs of the police, he nodded to the priest and pulled aside a sheet of rotting plywood. They entered the store and the priest clicked on a flashlight. He led them to the rear of the store and through a doorway, then down some steps into the basement. The scene that greeted them was a glimpse of hell. The darkened room was filled with people, injured people, groaning, some screaming and crying in agony. There were perhaps twenty of them in all. Others lay there dumbly, too shocked to cry out or perhaps accepting their fate. A fate that condemned to a dark and terrible end. A layer of dust hung over the room, like a heavy fog. Faith immediately made a start.

"Father, we need more light. Flashlights, candles, anything you can find. And water, warm water to bathe the wounds, disinfectant, let's get started."

"Here, you can use these." Father Juan handed the two

girls long cotton aprons that had hung behind the door since the business closed for the last time. They'd been used by the employees of the defunct hardware store, and they showed the stains and wear of much use. At least they'd keep their clothes clean of blood. As Faith bent down to attend to the first victim, she noticed the tunnel entrance, a dark hole that had been smashed through the concrete wall of the basement. It was about four feet high, and she shuddered to think of these innocents crawling through it, perhaps for a mile or more, to reach the promised land of America the other end.

An hour later the room was better lit, Father Juan had taken half a dozen candles from the church and others had fetched flashlights. They'd asked for a battery lantern, but it seemed that in this part of Mexico they were something of a rare luxury.

"Try and keep still, this won't take a minute," Galina murmured to a teenage girl who had suffered multiple abrasions and a suspected leg fracture. Deftly, she cleaned and bandaged the wound. There were no splints to fasten the leg, so she had to content herself with fastening a thick bandage around it to protect the wound from further damage. She turned to Faith.

"Where's the next one who needs looking at?"

But Faith was silent in the far corner of the room. She was watching the doorway that led from the store upstairs. Two men had entered, silent and unnoticed at first. One was older, perhaps forty years old. The other was younger, a man they both knew. Javier Garcia. The two men stood looking around the basement full of injured people, their faces mocking. Father Juan went over to them.

"Yes, what do you want?"

But he knew what they wanted. Both carried pistols in their belts, they were men who made a living through the misery of others. Trafficking drugs. And people.

"You are occupying our property. This building, this space, this tunnel, they all belong to us."

The priest choked down an outraged retort.

"Surely you can see there are injured people here? What are we supposed to do with them?"

The older man shrugged, Javier leered at Galina and Faith. He turned to the other man and whispered something to him.

"You are carrying a weapon?" he asked Galina.

"What is it to you? Are you a policeman?"

"Throw your pistol over here."

She glared at him. "No."

She was well aware that if she handed over her pistol, they'd be at the mercy of these men. And they would die. They'd rushed away in a hurry, she wasn't certain that Faith had brought her purse, so she may be unarmed, as her pistol was inside it. It meant that the weapon Galina had under her skirt was their only defense. There could only be one thing these men wanted. Their silence. Now that the tunnel had collapsed, the people who'd planned to travel through it to begin new lives in the US would have to return to Mexico. They'd want their money back, huge sums they'd paid to use the tunnel, and the traffickers couldn't allow that. They'd have to kill them, in Nogales it was the traditional way of buying silence. Abruptly, the two men both drew Colt .45 automatics, but Galina's hand moved in a blur and she had her own pistol in her hand. The older man smiled.

"Very well done, 'puta'. But you know that you can't

beat us, don't you? I have more men out in the street. If we start shooting they'll come down and you'll have a basement full of bodies. Hand over the pistol."

She didn't reply, just stood there, the gun pointed at the older man's stomach. It was rock steady. The man sighed.

"You want it the hard way, that's the way it'll be. Javier, come."

He nodded to Garcia and they backed out of the basement. The door slammed shut and they heard the bolt being slid across.

"I'm sorry," Galina said to the others. "I didn't handle that very well."

"They would have killed us," Father Juan countered. "You saved our lives."

She grimaced. "For now. But I shouldn't have let them live. They'll do anything to silence us, and we're stuck here without any way out."

"What do we do now?"

"I think the best thing would be to barricade that door. When they come back, they'll be heavily armed and they'll try to rush us."

They piled up old shelving and old timbers against the door to prevent it being opened. Father Juan surprised them by showing an expertise in woodwork. With a broken hammer and a few rusty nails he managed to construct a stout barricade that propped the door closed. Faith and Galina inspected his work when he'd finished and nodded approvingly.

"Where did you learn to do that?" Faith asked him.

He smiled. "I used to be a carpenter before I became a priest."

"You're following in illustrious footsteps, then."

"What? Oh, you mean Jesus Christ. Yes, some say he was a carpenter. Maybe it was true, I don't know. But he had bigger problems than the ones we face."

"Maybe. These are enough for the time being."

There was nothing else to do but carry on tending to the wounded. For the next half hour they did their best with the dwindling supplies in the basement. Then the men came back. The bolt slid back and when the door wouldn't open they pounded on it.

"You in there! Open up, otherwise we'll kill you all." It was Javier Garcia. "We won't wait forever. If you don't open this door we'll seal it shut from this side and you'll never get out."

Father Juan moved towards the barricade.

"What are you doing?" Galina demanded.

"We have to do as they say. If they shut us in we'll all die."

"If you open that door we'll all die. Don't you understand? They can't allow us to live and identify them as traffickers to the Federales, let alone be forced to hand back the money they took off these people."

"But if we don't open the door we're dead anyway. They'll seal us in here and we'll die of thirst and starvation. It would be better to try and deal with them. It's the only way out."

"It's not the only way out."

They turned to stare at Faith. She was inspecting the entrance to the tunnel.

"This would lead us out of here, and into the US."

But it collapsed in the center, that's why we're stuck in here."

"They dug it out once, it can be done again," Faith

snapped. "It would be better than staying here to be killed like sheep."

Father Juan waved his hands in protest. "That's crazy. Look at us, all we have is injured people and..." he stopped.

"You were going to say, 'and two women'," Faith finished for him.

"Well it's true," he shouted back. "It would need a team of fit, strong men to dig that tunnel. Look at them, they're in no state to even walk, most of them, let alone dig a tunnel."

"They don't need to walk. And we don't need to dig a tunnel. All we have to do is clear the earth from the collapsed section and we'll be through to the US side of the border."

"It can't be done," he snarled. He walked to the furthest corner of the basement and slumped against the wall.

"It can be done!" A girl stood up, a teenager. She was maybe eighteen years old. "I'm not waiting here to die. This gringo lady is right! They'll either kill us if we go out or starve us to death if we don't. We have no choice. I say we dig out the tunnel and complete our journey to the United States."

Her little speech seemed to ignite the huddled group of casualties. There were shouts of, 'yeah, let's go to America' and 'come on, anything's better than dying here.'

"What's your name?" Faith asked her.

"I am Conchita Ramirez, Señora."

"Well, Conchita, I suggest you explain to your people there is a way out of here. We'll go through and find out how bad the roof fall is first. Then you can organize them in teams to dig."

Conchita looked astonished. "But, you should take

charge, I'm only a girl."

"You're a brave girl with the guts to stand up for what you believe in. They'll listen to you. Let's take a look at this tunnel first, and then we can get started."

"Alright, Señora."

"It's Faith."

"Ok. Faith. But look at Father Juan."

She glanced across at the priest. After his outburst, he's slumped to the floor and buried his face in his hands.

"Father Juan," she snapped.

"Yes?" He looked up slowly. His face was agonized with the knowledge of their inevitable deaths.

"These people need your help. Go to them." Faith glared at him, and he looked away. But some part of what she said seemed to touch a part of his mind. He inclined his head. "As you wish."

He crawled over to the wounded, his movements like an automaton, to speak to the worst of the casualties. But he'd given up, they all knew it.

They took two of the flashlights and made their way along the tunnel. Conchita had hurt her leg in the roof fall, but the skin was only cut and bruised, there was nothing to stop her crawling once the wounds had been dressed. They reached the blockage after two hundred yards. The roof had collapsed, which was little wonder, considering the ramshackle nature of the props that had been used to support it. The wood was flimsy and rotten and had collapsed in a heap of broken timbers, soil, pebbles and sand. They played the flashlight beams over it just in case any part of it was not blocked. If they could have seen a narrow hole through to the other side, it would have enabled them to guess the length of the fall, but it was solid. Then one of the flashlight beams played on the ground and lit up a gruesome discovery. A limb stuck out of the earth and sand, it looked like part of the body of an older man. Conchita gripped Faith's arm as she was overcome with terror.

"I think it's Hugo, he was in our party and went missing after the fall. I recognize his pants and shoes. Could he still be alive?"

"No, there's no chance. When we start digging, we'll have to move his body out of the way."

"Can we get it back to the basement? Maybe he could get a proper burial."

Faith shook her head. "I don't think it'll be possible. It's hard enough crawling this far, it'll get worse once we start digging. We'll see what we can do, though."

They crawled back to the basement. Galina was busy putting more dressings on the wounds of the injured. She turned around as they emerged.

"What's the deal? Can we do it?"

Faith nodded. "We can. We'll need to find something to dig with. I doubt we'd manage with bare hands. Any problems with the men outside?"

"They banged and shouted a few minutes ago, but it's a standoff at the moment. It's a pity you didn't bring your gun. If they break in here, we'll have to hold them off with just my gun."

"But I did bring my purse, my gun is inside it!"

Faith rummaged in the corner of the basement where she'd thrown her coat. Her large purse was underneath. She reached inside and brought out the little pistol.

"If they try and come through that door we can hold them off."

But Galina wasn't looking at the gun. She was looking at a folded cloth; it was clearly the shroud poking out of the purse. Faith saw it and pushed it back.

"Is that what I think it is?" Galina asked, horrified.

She nodded. "I put it in my purse to carry with me for safe keeping. I was worried that Father Sebastian would steal it."

"At least he won't steal it down here. But we'd have been better off if you'd brought a folding spade."

Faith looked thoughtful. Then she stared at her friend. "I think this could be a lot more use than a spade. It's time that people knew what we'd found in their church."

"But, Faith, you don't know yet that it's authentic!"

"I know." She stared at Galina. "There was a time not so long ago when you used to have faith. Have you forgotten already?"

Galina sighed. "I'm just suggesting that we need to examine it carefully to see if it is authentic. As far as we know it could only be a couple of hundred years old, which makes it interesting, but not a religious relic."

"Believe me, it is authentic."

"You're really sure?"

Faith stared at her with an intensity that Galina could almost feel. "Trust me. I felt it, felt the power of something that was not natural. Then I prayed for guidance, and I was answered. It is authentic."

Galina smiled. "Perhaps you should have stayed a nun. Your faith could be catching."

"Yes, that's the idea. I want to talk to these people."

Father Juan was trying to comfort some of the injured who were in a great deal of pain. The cocaine that he'd assumed they had in abundance, for the traffickers made certain that the drugs went under the border along with the illegals, had been lost when the roof collapsed. He looked up as Faith raised her voice and asked for them to listen.

"Some of you have lost hope. I know that you don't believe we can get out of here." The weary, terrified and injured Mexicans looked up as her voice rang out. Clear, strong and confident. "Even Father Juan has lost hope. Yet you are not alone in this endeavor. We can get through the tunnel and still reach America. We are going to America!"

A man in his mid-twenties lifted himself from the floor to rest on one arm. The other was clearly broken. "If you're trying to tell us that you two gringo women are going to dig through that tunnel on your own and reach America, you're crazy, lady. We may as well let the traffickers kill us and finish it. The only thing that will save us now is a miracle."

There was a general murmur of agreement. Faith nodded.

"You're absolutely right. We need a miracle to do this."

They nodded and started to turn away.

"Wait! We have a miracle, I can show you."

They turned back with interest. The man with the broken leg sneered, "What miracle, lady? What miracle are you going to conjure up in this place?"

She pulled the cloth out of her purse. It was wafer thin, and had folded into a tiny package no bigger than a paperback book. She unfurled it, and at first the illegals looked puzzled.

"This is the burial shroud of James the Just. He was the brother of Jesus, the man who our Lord Jesus Christ intended to lead the Christian church after his death. I know this to be true. This is the most holy relic in the whole of the Christian world, touched by the body of the brother of Jesus Christ himself. I have prayed to our Lord, and he answered me. This shroud is the miracle we need to lead us. It has the power to work miracles, to restore faith, to heal the sick. We have to get it out of here and show it to the world to restore their faith. If you will join me in offering a prayer to give thanks for the miracle the Lord has sent us, we will make it through that tunnel. That is God's promise. It is my promise. That we will live this day to see America."

They watched her in astonishment. It was as if she had declared she came from Mars. The dingy basement was utterly silent, the only movement caused by the flicker of candle flames.

Then the man shouted. "I feel it. The pain, it is going from my leg."

He stood up, shakily. "I can stand on my leg. It is a miracle. Lady, I don't know where you got that from, but it's true. It is a gift from God. I'm going into that tunnel and I'm going to dig the earth out until I get through to America."

The room erupted in a babble of voices. The man limped to the tunnel entrance, picked up a bucket, crouched down, crawled in and disappeared. Five more Mexicans followed him, then five more. Ten minutes later the first bucket of earth from the roof fall appeared. Father Juan looked at Faith. His expression was angry.

"What have you done? You have only given them false hope. That man thinks his leg is healed, yet you know that it is only the adrenaline boost he got from believing in the miracle. In a few hours it will die away and he'll be back to where he was, in agony. Probably worse."

"And he'll also be alive and in America," Galina glared at him. "You're supposed to be a priest, yet you don't believe in the miracles sent by the Lord Jesus. You should be ashamed of yourself. You're a carpenter too, so get into that tunnel and start repairing the roof timbers. If your flock ever needed you, it is now. Go!"

He looked angry at first, and then he glanced around at his people who were looking to him for direction. The priest obviously felt embarrassed, he reddened, muttered something inaudible and disappeared into the tunnel. Faith thought of Gabriel, and wished he was here. He'd have got them out of this. And wherever Gabriel was, Jonas was never far behind. She looked at Galina.

"Any idea where Jonas is?"

She shook her head.

Faith knelt down. "We should pray. Galina, please join me, hold my hand."

* * *

Outside the derelict store, Javier Garcia held court with his gang of Nogales hard men. The boss had given him a simple order.

"Guard this door and make sure that no one comes out."

"How long do we have to wait here?" one of his men asked. It was Enrico, a sullen youth who was on the run from the Federales. Sometimes Javier wished they'd catch up with him, he never stopped complaining.

"As long as it takes them to die," he snarled. "The boss will be back later with a heavy excavator, he's going to smash the building down and seal it off. It's no use to us now, everyone will know about it. We'll have to find another building and start digging another tunnel."

Enrico pulled a face. "Javier, it took us weeks to build that one. It was hard work."

Javier glared at him. "Maybe you'd prefer to go back to the prison in Mexico City?"

He shook his head. "You know I can't do that."

"Ok. So shut up and make sure no one comes out of there."

CHAPTER EIGHT

"They're investigating the murder in that motel room."

Ricardo Valdez was feared by many in the city of Phoenix. In turn, he feared one man, the man he was talking on the phone with now. The man he had to answer to, who ran most of the criminal activities in Phoenix and throughout Arizona. He knew his identity, of course. He also knew that if he ever let it slip to another living human being, his body would be found in little pieces out on the desert. The man's power was enormous, his reach all-enveloping. The only way to deal with the guy was to be one hundred percent truthful with him. Lie, or conceal something important, and you may as well take out your gun and swallow it.

"What are you doing about it?"

"That kid I got to book the room, Manuel Duarte, I've asked him to come and see me for a chat. I'll find out what the cops asked him when they pulled him in."

"You're telling me the cops questioned him?" The voice sounded incredulous. "Why is the guy still alive? Find out what he told them and make sure they can't ask him any more questions."

"Right. I'll get on with it."

"Let me know when it's done."

He was about to reply when he realized the phone had gone dead. He sat waiting for Manuel. There was no need to call any of his men in. He decided he would deal with this himself. The trick was to make sure that Duarte didn't suspect anything. He'd found out long ago that a man taken by surprise was a man already disarmed. He took a spare pistol out of a drawer, checked it was loaded, took off the safety and put it under a cushion. Then he took his own pistol out of the shoulder holster and put it on the table, clip out as if he was cleaning it. He'd only just finished his preparations when Manuel knocked on the door.

"Manuel, come and sit down. How it all going?"

The man was nervous, but he glanced at the table and saw the gun there, the clip separated and visibly relaxed.

"Fine, Ricci, fine. I took care of those cops, they don't know anything."

"Yeah, you did well. What kind of questions did they ask you?"

He questioned the man for almost half an hour. By the end of it he knew that the cops hadn't got anything of value. Despite his protestations to the contrary, he also knew that the boss was right. Manuel could prove to be a liability, a link to the man at the top, as well as to himself. He smiled at the younger man.

"Get me a drink, there's beer in the ice box. Take one yourself."

"Sure, I could do with a beer."

He got up and went out to the kitchen. When he came back he was still nervous, but smiled when he saw that Ricardo hadn't moved. He began to believe that he was going to get out of this alive. He handed the beer to Ricardo and went to sit in the chair opposite. As he sat down, he saw that the Valdez was holding a cushion in front of him. When the shot came he felt a savage blow to his chest. The cushion had torn to shred, and smoke was curling out from inside it. As everything started to go black, he realized he'd been shot. He felt pain, terrible pain, he wanted to move but he couldn't. Everything went black as his heart stopped beating and the supply of blood ceased flowing to his brain. He slowly slumped to one side, and then rolled onto the floor. Ricardo picked up the phone.

"Jose? Bring some of your people, three will do. There's a disposal job, the usual place. Come here straight away."

He hung up the phone and dialed again. When it answered, he said two words. "It's done."

No words were spoken the other end. The receiver was put down, and he hung up his end. He heard a car draw up outside, he looked through the drapes and cursed. It was those two detectives. He'd have to go out the back way, but he had a contingency for this kind of problem. It would be a nuisance finding a new place but being here when those cops came in and saw the body would be much more of an inconvenience. He went into the kitchen and turned on the gas. Hidden inside a cupboard there was a small incendiary device, he set the timer for five minutes, picked up his gun and left by the back door.

* * *

Gabriel and David Whitehorse climbed out of the Cadillac. The address they'd been given was a shabby bungalow on a rundown lot. They knocked the door, but there was no answer. Gabriel looked at the other detective.

"What do you think? We really need to get in there."

"I think I can smell gas," David muttered.

He smiled. "We use that one in New York, I guess all cops do."

"No, I really think I can smell gas."

"Christ, we'd better get in there and see what he's up to."

Without waiting for an answer Gabriel shouldered the door. The lock caved in without a struggle and the door flew open. They rushed into the living and immediately came upon the corpse of a man they recognized. A corpse with a large hole blown in his chest.

"I guess they didn't want him talking to us anymore," David muttered. He felt the neck for a pulse, knowing that it was too late. "The body's still warm, so the perp could still be in here."

"I'll check around."

Gabriel walked in to the kitchen, with his Glock drawn ready to fire. He relaxed when the saw there was no one there, but the smell of gas was overpowering. The four gas taps were all turned on, he switched them off. But why the hell had someone left them on. Where was Ricardo Valdez? Or whoever else lived in this house? Maybe he'd left in a hurry. Then he recalled David saying 'the body's still warm'. Christ, a bomb, one of the oldest tricks in the book! He'd come across it more than once in Afghanistan, fill the house with gas and set off a bomb.

"David, there's a bomb, get out!"

He ran back into the living room and grabbed the detective and hustled him out through the door. They were just exiting the garden gate when it blew.

It was spectacular, a small explosion first, that could only have been a bomb. Then the gas ignited and the whole house went up in a massive ball of fire. Pieces of debris rocketed into the sky and landed around a hundred yard radius. The Cadillac alarm started wailing, a piercing shriek that he stopped with the remote key. He looked at David.

"You ok?"

The Indian nodded. "Yeah, I think so, that was a close one. You ever see anything like that before?"

"Yes. In Afghanistan, it wasn't that unusual. They'd rig an IED in a kitchen and set the gas full on. It wiped out a few of our boys before we got wise to it."

"Damn. I nearly died." He dusted himself, but he was shaking. "The guy in there is definitely dead and that was a mighty quick cremation. It sure wiped out any forensic traces we could have used. We'll have to hunt this Ricardo Valdez down the hard way now. He's got a lot of questions to answer."

They could hear the sound of sirens in the distance as the emergency service vehicles approached. He looked at David.

"Do you need to go to the emergency room?"

The detective was wiping blood from a cut on his forehead. The sleeve of his jacket had a black mark on it where he'd hit the dirt then the explosion went off. He looked at Gabriel.

"All I want to do is catch up with this mother. I don't

like people setting booby traps for me. We've got a place for characters like that."

"Maricopa?"

"Hell, no. Something far worse than that. Somewhere very deep and very dark, the state prison, it's a big hole in the middle of the Arizona desert. Always assuming that he escapes the needle, of course. I'll worry about a couple of cuts afterwards, when he's in custody."

"Remember, he's not the guy at the top," Gabriel warned. "That's the one we really want. Without him, the whole house of cards comes crashing down."

"Yeah, well maybe we can persuade Mr. Valdez to drop the dime on him."

"Maybe, but I wouldn't count on it. We've just seen what happens to people who talk to us. Besides, we've got to find him first. Where do we go to next?"

"Back to Phoenix PD. I want to see what our intelligence people have to say, they may have some idea where to look."

As they drove back into the center of the city, Gabriel had to stop for a moment. He was hit by a strong internal tremor that ripped through his body. David looked at him in concern.

"What's up? Did you take a knock when that bomb went off back there?"

He shook his head. "No, I don't think so, something hit me. I don't know what it was. I've got to make a call."

There was no reply from Faith's cell. He left a voicemail message and hung up. He tried Galina, with no reply, and then Jonas. Again nothing.

"What's the deal?" David asked.

"I can't contact the girls down in Nogales. They've

dropped off the radar, and I just know they're in trouble."

"Shit, that's not good. How do you know all of that?"

Gabriel stared at him. "I just know."

David was Navajo, he understood. "Like that is it?"

"Yeah, just like that."

"Got it. What are you going to do?"

"I'll let you know when I've worked it out."

Phoenix PD was a hive of chaotic activity. The calls had streamed in about the explosion and stirred up a hornet's nest. Chief Oliver Simpson was roaming the hallways and offices, bellowing an endless stream of orders. The man's bullying style was in full spate. He glared at David and Gabriel.

"What the fuck are you two doing here? I thought you were supposed to be out showing this guy around, Whitehorse."

"We got caught up in the explosion, Chief. I came back to report in and see what intelligence have on this Ricardo Valdez character, he's the one whose house went up."

"And you nearly got yourselves killed," he sneered. "Leave this to the ones that know what they're doing, Whitehorse. Make your report and then stay out of trouble. Detective de Sade is not down here to get himself killed investigating our problems."

"Chief, your problems could be linked with ours," de Sade reminded him.

Simpson sighed. "I doubt that, feller. But if you think so, get Whitehorse here to put it in his report. Then stay out of fucking trouble. Just look around at our operations for a couple of days, send in a nice, tidy report." He paused, and smiled cynically at Gabriel. "Then fuck off back to where you came from. Savvy?"

Gabriel returned his look. Eventually the Chief snorted and walked away.

"I'm sorry about him," David murmured. "He's not perfect, but he's got a real cactus up his ass over this business, first the murders and now the explosion."

"A pity he doesn't choke on it."

"I hear you."

Gabriel thought back to the times they'd run into trouble with the local law in Afghanistan. Most of them were on the take, from the Taliban and from the poppy growers and smugglers, who were responsible for a large chunk of the nation's income. Not that they paid much in the way of taxes. They'd been called in to meet the regional police chief at a small village in Helmand province. The man was smooth and well educated, fluent in English. The villagers complained that the Taliban had kidnapped some of their young children, to train them to become child soldiers. Or suicide bombers. It was a strange setup, on the one hand they'd requested assistance from ISAF, yet they seemed to be sullen and silent in the presence of the police chief. They decided to stay overnight and travel back the next morning. Afghan roads were at their most dangerous during the hours of darkness. Gabriel was suspicious of the police chief and watched him slip out of his quarters, a small village hut, and disappear into a narrow, dried up riverbed. He'd called Jonas and they followed the policeman. The man met with a group of Taliban fighters about a mile from the village. They couldn't make out what was being said, but the meeting was enough. Jonas slipped into the night to circle the group, while Gabriel waited and watched, with his Heckler and Koch HK 416, the new assault rifle that had just come into service.

Powerful and reliable, it was already proving to be a deadly ally in the battle against the Taliban irregulars. They had a simple plan. When Jonas was in position, he'd open fire on the group, driving them towards him. It worked like a charm. He was using a silencer and a flash suppressor on the weapon that made it difficult to establish where the shots were coming from at night. There were five in the group, together with the police chief. Jonas's first burst cut down three of them, the surviving men ran straight into his field of fire and he emptied a clip straight into them. Amazingly, the police chief survived that first burst. Gabriel remembered the man pleading with him, offering him power and riches if he let him live. Jonas came up on their position, without a second's thought he pumped a single round into the man's belly. He would die a long, slow agonizing death.

"He's a murderous, double-crossing piece of scum. That's part payment for some of the victims he's had killed."

Gabriel nodded once, he had no argument. They heard his screams for a long time into the night, but no one went to investigate. It was Afghanistan.

He snapped out of his reverie and watched Whitehorse finish writing up the events that led up to the explosion. Gabriel helped him fill in some of the missing data. David called up their intelligence section and spoke at some length. But Gabriel had something on his mind other than Ricardo Valdez. When he was finished, he pulled the Indian detective to one side.

"I need to run something by you."

"Yep, what is it?"

"You're a Native American, David, and a Navajo.

You're used to experiencing flashes of thought that white Americans are not party to."

"Like premonitions, you mean? Yeah, we do have those moments. Why do you ask?"

"Do you believe in them? You know, that they're real?"

He nodded. "Sure, of course I do. Our tribe is full of stories about stuff like that. It's part of our culture."

He explained about Faith Ward. That she had become deeply religious. And that she was prone to receiving messages.

"Messages? What kind of messages?"

Gabriel looked embarrassed. "I don't like to say."

David stared at him. "You mean like from God? Is that what you're saying?"

He nodded. "I guess so. I've never been really clear on how it works. All I can say is that there've been one or two times of extreme stress when she's had these messages and they've been right. Every time. Helped us out of some situations, in fact saved our lives."

"So what's the problem?"

"Back there, in the car, when I had to pull over. Something came into my mind. It was as if she was trying to tell me something. She was calling to me, she's in trouble."

"Right."

"The problem is this. I don't know what to believe."

"You say she was right in the past?"

"She was, yes. She got it one hundred percent right."

"In that case you'd better believe it and do something about it."

"Is that what a Navajo would do?"

"You bet your ass we would."

They left the building and Gabriel drove the Cadillac around the city, while David directed him to some likely addresses where they may find the man that might lead them to the killer, but they drew a blank. When Gabriel asked him why scumbags like Valdez were still running loose, David sighed.

"It's Chief Simpson, he's the big problem. All brawn, not much brains. He was an old time city cop, good at breaking heads and beating confessions out of suspects. As a Chief, he's a dead loss."

"So how come he made Chief?"

David grimaced. "Political connections, the usual."

But Gabriel wasn't really listening to the problems of the Phoenix PD. He had his own problems to work through. Could it be that Faith really was in trouble? He still wasn't certain if he was a fool, listening to a combination of Christian superstition and Navajo mysticism. It didn't seem sensible, somehow. And yet, if it was true...He stopped the car.

"David, I'm sorry, I've got to go."

"I kind of thought you might. To Mexico?"

"To Nogales, yes. If she's in trouble, she needs me. I have to help her. If I'm wrong, well, it's only my job. Can I take you back to Phoenix PD? I'm going straight on down there."

"Take me back? There's no need. I'm coming with you."

"Don't be stupid, it could cost you your badge."

Whitehorse stared at him. "Listen, Gabriel. There are a lot of reasons that made me decide to come with you. First, you saved my life back at that house."

Gabriel went to contradict him, but he waved at him to keep quiet.

"Second, I believe what you said about your girl. My guess is that what you felt back there was right on the nose. And if she is in trouble, you'll need an Arizonan cop to help you out. I've got plenty of friends in the Nogales PD, and they can get help from their Mexican counterparts. You're stepping into a world of trouble down there, believe me. It's another Ciudad Juarez. The Mexicans have taken gang murders to a new level, and they learned a lot of it in Nogales. So don't try to stop me. I'm coming with you."

Gabriel felt an overwhelming sense of gratitude. He knew that some of the Mexican drug gangs were as violent as the Taliban, some of them more so. They were just as well armed and incredibly vicious. He could use some help, any help. It was a pity that Jonas wasn't around. Where the hell was he?

He took David to his apartment, in a neat, modern block in downtown Phoenix. He waited on the street while the detective went inside for some personal things. Ten minutes later he came out with a large holdall, threw it in the trunk and climbed in.

"I'm good to go, do you know the way? Head south towards Tucson on Highway Ten then keep heading south for Nogales."

"I've got it, any problems we're likely to hit on the way? I want to avoid any potential delays and get down there fast."

David grimaced. "The only problems we're going to hit are when we cross into Mexican Nogales."

"I hear you."

They got stopped once by a county sheriff's cruiser. Fuming with impatience, Gabriel waited while the officer slowly climbed out of his car, hitched his gunbelt over his belly and plodded towards them. He leaned down to the driver's window.

"Don't you know about speed limits, feller? You were doing well over a hundred per back there."

David leaned across with his badge. "Phoenix PD, sheriff. We're on city business."

He looked across at Whitehorse. "They havin' something of a spending spree in Phoenix? This car ain't the usual police cruiser."

"We're undercover, sheriff."

"Really? Well it ain't much of a cover, this baby."

"It's fast, sheriff," Gabriel said quietly. "That comes in useful."

"I damn well know it's fast, you nearly broke my speed gun. You just take it easy in this thing. And good luck with whatever your assignment is. Where are you headed?"

"Nogales."

"Nogales, USA?"

"Nogales, Mexico."

He nodded. "Then you'll need a fast set of wheels to get out of there. You watch your backs in that place. They don't take kindly to Americans down there."

"Thanks, Sheriff."

"Nor Indians." He nodded at David. "You Navajo?"

"I am, Sheriff."

"Thought so. My sister married a Navajo boy."

"Is he ok?"

"He'd better be, he's my deputy. You take care now."

"You too, sheriff."

* * *

He was staring up at a light. It was blinding, hurt his head. He wished they'd turn it off. Where was he? It looked like a hospital room. He examined it some more as his blurred vision cleared. Sure, that's what it was. He blinked, and his eyes focused.

"You're awake."

He looked around. A nurse stood watching him. She was pretty, maybe about twenty three or four.

"How do you feel?"

He thought about that question. He tried to move his limbs, then his fingers and toes. They all seemed to be there, thank God. His head hurt badly, it was like someone was beating on it with a rubber hammer. Boom, boom, boom.

"I'm ok."

She smiled a pretty smile. "That's good to hear. I'll call the doctor and ask him to take a look at you."

She went away and came back a few minutes later with a doc in blue scrubs. The man checked him over with a stethoscope and a small torch that he shone in his eyes. He asked him the same questions as the nurse. The doc gave him the same answers. Jonas knew that something was wrong, but he couldn't put his finger on it.

"You're making a good recovery, Sir, with any luck you'll be out of here in a week or so. Do you know what happened to you?"

He shook his head. It was true, he didn't know. Why was that?

"What are my injuries, Doc?"

The man grinned. "A lot less severe than they could have been. Several bone fractures, contusions, bruising. We did a scan on your head, and we found a hairline fracture of the skull, that's what worries us more than anything. But at least you've recovered consciousness. I have to go and see another patient. The nurse will want to note your details."

"How long have I been here?"

"Of course, you wouldn't know. A week. You were brought in unconscious, today is the first day you've woken up. You had us worried there for a while, pal. I'll call in and see you later."

He strode of and the nurse came to his bedside, clutching a clipboard.

"Now, I need to take down some details, Mr. ?"

She waited with her pen poised ready to write. Of course, that was what was wrong. His name! What was it? Who was he? He felt an overwhelming sense of isolation, almost of panic starting to envelop him.

He looked at her. "I don't know."

She looked concerned, but tried to put a brave face on it. "You may only be suffering a temporary loss of memory. It's not that unusual in cases like yours."

"Nurse, tell me. What exactly did happen, what caused this?"

"You were brought in after a traffic accident. Someone called 911and the EMS people picked you up off the street. It seems you were hit by a truck. The cops said they'll call in to see you when you were able to answer some questions. But if you've lost your memory, I guess there won't be much you can tell them."

"I guess not. Was there anything on me that could identify me? Credit cards, driving license, something like that?"

She shook her head. "Nothing at all, that's why the cops though it may have been a mugging." She put the clipboard away. "Would you like some TV on? I'll put on the network news. Perhaps it will give you some visual cues. You never know, you may see some something that'll help."

She turned on the set fixed to the wall opposite his bed. Then she left him on his own to attend to her other patients. He watched the procession of images parade across the screen. First, a story about children in the White House, a smiling President and First Lady. He checked the date, the twentieth of December. Five days before Christmas. And he was in hospital, with no identity, no memory, nothing. He turned his attention back to the screen, but there was nothing that made any sense to him. Nothing that gave him any kind of a clue about who he was, or where he was from. What kind of job did he do? He'd no idea.

He lay back in despair. What if his memory never returned? How would he ever pick up his life, he'd be forever in the dark about his life's history. He dozed for a couple of hours, and then woke up with a start. Something had disturbed him, impinged on his subconscious mind, but he wasn't sure what it could have been. There was no one in the room, but the television was still on. The news anchor was talking about a series of drug killings. Nothing unusual there, the dealers were always killing each other off. So what had jarred his mind? He listened to the man recounting details of the murders.

"Local police report a number of bodies turning up on the outskirts of the town. Nogales, that's Nogales, Mexico, folks, not Arizona. The town is fast acquiring a reputation to rival that of Ciudad Juarez, the town that some say is the most dangerous in the world.'

That was it! Nogales, that name was important to him.

Could he have come from that town? But no, he was Caucasian American. It was the only thing he knew for sure. No way was he Mexican Hispanic. But the name was a start. Something nagged at him. He was certain that getting to Nogales was the most important thing in his life right now. He didn't know why, or what he'd do when he got there. Only that it was right, he should be there. It occurred to him that he could have been on his way there when he was injured. He painfully dragged himself out of bed and looked for his clothes. He had to clutch at a table for support when the pain shot through his head and he almost keeled over, but he regained his balance. He found his clothes in a closet and pulled then out. He had a leather holdall in there too, he opened it up but there was nothing inside that gave any clues as to his identity. There were some maps, a paperback book about the topography of the Arizonan border areas. He found little else, but when he put the bag down it seemed extraordinarily heavy. It must have been some residual memory that made him do it, but with both hands he groped to the bottom of the bag and felt for two particular rivets. He pressed them both at the same time. The bottom of the bag lifted a fraction, so that it exposed a lip that he could pull open. He looked inside, there were weapons in there. Two pistols, a Browning Hi Power and a Glock 17. Both 9mm, there was a spare clip for each and a box of fifty rounds of ammunition. There was also money, a bundle of fifty dollar bills, about ten thousand dollars in total. But no documents to give him any idea of who he was. The guns suggested he was something to do with law enforcement. Or working on the other side. Could he have been a hit man, paid money for killing people? Whatever he was, the guns looked and felt familiar. He picked up the Browning, ejected the clip, checked the rounds and slapped the clip back in. He made sure the safety was on and put the gun back in the bottom of the holdall, then closed the false bottom. He dressed slowly, painfully, but finally managed to get on his shirt and pants, lace up his shoes and pull on his jacket. He looked in the mirror and smiled. The top of his head was covered in bandages, and his face was cut and bruised. He could buy a hat to cover the worst of his injuries, for he didn't want to frighten any kids out on the street. He took a last look around, hefted the holdall and slipped out of the hospital ward. There was a crowd of visitors leaving, and he managed to insert himself into the middle of them and exit the hospital. He hailed a passing cab and asked the driver to take him to the airport. As they passed along the busy city streets, he began to recognize the city he was in. Washington DC. Now how the hell would he get to Nogales? He had money, that was obvious, but no documents. From somewhere inside his head, he knew that it wouldn't be difficult to obtain them, the money would buy everything he needed. How the hell did he know that?

CHAPTER NINE

The two detectives crossed the Mexican border without difficulty. The difference between the two Nogales was startling. On one side, a neat, dusty little town, basking in the winter sunshine. On the other, a nightmare. Streets that were unkempt, the roadways unrepaired and potholed. The cars that they passed were a microcosm of the country they'd entered. On the one hand, big, gleaming four wheel drive SUVs, all chrome and smoked glass. Most were undoubtedly the transport of drug dealers and people smugglers. Where they were stopped they were guarded by unsmiling, hard-looking young men. If the police that cruised past noticed the bulges in their coats that told of hidden weapons, they didn't give any sign of it. Probably they had been well paid to turn a blind eye. Gabriel didn't entirely blame them. In these lawless towns, they had a choice. Take the bribes from the mobsters, the drug-dealers and the people traffickers, or risk having their families killed. Most of the cars, however, were not worth tens of thousands of dollars. They were old and tired, dented and rusty. The people that drove them looked poor and resigned to their fate, as if they could do nothing to turn the tide of violence and poverty that was forcing Nogales to slowly sink into a morass of violence and despair.

"Where do we start?"

Gabriel thought for a moment. "They were due to visit the Church of the Blessed Virgin, so we'll go there. The priest is a Father Juan. I guess he'll know where to find them. I sure hope he does."

The Indian nodded. What he didn't say was that if the priest didn't know where they were, the two women were almost certainly in a lot of trouble. They passed groups of Mexican men standing on corners in rows, like terracotta warriors, waiting patiently like for someone to drive up and offer them a few hours work. They stopped the Cadillac to ask directions, a hopeful crowd surged forward and then fell back into dull inertia when it became clear that they had no work to offer. One young man, more enthusiastic than the others, gave them directions.

"Senores, I can help you in this town, believe me, you need me. Very cheap."

"How can you help? You don't even know what we want," Gabriel growled.

"I can show you the good parts of town and how to avoid getting into trouble. It is very easy to get into trouble in Nogales. I know everything and everybody in this town."

"Yeah, no doubt. But we can handle ourselves."

"Of course you can, Senores. But when you come back, your fine auto will be missing. I can take care of it for you. Believe me, whatever your business here. I can make it much easier for you."

Gabriel looked across at David. He nodded.

"Ok, get in the back. How much do you charge?"

The man climbed into the back. "Only fifty dollars a day, Señor. Is very cheap."

He nodded. "Your first job is to get us to the church. You're hired, we'll only be here for a few days, you'll get paid when the job's finished."

"But Señor..."

"Take it or leave it."

The man nodded. "I take it."

"What's your name?" David Whitehorse asked him.

"Rodrigo Diaz, Señor."

David introduced them. He tactfully avoided asking Rodrigo any details about himself. When he moved to get into the car it had been obvious that he had a serious limp. Whether that would prevent him from protecting their car remained to be seen. He was painfully thin, undernourished looking. Like many of the locals, his brown face was pockmarked with acne scars, under dark brown hair cut in a Mexican fringe. But he seemed cheerful and honest enough.

"We're both police officers, Rodrigo. I'm telling you now, don't try and screw with us. We're here on private business, but it wouldn't take long to check you out with the local police department."

Diaz nodded. "I understand, but I assure you I will earn my money. You will not have reason to go to the police about me."

"What do you do, Rodrigo? What is your normal occupation?"

"Occupation? This is Nogales, I live, and I survive. I do

anything to earn money. There is very little real work here, unless you are a smuggler or a policeman. They are often the same thing."

David grimaced. "It's that bad, huh?"

"It is that bad, and worse. It is very difficult to be honest in this town. If you want to earn enough money to eat, that is."

"Ok, Rodrigo, enough said. Is this the right way to the church?"

"It is, yes. Go to the end of the street and take a right. You will find it about four hundred yards on the left, it is the only church."

"Do you know Father Juan?"

"Of course I know him, it is my parish church. I was baptized there."

"Good enough. Maybe you'll be useful for more than watching the car. You can introduce him to us. Does he speak English?"

"He does, yes."

"Good, we shouldn't have any problems then."

They got to the church and started to look around. A monk came out of the gloom at the back of the church to surprise them. He was tall, gaunt, and quite old. "I am Brother Sebastian Braun, how may I help you?"

They'd been gazing at the building, in all of its faded glory. The church had once been an opulent building, typical of the Spanish Catholic style that was popular in Mexico. It had hit hard times, masonry that had once been finely carved and beautiful was now decayed. The stone flagstones that led up to the church door

"Nice to meet you, Sir. We need to speak to the priest, Father Juan. Two friends of ours came here to inventory some relics that the church is disposing of."

"Yes, of course, Faith Ward and Galina Polotsova, I spoke with them."

"Do you know where they are right now?"

He shook his head. "I haven't seen them since yesterday, or Father Juan. They seem to have disappeared. To be honest, I'm a little worried. But they may have just gone to visit one of our outlying churches, we have several rural parishes."

His accent was slightly guttural, Gabriel noticed. German, possible. The name could certainly be German.

"So you have no idea where we can look?"

The monk shrugged. "None at all. I wish I could help you more." Then he brightened. "I can direct you to their hotel if you wish."

"That'll be a start, thank you."

"It is the Hotel Plaza, one of the best hotels we have here in Nogales."

"Right." He turned to Rodrigo. "Do you know it?"

"Yes, Señor, I know it. Only a short drive from here."

"Good." Gabriel turned back to the monk. "We'll see if we can track them down. We may as well check into this hotel while we're here, we'll need somewhere to stay. Would you leave a message there if you hear anything more?"

Brother Sebastian smiled. "Of course I will. I wish you luck. But of course, they could be at the hotel even now."

Gabriel shook his head. "If they were there, they'd have answered their cellphones. If we hear anything, we'll let you know."

The hotel was like the rest of Nogales. A dirty,

crumbling shambles. The desk clerk looked up, appraising the newcomers. No doubt he had them pegged as Yankee cops before they got within twenty feet of the counter.

"How can I help you?" he smiled through broken, stained teeth. It was not a pleasant smile. Both detectives got the impression that he was already calculating which of his illegal scams they wished to question him about. Or maybe he was working out how he might pull a scam on them.

"We want two adjoining rooms, and we're looking for two friends of ours. Faith Ward and Galina Polotsova."

He seemed to breathe sigh of relief. "Of course, both of those ladies are staying here in the hotel. You would like rooms on the same floor?"

"Yeah, that's fine. Are they here now?"

"The women? No, I haven't seen them since yesterday."

"Yesterday! Exactly when and where yesterday?"

He looked thoughtful. "I'm not exactly sure when I saw them. I'll question the staff if you wish. Maybe they can recall when they last saw the two ladies. I'm sorry I can't be more helpful."

His look was one of pure avarice. Gabriel took hold of the man's coat and pulled him half over the reception counter. He stared into his eyes.

"I asked you a question, buddy. These women are important to me, I want answers. You'd better think again."

"Si, si, I remember now!"

Gabriel let him go and the man smoothed down his coat. He tried a look of aggrieved innocence, but when he saw the grim expressions of the two men in front of him he swallowed and started to speak.

"They were on the terrace having a drink. A priest came

to speak to them, they left with him. They appeared to be in a hurry."

"And you haven't seen them since?"

"No, Senores"

"Where did they go? I want the truth!" Gabriel moved closer to the man so that he was in no doubt about his the reward for lying.

"That is the truth, I swear, Senores. That is the last I saw of them, they left with the priest."

Gabriel stared at him, and then turned to Rodrigo. "Keep an eye on the car." He looked back at the receptionist. "I want you to open up the lady's rooms. You can come up with us."

They took their room keys and climbed the stairs. The receptionist went with them, despite his protests that he had important work to do, and he opened up the girls' rooms. Their possessions were there, but the rooms were empty. The two detectives dumped their bags in their own rooms and Gabriel made some calls, but there was no news of Jonas and none of his usual contacts had heard from his friend. He mentally shrugged. There was nothing he could do about that, not right now. Jonas was the toughest guy he'd ever known, if he couldn't get himself out of whatever scrape he was in, no one could. Then again, there could be a logical reason for his silence. Although he couldn't think what that could be. But he had more important things on his mind. Like two girls who were missing, and they were not as tough as Jonas. Wherever they were, they needed his help. He knocked on David Whitehorse's door and went in. The Navajo detective was sat on the floor, cross legged, as if in a yogic trance.

"What's going on, David? Are you busy?"

He didn't reply, so Gabriel sat down and waited. And waited. Ten minutes later, the Indian started to stir. Then he came awake, it was as if a switch had been turned, one moment he was in a trance, the next he was there, staring at Gabriel.

"I'm sorry, David, I didn't mean to intrude. If you want me to come back later, I will. I guess it's a Navajo thing you're doing, like yoga?"

"They're in trouble." David spoke slowly and precisely, almost like a chant.

"Excuse me?"

"The girls, they're in trouble."

Gabriel nodded. "Yeah, I expect they are, David. That's why we came here, remember?"

"No, you don't understand. The girl reached out to me. I don't know how, but I know they're in trouble. She said her name was Faith."

Gabriel was stunned. For a few moments he said nothing. He remembered the times in the past when Faith Ward had made similar statements and he'd disbelieved them. Yet they'd so often been proved true and even saved his ass on more than one occasion. Now there was this Navajo, David Whitehorse. This was a different story. The Indian had never even met Faith Ward. What was he trying to pull? Some kind of Indian trick to impress him? He began to wonder if he'd made a mistake in bringing him down here.

"David, I told you her name was Faith. We both know that she's probably in trouble, that's why we came here. What we need to do is get out and find her."

The Indian sighed. "You think I'm grandstanding, right?"

"I don't know what you're doing. All I know is that we're going to need more than Navajo fortune telling to find where they're hiding."

David stared at him intently. "She got through to me, my friend. I'm not bullshitting you. She's got some kind of mental power, I don't know what it is, or where it came from, but she managed to connect. It's extraordinary. I've never known anyone outside of the Navajo tribe who could do that."

"We're wasting time, my friend. We need to get out and find them."

"They're trapped, underground, de Sade. That's her, another woman named Galina, and the priest, Father Juan. They have a number of Mexicans with them too."

"You're serious?"

"Oh yes." David nodded emphatically. "Somehow, your girlfriend managed to get into my mind. I had a picture of her underground with her friend and the Mexicans."

"I don't understand it. What the hell are they doing underground? For Christ's sake, David, tell me exactly what you saw."

"It was only a brief glimpse. They're trapped in some kind of a tunnel, that's all I know. I got a picture of some kind of intense evil they're trying to escape from."

"Evil? What the hell kind of evil?"

"No idea. I'd guess they're still in Nogales. I can't think of anywhere more evil than this place."

Gabriel fumed inside. He didn't know whether to rely on what David thought he'd seen or not. Should he search here in Nogales, looking for some underground tunnel? Or should they broaden the search, maybe even go to the Federales? He thought for some moments, but he knew that the only thing that talked here in Nogales was money. They needed to talk to Rodrigo, for he'd know where to start looking, and who to start bribing. Or who to threaten. He decided to give David the benefit of the doubt.

"Let's see if Rodrigo makes any sense of this tunnel business."

"So you believe me?"

Gabriel paused. Then he turned to the Navajo. "I don't know, David. Let's just find the girls."

The receptionist scowled at them as they walked past, but they ignored him. Rodrigo lounged near the Cadillac, his hand stuck in the pocket of his coat. A group of ragged Mexican youths hovered nearby, waiting for the chance to get nearer the desirable Yankee auto. They seemed to be wary, and Gabriel thought he knew why.

"Rodrigo, are you carrying? A gun, a knife, something like that."

The Mexican stared back at him. "Something like that, Señor. This is Nogales."

"Show me."

Reluctantly, he brought out his hand, holding a slim, long blade. It was like a filleting knife, very thin and razor sharp.

"That's impressive, my friend. I imagine you find it useful."

"Yes."

"Ok. We're looking for a tunnel, whereabouts in Nogales would you find tunnels? Are there any old mine workings around here?"

"No, Señor, no mines."

"So why would anyone dig tunnels around here?"

"There is only one reason. To go to America. People,

drugs, Nogales is a smuggling center, there will be many tunnels that have been dug over the years. Most have been discovered and filled in. If any are still in existence, it is only because they have not yet been found by the authorities."

"Well, this tunnel still exists, and we think our people may be trapped down there. Who can we ask?"

"You can ask anyone you wish, but you are likely to end up dead."

"Maybe. I need a name, Rodrigo, someone to ask. I'll worry about who winds up dead afterwards, a lot of people have tried and I'm still here. But first I need a name."

"Javier Garcia."

It was David Whitehorse who'd spoken. They both looked around in surprise.

"Where did you hear that name?" Rodrigo asked. He sounded uncomfortable.

David shook his head. "It kind of came into my mind." He looked puzzled. "I really don't know, Gabriel. It just came to me."

"Does it mean anything, Rodrigo?" Gabriel asked.

"Yes. Javier Garcia works with the gangs here in Nogales. He is into everything, drug trafficking, people trafficking, and a number of scams on tourists who come here from the north. If there is money to be made, he's often involved."

"Is he a major player?"

"No, Señor. He is a kind of freelance. Always prepared to do anything for profit no matter how bad it is, but I do not believe he is totally trusted by the big time dealers and traffickers. Some of them think he may be a police informer."

"Do you think he is?" Gabriel asked.

Rodrigo laughed. "He is anything to anybody, provided that the price is right."

Gabriel grunted. "We can arrange that. We'll start with him. Where can we find him?"

"He normally hangs around the streets. We can cruise around. If we're lucky we'll see him."

"Let's do it."

For the first time since he'd hired the car Gabriel cursed as they drove through the littered and filthy streets. The Cadillac stood out like a sore thumb in Nogales. It wasn't a drug dealer's car, neither was it the property of some big shot politician on the make. It was an oddity. Wherever they drove it inspired curiosity. Gabriel was about to suggest they looked around for a more nondescript hire, somewhere that would garage the Cadillac for them for a few days, when Rodrigo called out, "That's him. Javier Garcia, he's down the street with a group of men. Don't stop, keep going, it is important that he doesn't know we're looking for him."

"Ok, ok, we're only a couple of blocks from the hotel. We'll take the car back and park it in the hotel car park. We can come back here on foot."

"You will not need me now?"

They could both see that the Mexican was sweating with fear. Javier Garcia obviously worried him. But they would need him. Or more importantly, they may need his local knowledge.

"You'll have to come with us, my friend," David spoke to him. "But we'll make sure nothing happens to you. You can stay back out of sight."

Rodrigo crossed himself. "I pray to God you are right."

Gabriel took him by the arm and stared at him. "You'll be ok, Rodrigo, believe me. We'll take care of you."

Fifteen minutes later they were back at the end of the street where they'd seen Garcia and his buddies, the car was safely garaged back at the hotel.

"What the hell are they doing?" David asked.

There was a mechanical excavator working at the site, it seemed to be an old building that was under demolition. The John Deere was using its hydraulic arm to smash down the building, then turning through one hundred and eighty degrees to use the heavy steel bucket to pile the debris into a huge mound.

"It looks innocent enough," David replied. "Just a simple demolition job."

"Simple? That doesn't explain why they need Garcia and a bunch of his hoods to keep an eye on it," Gabriel muttered. "Besides, wasn't it Javier Garcia's name that Faith got through to you about? Rodrigo, we need to get nearer and take a look at what they're doing."

The Mexican nodded uncertainly and they walked forward, using the decrepit buildings for cover, but when they got closer, they were no nearer to finding any answers. At least it was Garcia sure enough, they'd found him.

There was a shout from his men as part of the ground collapsed into some kind of underground space, and then the John Deere started to fill in the hole.

Rodrigo stared. "I think they're just filling in some kind of an underground hole, maybe a basement or something like that."

But David looked quickly at Gabriel, and de Sade felt sick. An underground hole, a basement. Or maybe a tunnel? He knew in that moment that they were too late.

"We need to stop them," he growled.

"How are we gonna handle it?" David asked.

"We'll take them down, every last one of the sons of bitches. If they've murdered the girls, I'll rip out their guts and hang them on their mother's washing line."

* * *

"The roof, it's starting to crack!"

The priest, Father Juan shouted a warning. They looked up at the ceiling. Something was banging repeatedly, trying to smash through. Trying and succeeding, cracks appeared in the masonry and a huge slab of concrete crashed down. Two of the Mexican women screamed. Another giant slab of masonry smashed into the room.

"Into the tunnel!" Faith shouted. "We'll be safe in there, quickly, get everyone in there."

Father Juan appeared at the tunnel mouth. His long black cassock was streaked with dirt from where he'd been working on propping up the hole.

"What's going on?" he shouted.

"They've got some kind of a demolition machine up there. They're bringing the building down on top of us."

"But…we'll be trapped. We're all going to die!"

"We're not going to die. We'll get everyone into the tunnel. Then we have to dig."

"To America? You must be crazy, it cannot be done."

She glared at him. "It can be done and it will be done. How far do we have to go, Father? Have you any kind of estimate?"

He sighed. "God only knows. Perhaps three hundred

yards. It could take us a week to get that far, in the meantime we've no food and no water. Even the air in the tunnel will start to become fouled with carbon dioxide when it is exhausted. We're on our own, no one knows where we are, I tell you, we're finished."

Galina was herding the rest of the Mexicans intro the tunnel. Faith was about to snap out a reply when something flashed inside her head. It was as if a warm, white light washed over her. As if some kind of force was there, something or someone to answer her prayers. They were here, with them, in this tunnel. She turned to the priest and spoke to him with absolute conviction.

"Father Juan, we're not on our own. You must help us get these people into the tunnel and carry on digging. You must have faith, believe me. We're not alone."

He gave her a skeptical look. Then he grunted a word, something unintelligible, and scuttled back into the tunnel, pushing two women and half a dozen children in front of him. Faith stared at his back. She'd felt the connection, she knew it was not a figment of her fevered imagination. It was true. It had to be true.

CHAPTER TEN

She checked her make-up in the mirror. For this one it had to be perfect. The guy was a bigshot, politics, finance, a real blue blood, the kind that had a season ticket to the Met in his wallet. A real catch in New York City. She'd spent half her month's salary on the dress, and it clung to her curves as if it had been molded for them. Bright, red silk, with a plunging neckline that displayed her smooth, creamy breasts and a high hem that showed off her legs. Jesus Christ, she chuckled to herself, she was almost naked. The doorbell rang and she quickly sprayed fragrance over her neck, seventy bucks a pop, he'd better appreciate the trouble and expense she'd gone to, then she opened the door with a shy smile.

"Hi, you've come. Welcome."

He was very tall and very distinguished looking. An older man, but what the hell? A faint odor of eau de cologne, his gray hair styled to perfection. The suit was classic Ralph Lauren, no sharp Armani for this guy.

He answered her smile. "I couldn't have stayed away for

another minute."

"Come on in. I'll get you a drink."

She poured bourbon on the rocks, but noticed he wasn't drinking.

"What's the matter, would you like something different?"

He was fumbling with something in his pocket, a thoughtful look on his face, as if he was undecided about something. That was unexpected, for a man like this to be undecided. Interesting. Maybe he would be more positive in bed.

"Look, Angelica, I hate to do this to you, but I have to get back to my office later tonight, I've got a conference call to Tokyo. These time differences are hell, but it has to be done. As much as I love that dress you're wearing, I'd love to see you out of it. What say we go to your bedroom?"

"You don't waste much time, do you?" she grinned. Inside, she felt annoyed. She'd spent a lot of time making herself and her apartment nice, and the meal she'd prepared would go to waste. On the other hand, if she did as he wanted, this could be the start of something big. Even permanent. She broadened her smile. "Only if you undress me yourself."

His voice shook. "Yeah, I'd love to. My god, but you're really beautiful. I can't wait."

She led him through to the bedroom. As he walked through the door, she noticed he used his elbow to push it further open. In fact, he'd done the same as he walked through the front door of her apartment. Perhaps it was some kind of hygiene phobia he struggled with. He could have any phobia he liked, when you were one of the most eligible bachelors in New York City, you could please yourself.

He helped her off with her dress, and she shivered with the anticipation of the approaching sexual ecstasy. He was attentive to her, very gentle as he slowly pulled down her panties and unfastened her bra. When she was naked, he lay her down on her back on the bed. His hand played between her legs, touching just short of the lips of her vagina, his other hand fondled her nipples and she shivered again.

She grinned at him, a saucy, lascivious smile. "Hey, are you gonna let me have all the fun? Take off your clothes and I'll return some of the pleasure."

"In good time, my dear. We need to make this as much fun as possible."

She noticed his voice was hoarse, choked with lust. Good. "I'm all in favor of that.

"I've got something for you to try. Is it ok?"

He'd reached into his pocket and pulled out a set of silken cords. So that was what he was thinking about earlier. She was slightly disappointed, for she'd been looking forward to a good, old fashioned, plain vanilla fuck. But if that's what he wanted, who was she to object.

"Sure, go ahead. But make it quick, I'm as randy as hell. You're really turning me on, honey, do you have this effect on all your girl friends."

"Only the special ones like you."

She shivered again. He was fastening the cords to her wrists, then her ankles. He fixed them to the bed frame so that she was totally vulnerable, at his mercy. Whatever he wanted to do to her, he could do, Christ, it had turned her on. Maybe this bondage thing wasn't so bad.

For Christ's sake make if fast, I'm soaking wet down there."

She closed her eyes and felt herself panting with arousal. These guys that liked the set piece sex thing, well, if only they could get on with it, make it a lot quicker. It was the unfamiliar click that made her open her eyes again and look up at him. She realized he'd put on a pair of latex surgical gloves. Now that was strange, but if that was his kink, so be it. *Just hurry up and fuck me'.*

But it was what he was holding in his latex gloved hand that started to worry her. He had a switchblade, it must have been the click she'd heard, when he opened it.

"Hey, I don't mind the bondage bit honey, but I'm not comfortable with the knife. Would you please put it away?"

He didn't answer, and she felt the first tremor of fear course through her body.

"Please, put away the knife, I don't like it," she repeated.

"You're not meant to like it," he murmured lazily.

He had a lazy smile on his face now. He pulled down his pants and underwear and put a condom on his erect penis. Then he lay on top of her, but held the blade of the knife against her throat. She felt him sliding into her and start pumping, but she'd lost her arousal. This was all wrong.

"Please," she whimpered. "Don't hurt me."

"Schh, keep quiet. Otherwise I'll have to gag you. Like I did the others."

Others? Oh my God, what was this, was he some kind of sexual pervert? Or worse? What was he going to do to her? But she was too terrified to ask, because he might go ahead with his threat to gag her. That would be awful! At least she was still free to use her voice, free to breathe. His strokes were more powerful now as he surged in and out of her, pushing hard against her vagina, she felt sure that she would be bruised when he'd finished, he was so rough, so powerful. Yet she bit her lip and made herself keep quiet. She had a feeling that anything she said would make things worse. She felt the blade pressing harder against her neck. It was a power thing, yeah, that's what it was. She knew that some men could only get off with that kind of hold over a woman, but if he slipped, Christ, he could slice in to her throat. She pictured herself in the Emergency Room, having a surgical team stitching up the cut in her throat, with a censorious look in their eyes.

"Look at me Angelica. Look straight into my eyes. I want to see into your soul."

She did as she was ordered, his eyes had a maniacal glare, she wanted to turn away, but she knew that he would be angry. She forced herself to stare into the glazed pupils. The knife pressed harder, now his penis was fully engorged, almost ready to climax inside her. It was hard, rough, and painful as his urgency overcame him and battered her with his powerful body. The knife pressed even harder, he banged his prick in even harder and harder. He was almost there. "Look at me, Angelica. You must look into my eyes."

She looked, and felt his semen spurting inside her. The knife was hard on her throat, there was something wet there. Was she drooling? No, it was blood. She realized it was her own blood, for he'd cut her at the moment of his climax. She started to feel faint as her blood pressure dropped lower. As his face started to fade, she was puzzled to see that his eyes were wide open, staring into her own. Yes, it really was as if he was staring into her soul. Then everything went black.

When she was still, he climbed off her. The trick of

course was to make certain that he left no traces for the cops to pick up crime scene residue. Especially DNA. But it was worth it, it was so good. A feeling beyond anything in this world. As long as you didn't get caught, of course. He worked slowly and carefully, as always. His brain seemed to fizz with the incredible energy, the life force that had drained out of the girl at the moment of climax, the moment of death. He made a conscious effort to control himself, he had to be careful. This was the moment of maximum danger, when he could make a simple mistake that would bring him down. He reviewed his actions so far. Had he touched anything that he shouldn't have? He didn't think so. It was time for the next move. Using the switchblade, the edge lovingly honed to a razor's edge he cut through her wrists and removed the hands. He put them on the floor, careful to avoid any drops of blood falling on his clothes. Then there was just the finishing touch. The chess piece, artfully displayed on the body, between the two breasts. A bishop for this one, she was class, sheer class. Nothing less than a bishop. He'd considered a queen, even. But that would need someone more than this girl, someone who truly would be a major conquest. Had the cops worked it out yet, he wondered? Probably. It was a game, which was all. Chess was supposedly the greatest game in the world, or so many people said. They may have worked on their complicated psychological theories about the deaths, about cutting of the hands, too. He laughed to himself. That was an easy one. He made a mental note to burn all his clothes when he got back home. He left the apartment block and climbed into his car, European, a Mercedes S500, of course. He always drove a Mercedes, always had. He used his cell on hands-free to make a call.

He didn't want to break the law and use a cellphone in his hand, did he? He laughed again. The ringing stopped as the number answered.

"Yes?"

"It's me."

"Another one?"

"Another."

"Ok. I'll see you in the house."

$$* * *$$

"Rodrigo, stay out this. I'll handle this."

The Mexican moved several paces back. David raised his eyebrows.

"What's this 'I' thing? I'm coming with you, buddy."

"You don't need to risk anything for me, David."

The Navajo nodded. "I guess not, but I'm not waiting here staring into space while you get your ass shot off. Count me in."

"Ok. We'll just wander down the street, two innocent Gringo tourists. When get up with them, I'll take them, you back me up."

"What do you mean, you'll take them? Not what I think you mean?"

"I'm pretty sure that my partner is under that building they just collapsed. What do you think I mean?"

"Christ, you mean you're going to kill them."

"Right. Does that cause you a problem?"

He thought for a few moments, and then nodded. "I guess not, but we ought to call the cops."

"Yeah, right. In Nogales?"

David nodded. "Understood. Ok, so we'll kill all of

them."

Behind them, they both heard Rodrigo groan loudly in terror.

"Except one. I want one left alive, the leader preferably, Javier Garcia. Only until we question him, then he can keep the others company."

Rodrigo came up with them. "Senores, this is madness, the police…"

"Are corrupt and useless, my friend. Stay out of the fucking way. And don't think about doing anything stupid. I do this for a living. Clear?"

The Mexican nodded miserably and stood in a nearby doorway.

"Right, let's go."

Gabriel and David walked side by side along the narrow street. Rodrigo ambled along a few paces further back. They chatted to each other like anyone who was going about their normal, lawful business. They saw Javier Garcia glance in their direction and then turn back to the business at hand, the demolishing of the building. They walked on, watching the group of Mexicans carefully. Apart from Javier, there was a man controlling the John Deere, using the mechanical arm and bucket to pile more and more masonry on top of the already substantial pile he'd collected. There were four more of Garcia's men, they were holding shovels and standing to one side while they watched the machine do its work. They were all obviously armed, bulges inside their coats showed that they carried pistols. An assault rifle leaned against a low wall within easy reach. Without hesitation, Gabriel walked up to Javier.

"Hey, friend, we're looking for the Plaza hotel, can you

help us? We're new here."

The Mexican smiled. "Yes, Senores, I'd be more than pleased to help you. You've come to the right man. How long are you in Nogales?"

"About a week, but it's difficult to find out way around here."

"Perhaps I can offer you my services as a guide? My work here is finished. Pepe, come here, I need to help these two Gringos, they're lost."

"Pronto estarán," they heard him mutter. *They soon will be.'*

"Come, let me show you the way," Javier smiled.

His smile faded as Gabriel's Glock seemed to appear as if by magic and its barrel was screwed into his skull.

"What's this, what's going on?" He screamed the words out in alarm.

The John Deere operator had slowed the engine to an idle, so the other men heard him shout. Three began to drag out their pistols, the fourth man ran for the assault rifle. The Mexican in the excavator ducked down behind the steel plating of the engine cover. They reacted fast, Gabriel realized. But he'd known faster. And he was quicker still.

"David, take care of this one, try to keep him alive."

He threw the terrified body of Javier Garcia at his partner and fired twice at the man diving for the rifle. That was the real danger; if he cut loose the steel jacketed military rounds could shred him and David. The guy tried to weave as he realized the danger he was in, but Gabriel anticipated him and the double tap scored with both bullets. The first hit him in the shoulder, not enough to stop him. But it slowed him. The second, fired as he was reeling from the first shot, took him in the head. He wasn't about to get up. A round whistled past his hair and he glanced in the direction of the other three Mexicans. The quickest had his pistol out and had fired a snap shot that came close. Too close, he jerked up the Glock, lined up the barrel instinctively and let fly another double tap, another man went down. Another bullet zinged past, from the direction of the John Deere. The guy was firing from behind cover. He could hear someone shouting, but he didn't have time to assimilate that data. As ever, when the action started, he went into a kind of trance. A killing trance, when he ignored everything around him except for the targets. He became a killing machine, remote and unstoppable. He ignored the excavator, by the time he rooted out the shooter hiding behind it the other two would have drawn a bead on him. He crouched down just as two more shots zinged past, then he sighted on the two Mexicans. Both were firing at him wildly, shots that peppered the ground around him, but he coldly took aim and fired, once, twice, three, four times. Both men went down, flung in a bloody heap on top of the dusty pile of rubble they had created. Only one man remained, the John Deere operator. Gabriel looked for him. Yes, he was there, crouching behind the steel track of the vehicle. Only a tiny part of his body showed, de Sade had to get nearer. He moved towards him, the man fired a snap shot and by a thousand to one chance it hit the barrel of his Glock and ripped it out of his hand. The Mexican stood up, a triumphant look on his face.

"Now it is your turn, Gringo. Time for you to die."

Two shots cracked out, then two more. Gabriel tensed, but he wasn't hit. The gunman crumpled to the ground.

David stood nearby, holding his pistol in one hand and Javier Garcia in the other.

"I couldn't bring the cavalry, my friend, so I thought you might appreciate the Indian helping out for once."

He nodded his thanks. "You're right, David. When it goes to the line, it's no time to be fussy about who saves your ass. Nice shooting."

"You should see me with a bow and arrow."

"I'd sooner you stayed with the pistol," Gabriel smiled. "It's technology I understand. Let's get that guy out of sight and we'll have a chat with him."

They found a space between two mounds of masonry that were hidden from the street. Gabriel spoke to the Mexican just as Rodrigo came around the corner and stood to watch.

"I'm looking for two American women. Tell me what you know about them."

"Two women?" Garcia was terrified, but this was more familiar ground to him, North Americans looking for information. "I don't know anything about two women, but if you wish I can…"

He stopped because Gabriel had taken hold of his testicles and squeezed. Hard. He held his other hand over the man's mouth to stop him from shrieking. He stared into the Mexican's eyes.

"Listen to me, Javier. I want you to listen carefully. The only way for you to live any longer is to tell me everything you know. You lie again and it'll hurt bad, real bad. So bad that you won't be any use to your women any more. You comprehend what I'm saying?"

He increased the pressure and then released it. Javier nodded in desperation. "Si, si, I will tell you everything."

"I know you will, Javier. I know. The only question is how much pain it will take to persuade you. Now, the women, where are they?"

Javier looked at the piles of broken masonry. The glance was unmistakable. "They're under there."

"Both women, and the priest too? Is there a way out?"

Javier shook his head. "The tunnel, its roof caved in somewhere over on the American side. There is no exit."

Gabriel felt waves of grief threaten to overtake him. So they were dead, Faith was dead. Then his anger took control of him, but it was not an anger of heat. Rather it was a cold fury that possessed his mind absolutely. He would pay. They would all pay.

"I see. Now, Javier. Who ordered you to bury those people?"

He jerked in even more fear. "If I tell you, he will kill me. Please, if you want more women, I will find some for you. Young and beautiful, too, I can...aarrrgghhh!"

The New York detective had taken hold of his testicles again in an iron grip. He was trying hard to control his fury, for otherwise he'd kill this man before he got the information from him that he required.

"Last chance, Javier. I want the name, or I twist them off. And then I'll start on the rest of you. Maybe I'll take out your eyes."

"No, no. I tell you, he is Ricardo Valdez."

David's eyes narrowed. "Ricardo Valdez? Where is he from?"

"Phoenix."

De Sade glanced at David. "Isn't he that guy in Phoenix? The dealer in the Hummer?"

David nodded. "Yeah, that's the one."

Gabriel turned back to Garcia. "Is Valdez the guy at the top? The one who runs your organization?"

"Yes, yes, he is the one."

But Gabriel had seen the momentary hesitation, the flicker of the eyes. There was someone else, someone higher up the totem pole.

"Who else, Javier? Last chance, I warned you."

The Mexican didn't reply, and his eyes shed tears of agony. The hand on his balls had twisted and wrenched them beyond recovery. The hand clamped over his mouth stopped him from crying out. When de Sade was satisfied that the man wasn't going to scream, he gently eased off the pressure.

"David, lend me that big knife you carry. It's your eyes next, my friend. I did warn you."

"No, no, listen, I will tell you everything I know. I don't know a name, but I might be able to describe him to you."

"Go on."

"I have only seen him once. He is white, like you. Norte Americano. Tall, slim, very fit. Older than you, I would guess he is about fifty years old."

"Yeah, that describes several million Americans. I'm sorry, Javier, you just lost your eyes."

"No!" The word was screamed out in abject terror. There is one more thing, the only one I know. His boots."

"His boots? What about them?"

"They are very expensive, snakeskin, handmade. He is very proud of them, said they cost almost a thousand dollars."

De Sade looked across at David. "Are you thinking what I'm thinking? It has to be him."

The Indian nodded his head. "Congressman Carson.

But it doesn't make sense. Wasn't it Carson who wanted you to come down here to look over the department?"

"It makes perfect sense to me. If the guy thought that the cops were getting close to him, wouldn't he do something like that to avert suspicion? It means that he's central to the operations of the Phoenix PD now. He can argue that he has an interest in how things are going. He's put himself into the middle of the investigation."

David nodded. "It does make a certain sense. But we'll need evidence."

De Sade laughed. "Evidence? The bastard gave the orders that got Faith murdered. He isn't going in front of any jury."

David opened his mouth to object, but Gabriel took Garcia by the throat with both hands and twisted violently. His neck snapped and the body fell to the ground. Behind them, Rodrigo moaned again in terror. "You shouldn't have done that, Señor."

"I did nothing, Rodrigo. Do you understand what I'm saying? Nothing!"

The man stared into de Sade's eyes and saw the tortured depths of a man who had embarked on a mission of revenge.

"Yes, Señor. I saw nothing. Nada! Nothing at all."

"Good. David, we need to get back to Phoenix and find Carson."

But David had squatted on the rubble, and his eyes were staring into infinity.

After a few moments, Gabriel thought he had to move him along. If the cops came along, and sooner or later they would, there were too many dead bodies lying around to explain away.

"David, what is it?"

But the Indian didn't move. He just sat, staring, motionless. Rodrigo looked at Gabriel.

"Señor, is he ill?"

"No, not ill. Just wait, give him some time."

"But, the police..."

"We wait."

They waited for ten minutes, and then David Whitehorse stirred. "They're alive."

Gabriel felt a surge of hope, but then squashed it. It was crazy; they were buried under hundreds of tons of masonry. "How the hell could you know that?"

David stared at him. "You're just not a believer, are you? No matter what stares you in the face. I'm willing to bet that there've been many times with that girl that she's come through, and you haven't believed her."

"I guess there have been a few times when it was a bit..."

"Has she ever been wrong?"

"No."

"I didn't think so. There are some people in our tribe who have that kind of power, but she's got something more. It's as if..." he tailed away. Then he spoke again. "Our medicine men would have said she was able to speak to the spirits."

"The spirits?"

"What you would call God, I guess."

"David, this sounds crazy to me."

"So when she comes through, and she's proved right on every occasion, you still don't believe it. What the fuck would it take, Gabriel? A shooting star? Or an eclipse out of nowhere?"

"David, she's dead, we know that. Whatever she was able to do when she was alive. She can't do it when she'd dead."

"But she's not dead. They were in a basement room, when it collapsed they'd already moved into a tunnel. The tunnel under the border, I guess. I imagine that can only mean one thing, they're moving along the tunnel into the US. Except that it's blocked with a roof fall."

De Sade hesitated, now knowing what to say. Then he looked at David. "So what do we do now?"

"If she's heading for the US of A, that's where we need to be. We need to get back over there and help them from that side."

"Where would this tunnel come out?"

Whitehorse shook his head. "I've no idea. It could be anywhere in a hundred square miles of territory."

"Then we'd better start looking."

"I guess so. But we'll need help. Rodrigo, how would you fancy a trip to the US?"

"But, Señor, I have no visa."

"I'm a Phoenix cop. I guess I'll have to arrest you, which should do it."

* * *

The air was already becoming stale and difficult to breathe. The tunnel was cramped, and there were far too many of them and not enough air. They were still struggling to clear the roof fall and there was no sign that they were any nearer to getting past the blockage. In the meantime, they'd formed a kind of chain. Those who weren't digging or helping to fix the roof timbers squatted on the floor of the tunnel passing buckets of earth and sand back along where they could be emptied at the Mexican end of the tunnel. In the dim light of their flashlights, the two girls could see the grim faces of the Mexicans.

"They think they're digging themselves further into their own graves," Galina murmured.

"I guess that's exactly what they are doing, if we can't get past the roof fall."

"How can you say that? I thought you were confident that we were going to make it."

"I'm confident that we 'can' make it, Galina. It doesn't mean that we will. There are many problems we need to resolve. To start with, these flashlight batteries will fade before much longer. These people may start to panic then. That'll make it more difficult for us to dig and repair the timbers. It will also consume more of the air."

"It's getting bad."

"Yes, it is."

"If only they could start digging from the other side," Galina whispered. "It would give these people hope."

"They know we're down here."

"Who knows we're here?"

But Faith shook her head. "I'm not sure. We need to have faith."

"In God?" Galina asked with a degree of exasperation, laced with a tinge of fear.

"Is there anyone more powerful than God, Sister Galina Polotsova?" Faith asked.

The Russian inclined her head in agreement. "You're quite correct, Sister Faith Ward."

Faith nodded. "Yes, I am." She looked at the line of Mexicans squatting along the length of the tunnel. "We must pray, again. We're getting out of here, but we must pray. It is our only hope."

CHAPTER ELEVEN

The journey over the border was a breeze. David Whitehorse showed his Phoenix PD credentials and there were no questions about the handcuffed Rodrigo Diaz. Night was falling when Gabriel drove into a motel outside Nogales, Arizona. As David had patiently explained to him, searching the Arizona desert at night for a remote tunnel was a sure way to court disaster.

"It's like this. You've got drug smugglers, people traffickers, border patrols that'll shoot first and ask questions afterwards, and any number of gullies waiting for you to drive into and break all of our necks. And that's another problem, the car."

"The Cadillac?"

"The Cadillac, sure. You won't get more than a hundred yards off the main track before this beautiful piece of machinery bogs down. If we're going looking for this tunnel, we need a four wheel drive SUV. It's almost ten at night, there's no way we'll find a rental company until first thing in the morning."

"I'd prefer to keep looking tonight," Gabriel replied. He felt uneasy at the prospect of leaving Faith and Galina in the tunnel any longer than necessary. But he understood David's logic. Until had an off road vehicle and some daylight, they had no chance. He glanced in the back as Rodrigo spoke for the first time since they'd crossed the border.

"Excuse me, Senores."

"Yeah, what is it?" David replied.

"The handcuffs. Must I keep them on?"

They both laughed and David dug out his key and unlocked them. "Sorry about that, I clean forgot about them." He looked ahead. "That motel there, it looks good enough."

Gabriel drove into the courtyard. It was thirty year old architecture that had not borne well the attacks of wind, sand and rain. The thirty year old paintwork was peeling, so that it gave the front of the building almost the appearance of camouflage. At least there would be a degree of anonymity here, all three men were conscious of the heap of bodies they'd left lying in the rubble back in Mexico.

They managed to check into an adjoining pair of rooms, one for Rodrigo and a double for the two detectives. The clerk looked puzzled at the white man and the Indian sharing, whilst the Mexican had his own room. It was hardly the norm for this area where Indians and Mexicans formed a sizeable underclass, but he wisely made no comment. He was probably the owner. His appearance was a caricature of a rooms by-the-hour motel, displaying a huge paunch which suggested that he spent most of his time behind the desk eating Twinkie bars. Maybe he'd have been better off on a ladder, tidying the paintwork. When they'd walked in, he'd just tossed the latest wrapper into a bin where they could clearly see another dozen used wrappers. He was almost bald, with a transparent comb-over that failed to hide most of the top of his crown, and he wore a stained, white wife-beater shirt. Were they 'de rigeur' for seedy motel clerks, the detectives wondered?

"Excuse me," Gabriel caught his attention, "I need a vehicle in the morning. Can you arrange it? A four wheel drive, we'll be heading into the desert."

The man shook his head. He adopted a calculating look. "Ain't none of the local hire companies going to be too pleased to let you have a shiny new rental to take out there. The desert is hell on autos. I tell you what, my friend. I've got an old Jeep out back. I can do you a deal on that. She drives real well. Hundred dollars a day."

David looked up in astonishment. A hundred dollars a day was extortionate for an old Jeep, but Gabriel agreed immediately, subject to it having a full tank of fuel. The only thing that mattered was lives. Money didn't figure. They managed to get troubled night's sleep, and in the morning Gabriel took a cold shower, dressed and went to check out the Jeep. He'd expected to see a scratched and rusting Jeep Wrangler, a common workhorse in the southern deserts. Instead the clerk pointed him to a battered World War II vintage Willys Jeep. It looked as if it had driven ashore at Omaha beach and carried on through shot and shell all the way to Berlin. Not a single panel was undented or without patches riveted over whatever lay beneath. Neither had it weathered the Arizona climate any better than the war. The paintwork had been sandblasted in some places to bare metal. There was no canvas roof, so the vehicle was totally open to the elements. At least the all-round visibility suited their operation to hunt for the tunnel. When he climbed into the ripped driving seat, the engine turned over well enough. It would do, it would have to do. He went back to their room, called for the other two men to join him and they went across to the greasy dining room for an unappetizing breakfast of ham, eggs and French fries.

"I guess we should check the oil on the Jeep, I get the distinct impression the motel kitchen has been using it to fry their breakfasts."

"Yeah, it sure tastes like that."

Rodrigo had wolfed down every scrap of his food. "I thought it was very good. Many people in Mexico would like to eat a breakfast such as this one."

"Yeah, many people in Mexico had better be able to afford plenty of Alka-Seltzer," David smiled. The Mexican looked puzzled, and he didn't enlighten him.

"What's the fuel situation?"

"The gauge is broken. I guess we'll have to look at the level in the tank."

On the way out, Gabriel questioned the clerk about the fuel. The man chuckled at the question.

"Don't expect any modern amenities in that baby. The filler is under the seat, and you'll find a stick next to the cap. You use that to dip into the tank to check the level. But she's full, I did it last thing after you left. By the way, there's no key, you start the engine using a button on the floor."

"We'll need drinking water, do you have any containers? I don't want to go out into the desert without enough to drink."

He looked surly. "What do you think I am? An expedition supplies store? The only drinking water I have to take away is over there."

He pointed to a vending machine. "It's one dollar a pop, do you want some change?"

Gabriel gave him a fifty dollar note and took the bucketful of coins. They left Rodrigo inserting them in the machine and removing the bottled water while they went out to the Jeep. The climbed in and Gabriel found the button that started the engine. It sounded sweet enough, so they swung around to the front of the motel and helped Rodrigo load fifty bottles of cold water into the back. He climbed in amongst the heap of plastic bottles and the two detectives boarded the front seats. There were no seat belts. Feeling like he was about to invade Nazi Germany, Gabriel managed to juggle the clutch and gear shift to get the Jeep moving. They swung out of the motel and he drove along the road that led back to Nogales and the border. Alongside them the vast expanse of the desert stretched away into infinity. His spirits began to lift, with this game and tough little vehicle and the two men who were with him. He felt they had as good a chance as any of finding the tunnel. David Whitehorse had proved his competence again and again, and Rodrigo, despite his obvious physical limp, was always ready to pitch in and help. But it was still not much of a chance, he reminded himself. Unless his partner had any more thought flashes, any more connections with Faith. Could they truly be coming from Faith, he wondered for the hundredth time? He had to believe they were. If they were not, she could be dead, buried beneath the rubble in Mexican Nogales.

"There's a cop car, about a hundred yards behind us,"

David interrupted his thoughts.

There were no rear view mirrors on the Jeep. It was just four wheels and an engine built onto a metal bathtub. Perfect for taking soldiers into a battle zone, but a sitting duck for an Arizonan traffic cop to pull over.

"If he stops us, he may impound this old tub on a score of traffic violations. I doubt it's legal."

"No. But we're heading into the desert, right?"

Gabriel nodded. "Yeah, of course we are."

"Ok. There's the desert, right next to us. He can't follow us there in that Chevy sedan. Just make sure you're in four wheel drive, the Willys has selectable two and four wheel drive as I recall. It's one of those levers next to the gearshift."

Gabriel looked down. "It's already pointing at the four wheel drive indicator."

"That should do it. Let's get out of here," David shouted above the engine noise.

"Are you sure you're a real cop?" Gabriel smiled. "I mean, your first instinct is to make a run for it."

"I was an Indian first. I learned to run from the law before I learned to talk."

Gabriel heaved on the steering wheel and the Willys left the tarmac and bounded across the sand. The police cruiser stopped and a cop got out. He wore a Stetson, mirrored shades, and he watched them for a few moments. Then he climbed back into his vehicle and drove away.

"He'll call the border patrol to keep an eye out for us," David pointed out.

Gabriel nodded. "Ok, if they come after us with SUVs or helicopters there's not much we can do. But we're not breaking any laws out here, are we?"

"Not now we're off the highway. They may peg Rodrigo as an illegal, though."

"We're peace officers, so we can always explain the situation. Besides, Rodrigo's going back home to Mexico when this is all over, aren't you?" He looked back at the Mexican, who glanced away with a guilty expression. "Oh Jesus Christ, you're not intending to become an illegal immigrant?" He looked across at David. "What the hell are we going to do? We're supposed to enforce the law."

"We do what cops have always done when necessary. Turn a blind eye. Rodrigo, if anyone asks, you intend to go back home. Savvy?"

The Mexican nodded. "I understand. Thank you."

Gabriel drove across the desert to a point where they were directly opposite, as near as they could tell, from where the demolished building lay across the border in Mexican Nogales.

"Rodrigo, about how far away would you say we are from the start of the tunnel, the demolished building?"

He shaded his eyes from the sun and looked back and forth, making his mind up. "I guess about six hundred yards."

"Yeah, is that about what you would expect for a tunnel?"

"Yes it is, but some are longer, much longer, as much as half a mile long or even more. A few are short, they come out just on the American side of the border, but they are easily detected."

"There's another factor," David said. "You're assuming the tunnel runs in a straight line. If it's at an angle, it could be anywhere."

Gabriel felt the dead weight of the impossible task

they faced crushing him. He'd been in many life and death situations, but the consequences for failure of this one were too horrific to contemplate.

"We can only make our best guess, in the light of what we know. We'll start here, directly opposite the wrecked building. What are we looking for, David? You're the man with the local knowledge."

"I've done a few stints down here, looking for fugitives. The officers I worked with talked about any number of disguises for tunnel entrances, but there always has to be some feature that stands out in the desert. Piles of rocks built up to make an artificial feature of the landscape. They plant bushes and such. Clumps of mesquite are one of the old favorites. An old building, even a wrecked vehicle could hide the entrance. It'll be here somewhere."

"Right, I suggest we…"

He stopped as his cell rang. "De Sade."

He listened for a few minutes. Then he pulled a face. "I'm busy right now. I'll get back to you later. I don't care that the chief wants me right back, I'll call you when I can. Try and stall him, Carlo. Anything you're not sure about, talk to Frank Willard, he'll know what to do. I'll talk to you later."

He clicked off the phone.

"Trouble?" David was watching him.

"There's been another one in New York City, they want me back. The Feds are getting rattled."

"Another what?"

"Another serial killing. Same M.O.. Chess piece, hands cut off, the works."

"Jesus. What are you going to do?"

"Find that tunnel. Let's get moving."

* * *

Jonas climbed out of the taxi that had driven him into Nogales, Arizona. Every time he asked the driver about taking him all the way into Nogales, Mexico, the man laughed. Even though he was Mexican himself. "Señor, you should stay away from Nogales. No one goes there, not if they want to live a long and healthy life."

"It's important, I need to get there."

"What is so important that you need to get to that terrible place?"

But Jonas shook his head. "I don't know."

The man gave him an odd look. "Are you well, Señor?"

"I had an accident, and I lost my memory. All I know is that it's important that I get to Nogales, Mexico. I think I must have some friends or family there that is in trouble."

"If they are across the border they are indeed in trouble. You could even be mistaken. Take my advice and don't go there."

"Just drop me off at a hotel in town. I'll work out my next move from there."

The man shrugged. "Whatever, it's no problem. There is a Holiday Inn, it is very good there."

"That's fine."

The man took him to the door, and he paid him and carried his bag inside. The clerk gave him a room for one night, he didn't intend staying on the American side of the border for any longer. He checked the room. It looked fine, he was certain he'd stayed in many like it before. He put his back in the closet, then took it out again and removed the Browning Hi Power from the hidden compartment. He didn't know why he did it, but it seemed like the right thing to do. The tucked it into his waistband and donned a loose fitting windcheater jacket. Then he set out to look around the town, he didn't know why. It just seemed like the right thing to do. When the accident happened, it took him by surprise. The guy was crossing the street, an American, when a Hummer drove towards him at high speed. The driver evidently hadn't seen him. He only saw the guy at the last moment and banged the horn several times. The man stumbled as he tried to avoid the onrushing SUV, but Jonas could see that he wouldn't make it. He appeared to have a disability, for his movements were slow and jerky. He tripped again, and without thinking, Jonas launched himself across the street and knocked the guy out of the path of the speeding Hummer. The front fender clipped his body and threw him into the curbside, his head hammered into the concrete and everything went black. A few seconds later he came around to see that the guy was lying prone on the sidewalk. He checked the man and found that he was still breathing. His own head hurt badly, but he ignored the pain, it was nothing new, he remembered when... Christ, it was all coming back. He'd been a soldier. He looked at the unconscious victim again, he could see a tattoo on the man's arm, and he recognized it, a Delta force unit patch. As his memory came flooding back to him he saw the Hummer had halted a hundred yards away, two faces looked out of the windows back at the man they'd knocked down. A cab had stopped opposite him, Jonas gestured for the man to come nearer.

"This guy needs to get to the emergency room as fast as possible, would you call 911?"

"Sure buddy, it's already done. I used my cell to put the call in, they'll be here soon."

Jonas felt his anger surge into a white hot killing rage. They'd almost killed a man, obviously a vet, and a disabled vet as well. He couldn't let them get away with it. The cab driver looked ex-military; he had the look about him. Erect, upright bearing, crew-cut, a calm and measured way of dealing with an emergency.

"You're a vet?"

The man nodded. "Sure am. Marines, I saw service in Afghanistan."

"Yeah, I was there too." He gestured at the injured man. "This guy's tattoo says he's a vet too. Those guys nearly killed him and they drove away and sat watching him bleed out. I need to have a word with them. Can I hire your cab?"

The driver's eyes narrowed. "What have you got in mind? No rough stuff, this is the way I earn my living."

Jonas brought out a wad of notes. "A thousand dollars should take care of it. And I'll pay for any damage on top. It's either that or we let those bastards get away with it."

The guy took the money and held out his hand. "Art Fisher, Gunnery Sergeant. Let's go and have a word with those Mexes."

An ambulance screamed up to the curb and two paramedics jumped out and started to take care of the injured man. The Mexican's Hummer drove away just as the two men climbed into Art's taxi. Former Gunnery Sergeant Art Fisher started to follow.

* * *

They were finished. All of them were gasping for air, their faces were turning blue, and even Faith was beginning to doubt her earlier optimism, he faith in the power of the supernatural. Of God. Yet she'd been so certain. Someone was out there, she knew that now. Someone was looking for them. It was the message that was given to her. She'd felt it, in that innermost part of her mind. The place where she only went to communicate in the way that she still couldn't understand herself. Why hadn't they found them? Where were they? Or was it that the tunnel couldn't be found.

"We're on our own, so we'll have to dig this out ourselves. It's our only hope," she whispered.

"What was that?" Galina looked at her sharply. Faith felt annoyed with herself, she hadn't meant to speak out loud.

"Don't say anything to the others."

Galina's eyes narrowed. "You were so convinced that help was on its way. What's changed?"

That was the question, what had changed, Faith thought to herself? Yet everything had changed. They were in a dark, airless tunnel. The flashlights were on the last of their battery power, only putting out a feeble glow. The air was foul, there were too many people in such a confined space, and if there was any way for fresh air to get into the tunnel it wasn't apparent to her. They were desperately thirsty, as none of them had taken a drink in many hours. They were hot, far too hot. They were surrounded by the hot desert, and their own body heat was making the tunnel even hotter. There was no sanitation, Father Juan had organized a rudimentary way for them to relieve themselves, just a hole in the floor of a shallow side tunnel he'd insisted they dig out. The stench was terrible, overpowering. Yet none of it was as awful as the fear. The cloying miasma of terror that surrounded them seemed to make their every movement an agonizing and painful effort. Faith was partially glad that the feeble light made it impossible to see their faces. It was enough to smell them, to hear their frightened words, their desperation, but for most it was more than that. It was resignation. Many of them knew that they were going to die down here. Then something touched her mind, something that was not of this tunnel, something that did not carry the taint of fear, the stink of sewage and body odor, something that was very alien to this earthy prison. It was like a cool mountain stream, reassuring, gentle, pure and clear. Something free. It was outside, out there, close. Looking for them.

"Please!"

Her scream made them all stop. The noise of digging died away, the women and children stopped their wails and efforts to calm frightened babies. The constant hammering of wooden props into the sandy roof of the tunnel was silenced. Galina peered closely at her face.

"Are you ok?"

They're near to us, I felt them."

Galina sighed. "I don't know, Faith. You've been saying that for some time, and everyone has worked hard to clear the roof fall. But maybe you were mistaken; it could be too much for us to do. We still don't know how far we have to dig."

She spoke in a confident tone. Whatever their situation, panic would make it much worse.

"They're near, very near. We're going to get out of here. Soon."

"How can you be sure of that?" Father Juan had spoken; he'd crawled back along the tunnel to find out what the problem was. "You keep saying that

"I'm not wrong. They're near, very near. We're going to get out of here."

"How can you be sure of that?" Father Juan had crawled back along the tunnel to find out what the problem was. "You keep saying that you've heard some message. Yet we never see any sign of it. Do you think that you have some kind of personal telephone line to the Almighty? Is that what it is?"

"No, Father, I do not. For some reason, I have been blessed with some kind of supernatural ability. It started when I became a nun. I don't…"

He looked at her sharply. "Yes, you said you were once a nun. But the nuns I have known do not have any kind of supernatural ability. I wonder if you are misguided in some way."

Galina snapped at him. "Father, I was a nun too, and of course I do not have that kind of ability. But if Faith says she had been in contact with someone outside, then we must believe her."

"Is that so?" he snarled. "Why should we believe her?"

Galina looked around desperately. "These people, Father, look at them. They're all in, finished. They need a miracle to save them. Or at least, they need to believe in a miracle. Do you want to see them start to panic, a panic that can only end in them destroying themselves, tearing themselves apart? As long as we are still alive, we must believe in her."

"So you think this miracle really is true, that it's going to happen? You think that she knows our rescuers are near?"

She knew she needed something powerful to convince him, so that that he could convince the others. "You know of the Church of the Resurrection in Jerusalem?"

"You mean the Church of the Holy Sepulcher?"

"Yes, that's the one. We call it by a different name, that's all. We were trapped inside there with a terrorist bomb about to explode and destroy the church and us with it. Faith was able to save us."

"You mean, she really did communicate with, well, something?"

"That's what I mean, yes. To this day none of us know how she did it, or who was giving us guidance and help. But she saved us, and saved the Church of our Lord Jesus Christ."

"Who did she think she was in contact with?"

Galina drew a deep breath. "We were next to the tomb."

The priest crossed himself. "THAT tomb? I find that very hard to believe it was..."

"Yes, no doubt you do. But I was there, and it's true."

Father Juan looked thoughtful. Then his face cleared, as he came to a decision. "It seems that we have no choice but to accept what she says." He raised his voice for all of them to hear. "Listen, everyone. We are not alone. Sister Faith had had a message. A voice has spoken to her. It tells her that we will all be saved. It's a miracle!"

The tunnel erupted in a hubbub of voices, as tired, desperate and stinking people, women, children, men, many of them old, dared to hope once more.

"I am no longer a nun, you should not call me Sister," Faith said quietly to Father Juan.

"Right now, they need a miracle, and you're all they have. Do not disappoint them. Sister Faith."

She nodded. "Very well, I will do my best."

"Thank you, on behalf of all of us here. What would

you have us do?"

Faith glanced around. Those nearby were staring at her expectantly. She sighed; it seemed she had been cast as their leader. She spoke loudly, so that they could all hear. "Those that can dig, I want you to dig. All of our lives depend on it, and God will only help those who help themselves. Those that cannot dig, we must pray."

"Will that help?" a Mexican woman asked, her voice filled with doubt. She was sitting nearby, trying to comfort a frightened child of perhaps two years old. Faith stared at her.

"You ask if it will help. Yes, more so even that the digging. Our prayers will be a thousand times more powerful than the digging. And they will be answered, I promise you that. I tell you they will be answered. That is enough questions. It is time now for prayer."

CHAPTER TWELVE

They'd been hunting all morning, four hours had gone by. It was hopeless, they crisscrossed the desert floor repeatedly, checked every bush, every abandoned and rusting vehicle. Every rotting timber hut left by long-gone settlers and drovers, every pile of rocks or ruined dwelling, but there was nothing.

"They'll be running out of air," Gabriel muttered, half to himself. The others glanced at him and said nothing. "We need to try something different," he continued. "We have to get into that tunnel and find a way to get through to them. Rodrigo, haven't you got any ideas?"

But the Mexican shook his head. "I'm sorry, Señor. I have been looking everywhere. Perhaps if we went on foot?"

"No. We can't cover enough ground on foot. We'll have to…David, what's the matter?"

The Indian held up his hand for quiet. He climbed out of the Willys. When Gabriel made to follow he gestured for him to wait. "No, leave me for a few moments. I need to be alone."

They watched as he walked a dozen paces away from the Jeep and squatted on the desert floor. Then he went still, totally motionless. His eyes were wide open, Gabriel could see them clearly, but he knew they could not see him. He was far away, in some kind of a trance. For a long time Gabriel kept his patience, not daring to hope that some combination of his partner's innate Indian mental abilities and Faith's mental powers, whatever they were, could somehow connect and help find them before it was too late. Unless it already was too late. He looked at his watch, they'd been here a half hour and he was tempted to go to David and tell him they needed to move on. He was more desperate that he'd ever been in his life. Then David got up and started to walk. Gabriel nodded at Rodrigo and the two men followed the Indian detective. He walked for almost half a mile, finally they saw he was heading towards an old, stone hut. At least, it had once been a hut. At some stage the walls and roof had been dismantled and it was now just a stone slab floor, with a low wall around it, about a foot high. David walked into the remains of the hut and stood staring down at the floor.

"We need to lift these flagstones," he said abruptly.

"Are you sure, it could take all day to lift them? We'll lose the chance to search anywhere else."

"We must lift the stones."

They started to prize out the first flagstone, and it came out with ease, surprising both of them. It struck them that it had to have been loosened and removed recently. David had found the tunnel entrance!

They flung themselves on the stone slabs, ripping them up and tossing them to one side. Beneath the layer of stones there was a layer of heavy timbers. Gabriel ripped them out, frantic to find the tunnel entrance. And then it was there, a funnel-like hole that disappeared into the ground beneath the desert.

"How can we be sure this is the right tunnel?" Rodrigo enquired. Gabriel felt a flash of despair at the thought that they could be in the wrong place, but David dispelled their doubts.

"It is the correct tunnel, there is no doubt. You can believe me."

"Some kind of Indian thing?" Gabriel smiled to make it clear he was joking. He felt almost drunk with renewed hope now that they'd found something. But David just shook his head.

"It's hard to explain. An Indian thing, maybe. But that girlfriend of yours has the power, believe me. It's like nothing I've ever know before."

Gabriel didn't ask him to explain, he only had one concern. To reach the blockage in the tunnel and clear it to allow them to escape. Assuming that David was correct, and what he thought he'd communicated with Faith proved to be the case. And that this tunnel, out of the hundreds that had been dug across the border, was the right tunnel. But he had no other options. There was nothing else to try, nowhere else to look. Rodrigo went and brought the Jeep closer. He found a pair of big, old flashlights in the back of the Willys Jeep, together with an oil lamp. Just as importantly, there were two spades strapped to the side of the vehicle. David lit the lamp and they climbed down a rotting wooden ladder to the floor of the tunnel, almost twenty feet below the surface. He led the way through the stifling, almost airless space lighting the way with the oil lamp. Rodrigo switched on a flashlight too, but he ordered him to turn it off.

"We don't know how long we'll be down here, so we have to conserve the batteries. If the oil lamp starts to run low we can use gas out of the Jeep."

The tunnel was narrow and too low for them to walk upright. They had to move along with their shoulders hunched over, bumping into rocks that stuck out of the sides. He held the lamp up to inspect the roof.

"Jesus, no wonder it collapsed. The timbers are rotten. If we had the time we should find some timbers to reinforce these supports."

Gabriel nodded. "It's bad, but it's a risk we have to take. I only hope to god they have enough air to keep them alive."

David didn't reply with the obvious. They were with a large party of Mexicans, whatever air they were breathing had to be almost pure carbon dioxide by now. Then they came to the roof fall. A ragged heap of broken timbers mixed in with earth, sand and gravel. Without a word he set the oil lamp in a recess in the side of the tunnel and set to work with the spade.

There was only room for one man at a time to work. David dug for five minutes while the other two men used the remaining spade to toss the earth back out of the way. Then Gabriel took over, he was like a man possessed.

"You need to pace yourself, buddy. This could take all day, and then some."

"If that what it takes, that's what I'll do. You know they must be almost out of time."

"Yeah, I know."

He worked with a fury, so that the others had to work

at speed to remove the earth he shoveled away. Half an hour went by, and still he wouldn't let up.

"You've gone about five feet, I'd guess. Let me take over," David suggested.

"Not yet," was the stubborn reply. "We may not be far away. I'll keep going."

His speed increased, earth, sand and pebbles flew back along the tunnel. Then he stopped.

"You want me to take over?" David asked, moving forward.

"Quiet! I thought I heard something."

They stopped dead, hardly breathing. There was nothing.

"Señor, I do not..."

"Wait! I heard it again."

"What did you hear?" David asked.

Gabriel listened, yes, there is was again. A scraping noise. "It could be someone digging. I think we've found them."

David joined him and shoulder to shoulder they clawed at the soil, using both spades and their bare hands when they couldn't use a spade in the tightly enclosed space. Rodrigo held the lamp high so that they could see to work, the soil they threw behind them was forgotten now. Only one thing mattered, to break through the last of the blockage. Then Gabriel jabbed the spade into the mass of earth, it went in a few inches and stopped as it hit a small rock, he pushed harder, and then staggered as it went all the way through.

"We've made it, we're through!" he shouted.

David was clawing at the earth, pulling away the soil to widen the gap around where the spade had gone through.

A small hole became visible, just a narrow slit little bigger than the spade. Both men ripped at it, breaking their nails as they battled to break through the final barrier. Both men heard the woman's voice at the same time.

"Gabriel? Is that you?"

Faith! They'd made it. They ripped out the last of the earth and widened the hole until a person could fit through it. It happened in a rush, one moment they faced a blocked tunnel, the next there was a rush of loose sand, soil and pebbles, a blast of stale, fouled air, and they were staring at the filthy, bedraggled faces of Faith, Galina and the Mexicans. Seconds later, Gabriel was holding Faith in his arms. She was weeping tears of relief, but she still had the presence of mind to call out to Galina to help the others through. But the Russian woman was already pushing the first of the children through. They had arrived. In America.

They helped the priest and the rest of the Mexicans to clamber through. Rodrigo led the way back out to the surface, they were a hundred feet from the tunnel entrance where they'd left the Jeep. Galina went on ahead, David escorted her and Gabriel lingered in the rear with Faith. They'd switched on the flashlights and he could see the filth on her face, the sand and soil in her hair. She was grinning from ear to ear.

"I thought we'd had it that time. Who was it that found us? I know it wasn't you," she grinned.

"How could you know that?"

She shrugged. "It had to be someone who had some ability to understand supernatural power. I know that you've got your feet planted too firmly in reality. You're not a believer. It was someone who lives and breathes the old ways."

"Maybe I could learn someday."

"No, I don't think so. I don't know what it is, but I believe that it has to be part of the very core of your being. I know you, Gabriel de Sade. If you can't shoot it or make love to it, it doesn't exist."

"I guess that about sums it up, yeah. If you can't shoot it or make love to it, what's the point of it existing?"

She smiled. "So who was it?"

"You mean the person that worked out where you were?"

She nodded.

"It was a detective from Phoenix, David Whitehorse."

"An Indian! Of course, that makes sense."

"Yeah, he's a Navajo, that's right. He's one of the good guys."

"I hope you won't be jealous, I owe him a huge hug and kiss for finding us when we get out of this tunnel."

"I'll try not to be. Provided it's just the once."

They held hands tightly as they worked their way out of the tunnel. She was weak, the first thing they'd all need when they got out would be the bottled water. They reached the tunnel entrance, the others had already all disappeared up into the open air. He found it strange. There was no noise, no sounds of joy and jubilation. Maybe they were plumb exhausted, they'd be better when they'd drunk plenty of the water. Better still when they'd had some food. He pushed Faith ahead of him, and she clambered out of the hole. Then he followed. The reason for their silence became apparent. He was staring into the barrel of a gun.

"Well, another gringo. We've got all of you, a clean

sweep."

The man who spoke was holding an Ingram in his hand, the barrel pointed at the group who had escaped from the tunnel. He wasn't alone; there were five other men with him. They were all Mexicans, and all armed. Two more carried Ingram sub-machine guns, the other three held scatterguns. They looked as if they were ready to start shooting. Gabriel said nothing, just waited.

"So you're the other cop who killed my people? It's nice to meet you, and even better that you've brought these people along with you. Now that you're all in one group we can finish up this mess and get ourselves home."

"Who are you?" Gabriel hadn't a clue about how to deal with them. On his own he would have taken a chance and maybe even taken some of them down, he knew his Glock was still in his belt. He realized that covered in the dirt and filth from the tunnel, it wasn't so obvious that he was armed. He wondered if David had managed to keep his weapon. Even so, with the women and children it was out of the question to start a shooting war. He needed time. Time to work a way out of this. The Mexican smiled.

"Of course, you wish to know who is about to kill you. My name is Ricardo Valdez."

De Sade had already recognized the Phoenix drug dealer. He began calculating the odds of taking the Mexicans down. They weren't good, but if they were to be killed anyway he'd have to chance it.

"You're the pervert from Phoenix who rapes and murders women and mutilates their bodies, are you?"

Just as he'd hoped, the man's face flared into anger.

"That's a lie. I had no part of killing those women!" Then he smiled. "So you think it was me, do you? I must tell the Congressman, he will find it amusing."

"So what are you, his bum boy, Valdez? Just clean up after him, run his errands, that's all you do is it?"

"You fucking gringo, no one speaks to me that way." Valdez stepped up to him and clubbed him to the ground with his Ingram. De Sade rode with the blow and dropped to the sand. Valdez stood over him, then drew his foot back and kicked him hard in the stomach. He rolled again with the blow, but it still hurt like hell. He was waiting for an opening when he could get close to the Phoenix drug dealer and use his Glock. But the moment hadn't yet arrived. If he drew his gun now the Mexicans would mow the civilians down. He had to wait. Valdez slashed across his face with the barrel of the sub-machine gun. He felt the skin split and the sticky wetness of blood pouring down his face. It would have to be soon, or the guy would kill him before he got a chance to move. The guy was in a rage now, spitting balls of phlegm as he gave vent to his anger.

"You fucking Yankees think you can come down here to Mexico and interfere with my operation, you're crazy if you think you're getting out alive. You still think you own the fucking place. I've got news for you, American. We own the place. Me and my buddies. Not fucking cops. When you're dead I'm going to send your body back to where you came from and they can see how we deal with fucking interfering Americans. It's time for me to kill you."

He brought up the Ingram and Gabriel saw his finger whiten as he prepared to pull the trigger. The patch of desert they were in went very quiet as if it was holding its breath. Until a voice rang out. Loud, clear and menacing.

"I reckon not, buddy. You pull that trigger and I'll fill

you full of holes."

Valdez whirled around to see who'd spoken. Gabriel glanced in the same direction, but he's recognized the voice. It was Jonas; he'd appeared like a miracle. Valdez's men had already been disarmed, their weapons lay on the ground, and they cowered under the threat of the big Browning.

"Jonas!"

Galina, despite all of her training, ran to him. She was hysterical with happiness, after the hell of their entrapment in the tunnel, without hope of ever seeing her lover again, to be saved only to be threatened once more with death, it was too much. It was also the wrong move. Valdez calculated when her body was shielding him from Jonas' Hi Power and made his move. He whipped up the barrel of the Ingram and pulled the trigger. Gabriel felt helpless, he knew that the Mexican would stitch a volley of bullets across the back of Galina, some would undoubtedly hit Jonas. But the gunfire went wild, the gun barrel jerked upwards as a piece of rock the size of a tennis ball thumped into the side of the gunman's head. Thirty feet away, the cab driver, former Gunnery Sergeant Art Fisher, stood in the classic pose of the baseball pitcher. In the stunned silence, they all saw him shrug in response to their astonished glances, he drawled, "I used to pitch for my unit in the Marine finals."

Valdez was recovering, he look again for his target. But the opening was more than enough for Jonas, the kind of opening that soldiers dream of when everything has hit the fan. He gave Galina a mighty shove and sent her sprawling to the ground. Valdez was bringing his Ingram back around to bear, but the former Delta specialist flung himself away from Galina and fired a double tap that took the drug dealer in the chest and head even while he was still moving. Valdez's men saw the opportunity to grab for their weapons, but Gabriel was a mile in front of them.

"Not now, boys. Touch those guns and I'll start shooting."

He'd drawn his Glock and trained it on them, he held it rock steady. They eyed him sullenly, and then slumped as they realized that the odds were too long for them. Galina was on the ground, but she'd drawn her tiny Beretta to cover them, but the Mexicans backed away. She got up slowly and went back to Jonas. They hugged each other, neither spoke. Gabriel kept the Mexicans covered and walked across to the man who'd thrown the rock.

"I don't know who you are, my friend, but we owe you a lot."

"I'm Jonas's cab driver. Former Gunnery Sergeant Art Fisher."

De Sade shook his hand. "A cab driver? Gunny, you were wasted in uniform. The Mets would have paid anything to have you on the squad."

"I'm strictly a Diamondbacks man myself, but thanks for the compliment."

"But a cab driver, out here in the desert? What's that all about?"

"It's a long story. Those guys upset your friend Jonas in town. Bad mistake, they ran over a disabled vet."

"Ouch. Yeah, that was a big mistake."

"Too right. He persuaded me to follow them, and the trail led out here."

"Glad you could make it, Gunny."

"Anytime. You were in uniform?"

"Delta Force, with Jonas in Afghanistan."

"A hellhole, I was there. Well, I guess we'd better start ferrying these poor folks into town, they look all in."

Faith was clinging to him, and with difficulty he turned and glanced at the escapees from the tunnel. They resembled walking corpses.

"I guess there's no time to waste, some of these people are going to need treatment."

"Yeah. I can take half a dozen if I turn a blind eye to the rules. More, if it's the kids. I'll make a start."

"Thanks, Art."

"You're welcome. What are you going to do about the bad guys?"

He nodded at the Mexican hoods. David had his pistol out and pointed in their direction.

"I want to have a word with them first. Then we'll call the Border Patrol, I'm sure they'll know how to handle them."

He left Art to start rounding up the women and children. He and Jonas hugged each other, in the way of long lost brothers. Faith stood back and she and Galina smiled proudly at their men, they were more than brothers, these two. They shared a steel bond forged in the white heat of combat, where you never knew if you'd be going home to a homecoming party or your own funeral.

"What the hell happened to you? You had me worried."

Jonas shook his head. "Damned if I know. Some sort of an accident. I only recovered my memory a short while ago."

"So how did you know where we were?"

Jonas struggled to marshal his thoughts. He shook his head. "I just don't know, and that's all I have. I wish to god

I knew myself."

Gabriel shook his hand again. "We'd have been finished if you hadn't arrived. Thanks again, Jonas, I owe you another one."

"Don't forget Gunny Fisher. If anyone deserves the title, 'killer pitcher', it has to be him.

"I won't forget him. He's one mean guy."

Art came up to them at that moment. "I'm loaded, ready to take the first trip into town."

"Yeah, Art, they're probably all illegals. Whatever they need, let them have it, give 'em a chance to get clear of the cops."

"I hear you. Were you just talking about me?"

"Yeah. I said you were a helluva guy. For a Marine."

He smiled and went away whistling. David came over to them. "We need to contact the Border Patrol about these people. There's a raft of charges they'll have to face, I don't want any of them to escape justice."

"Give me fifteen minutes, David. Then you can call whoever you want."

These drug smugglers and people traffickers were not the first murderous parasites he'd tangled with. His mind raced back to his service in Afghanistan. They'd intercepted a gang of smugglers late at night, trying to slip across the border to Iran. They'd used the radio to call in the local Afghan police to round them up, as procedure and protocol dictated. But the smugglers weren't working alone, their Taliban minders were not prepared to allow a valuable cargo of opium to the Americans. And the policemen who were supposed to be in position to meet them had failed to arrive, as so often happened. A curtain of red and green tracers rose from the ground a hundred yards away. Thousands of tracers told them that they were faced with a well-armed force of enemy fighters. They ducked into cover and de Sade used his radio to call for air support, it was a heaven sent opportunity, the tracers pin pointed the enemy and made them a sitting duck for the air force. Except that a round had smashed the radio and they were out of contact with their headquarters. Two of the team were hit, one was killed outright and the other seriously injured. He'd sent two men to flank the enemy to the right and two to the left. Both were carrying the M249, an American version of the Belgian FN Minimi. Fitted with a one hundred round box magazine, the weapon was devastating. Brave and reckless though the ambushers were, their commander did not know his business and he had no flanking sentries out. The Team Bravo machine gun teams set up and went to work pouring fire onto the enemy machine gunners. The rest of them advanced in a frontal attack while the enemy was trying to cope with the flanking fire. Faced with a three sided attack, the rebel fighters pulled back. Into a closed ravine, from which the only escape was a climb up a two hundred foot sheer cliff. De Sade had shouted for a cease fire, and offered the enemy a chance to surrender. He was rewarded with a fusillade of bullets and an RPG rocket aimed in his general direction. It was badly aimed, and when the smoke cleared he'd ordered them to finish the job. They'd been left no choice but to slaughter the enemy, who fought like wild savages rather than surrender to the infidel. Afterwards, he counted up the cost. One of the team dead, one would never fight again, and the smugglers had escaped. The only plus side was that they'd left their load of opium. The sickening smell as it burned stayed with them for a

ERIC MEYER

long time. As would the knowledge that when the next crop was in, they'd have it all to do again. They deserved everything they got, for the callous misery and death they brought to everything they touched.

CHAPTER THIRTEEN

The interview with the Mexicans started badly. They'd found several lengths of wire in the Willys and used them to fasten their hands behind them. Gabriel and Jonas made them lie flat on the flagstones, close to the tunnel entrance.

"Mister, it's hot on these stones, we need to stand up."

"No problem, we're just fine. Tell me about the guy in Phoenix."

The man who twisted round glared at him. "He is dead! You know that, you just killed him. Ricardo Valdez. What more can we tell you?"

He glared at Gabriel. He had a twisted lip that turned his glare into an ugly snarl. Medical care in Mexico obviously left a lot to be desired.

"I need to know who called the shots for Valdez. El Jefé, the boss. When I've got some answers, I'll maybe let you go."

"But we know nothing about another guy. Ricardo was our Jefé."

Gabriel stood over him, and used his shoe to press the man's face against the hot flagstones.

"No, Señor, stop!" His voice was a shrill scream.

"The guy in Phoenix, talk to me about him. The guy in the snakeskin boots."

The man's eyes narrowed. "You know about him?"

"Yeah, I know. Maybe not all of it, so you're gonna help me fill in the gaps."

He pressed the Mexican's face back against the ground. The screams started again, but within five minutes, he had everything that the Mexican knew. Although they didn't know the exact name, the description they gave could only be Max Carson. They also knew about his little hobby, the perverted raping and killing of women. They'd even helped on occasion to round up victims for his to abuse. There could be no doubt now. He called David Whitehorse over.

"You can call the Border Patrol now, I'm done with them."

"You said you'd let me go!" The Mexican screamed and struggled against the wire that held his wrists.

Gabriel smiled. "Yep, that's true. I'm letting you go to the Border Patrol. I reckon you've got a few counts of murder and attempted murder to face, not to mention drug related charges. I reckon you'll be a guest of the state for the next twenty five years. Unless they transfer you to a Mexican jail."

The man shouted curses, and his companions joined it, until Gabriel stepped on the leader's face again. Then they quietened down.

David finished talking on his cell to the Border cops. "They say they'll be here in less than a half hour, they'll take these characters straight to the lock up. I guess they'll want to fill in that hole. Not that it'll make much difference. They've probably already started to dig another one."

"They should fill it up with those Mexican smugglers, I'm pretty sure they're responsible for a lot of innocent lives. They were doing their best to kill these people, that's for sure."

"Yeah, I'll make certain they have all the details. What's the plan now?"

"We need to get back to Phoenix. When Art has finished ferrying the people away from here, we need to return the Willys Jeep and I'll ask Art to take a fare to Phoenix. There isn't room for all of us in the Cadillac."

"You're going to see Carson?"

"Yes."

David stared at him for a few moments. "Detective, you can't just bust into town and kill one of our Congressmen. This needs to be called in and dealt with officially. Chief Simpson may be an asshole, but he won't just let this go. No way."

"How will you connect him to the Mexicans? Your chief won't take the word of a bunch of Mexican drug dealers against a US Congressman. You know as well as I do that the chances are that he'll go free."

"I don't believe that would happen," David objected stubbornly. "But even so, it's a Phoenix case, not one you should be involved with. I appreciate all you've done, de Sade, but now it's time for our people to take this one on board."

Gabriel reminded him of the New York homicides. "It's connected to our investigation in some way, I need to talk to Carson and find the connection."

"Even if Carson has been killing women in New York,

it's still our case, he's an Arizona Congressman."

"That's the problem," Gabriel objected. "I don't think he could possibly have killed all of those people in New York and operated in Arizona as well. No, it's a different killer, I'm sure of it. But they're connected in some way, I just don't know quite how. The only way I have to find our local killer is to talk to Carson before your people arrest him and he lawyers up."

David sighed. "I've seen you talk to suspects, de Sade. You play rough, de Sade. You can't do that with a US Congressman."

"So what would you have me do, David? Can you look me in the eye and swear that your Chief of Police will take the bastard down?"

"Of course he will, he'll…"

Whitehorse tailed off and he looked sheepish. "You're right. Yeah, the bastard'll give him an easy ride. Carson could get away with it, with a good enough lawyer and if Simpson doesn't push hard enough. What are you going to do?"

"I told you, I want to talk to him."

"Talk to him, right. And then?"

De Sade's lips formed a half smile, but it didn't reach his eyes. "It'll depend on what he says. But I've got one or two ideas."

Whitehorse nodded. "I guess you have. Do me a favor, keep them to yourself."

There were a few tricky moments with the Border Patrol, as Galina and Faith had no documents, having left everything in Nogales. But they accepted the word of the two cops, and just nodded when David told them that Rodrigo was his prisoner. He was wearing cuffs, and they didn't seriously question it. The lieutenant, a desiccated, stringy twenty five year veteran of the struggle to stem the tide of illegals into the state, spoke to the two detectives before he left.

"I'll take these hombres back with me and process them through the system. Just to be clear, they attempted to murder these two ladies, is that correct?"

"The two ladies and a bunch of Mexicans, yes," Gabriel asserted.

"Right. And these Mexicans are where, right now?"

"I've no idea, Lieutenant. When the fight started they scattered, I guess they took off further into the desert."

"Not towards the town of Nogales? I can't see them heading deeper into the desert."

"No, they headed away from the town. If they were going towards the town, you'd have seen them when you came in."

He nodded thoughtfully. "Yeah, I guess that's true. I've got your card with your New York address, so I'll contact you when I need statements from these two women. Maybe I'll come up to New York myself I haven't been there in a few years."

"We'd be happy to make you welcome, Lieutenant."

"Right. So deeper into the desert, that's where you reckon they went?"

"Sure."

He nodded. "Then I guess we'll never find them. They don't have it easy over the border. Being poor in Mexico is a state of mind. I've seen cases when I've been over there. People have their four year old kids out on the streets begging. I was in Nogales a month ago and I saw two shootings in the same day, I kid you not. The drug lords run the whole darn country. They own the military, the police, it's insane what the government let's them get away with. Some places are calm, but other places like the ones near the border are a warzone every single day. In some towns the cops have quit their jobs because they're scared of the drug lords. Then they try to come here for a better life and they're hunted like dogs by us, or the get lost to die of thirst in the desert. Jesus! What a life!"

He realized he'd been ranting about a pet subject. He smiled. "Have a safe journey back."

They said their goodbyes just as Art returned in his cab. He took Jonas and the two girls back to Nogales, USA, and Gabriel followed in the Willys with David and Rodrigo. When they got to the motel they released him to make his way to relatives he said he had not far outside the town. They settled accounts with the owner and an hour later they were on the road back to Phoenix. Gabriel drove the Cadillac with Faith in the passenger seat, and the others rode in Art's cab. They were silent for the first few miles, and then Gabriel asked Faith about getting their personal effects back from Nogales.

"We have to go back to finish the job, we need to arrange the shipment, so we'll get our things then."

"Going back!"

He almost crashed the car, the shock made him stamp down on the gas and the supercar charged forward, reaching over a hundred miles an hour within seconds.

"Yes, of course, we have a job to do."

He turned towards her. "Faith, for Christ's sake, do not go back to that place ever. At least, not without an armed guard."

She was silent for a few moments, and then she smiled.

"Well, that's what we have you and Jonas for, isn't it?"

He let out his breath. "Of course we'll go with you. But I'd sooner you never set foot in that place again. Jonas and I can go and get your stuff. Or maybe that monk, Brother Sebastian, he could pack it all and send it to you."

"You're forgetting something. The antiques, the relics that the church is selling to us. They need the money and we need the stock for the gallery."

"Jesus, it's a load of junk. Can't you find stuff somewhere else, somewhere not so dangerous?"

"Not like this, no. Although I did recover the burial shroud, which I know is genuine."

"You mean you have it with you?"

She nodded. "Yes, I have it. I believe its power saved our lives in that tunnel."

"Is it worth a lot of money?"

"Yes." She hesitated. "But in this case, it is not money. The shroud was used to bury the founder of the Christian Church."

He jerked around. "You mean Jesus? That's ridiculous."

She pursed her lips and frowned. "I don't see that it's ridiculous at all. In fact it's not the shroud that was used for Jesus, but why would it be so ridiculous?"

"Isn't that shroud in Turin?"

"No, the Turin shroud has generally been proven to be a fake, made in the eleventh or twelfth centuries."

"So what's the deal with this one in Nogales? I thought Jesus was the founder of the Christian Church."

"Jesus was a Jew," she continued. "Evidence suggests that he had no intention to create a new church. Many people credit the founding of the Christian church to Paul, but in fact the church Paul left us with bears little resemblance to what Jesus wanted. The true legacy of Christ was left in the hands of his brother, James. Some would say Jesus' wife, Mary Magdalene, too, was one of the early church founders."

"So you think they were married then, Jesus and Mary?"

She shrugged. "Maybe, maybe not. Who can tell? But after the crucifixion, there were competing strands of Christianity, all with their own differing agendas. It is my belief that James set out to continue the work of Jesus and was forced out by the other disciples. Peter of course was his main opponent. But it was James who directly carried Christ's legacy and whose shroud I now have in my possession. You see how important it is to recover it."

"If you believe all this stuff."

She glanced at him. "So you don't believe?"

"Believe what? Isn't it all a tissue of superstition, some of it undoubtedly true, much of it made up over the centuries?"

"Your friend, David Whitehorse, he believes."

"He's an Indian, so he's steeped in all of that supernatural stuff. You know, visions, seeing the future, all kinds of weird stuff."

"Isn't that the essence of God? A supernatural force that exists for good? Perhaps David's belief is not very different to mine. It's just that he calls it by a different name."

"That's a bit of a jump, Faith. You'll upset a few million Christians comparing their beliefs to those of Native Americans."

"Perhaps so. But I believe it to be true, up to a point. Good and evil, that kind of thing. And talking of that, how do you think you and David found us?"

"I, er, well, I don't rightly know. Luck, I guess."

"You know that someone or something up there was taking care of us, sending the right messages to your Indian friend?"

"You don't mean God, surely?"

Her eyes narrowed. "Gabriel, you've sure had some doubts since I've known you. For some reason I've been chosen to communicate with some kind of power, I don't know what it is. I call it God. Other people call it other things. Whatever, it's a force for good, and it saved mine and Galina's lives. Other people too, you included on at least one occasion. Why don't you believe still?"

"I've seen too many bad things, Faith. If there was someone up there who cared, this 'supernatural force', they never would have been allowed to happen."

He thought about Afghanistan, of the dead eyes of the locals as they passed through bandit country. Eyes that betrayed the hatred these people had for Allied soldiers. Their eyes were black and empty, and the very pressure of their loathing crushed you to the size of a walnut.

"We went on patrol in Afghanistan, we bumped into some kids," he explained. "They should have been in school, but instead they were being used to harvest and transport the opium crop. The Taliban had prepared and ambush, they were dug in on a low hill about two hundred yards away. The problem was that these kids were walking past ambush at the exact time we came along. As we walked into their lines of fire, so the kids walked between us and them."

"What did they do?" Faith asked. But she knew the reply before he answered. It was etched into his face.

"They opened fire anyway. I guess their intention was

to blast the kids out of the way so that they could shoot us. Their own kids! They weren't collaborators or informers. But it made no difference, because they were shredded in a burst of machine gun fire. Of course, we're trained for that kind of thing and we were all wearing body armor. The kids froze in panic and were cut down by the gunfire, dozens of them. They were taking bullets intended for us. We went to ground, but we couldn't shoot back because the kids were in the way, although most of them were dead or badly wounded. In the end, we called in a couple of gunships and they blasted those suckers out of that hillside. We gave what help we could to the children, but in the end only two survived. We all had nightmares for a lot of nights after that particular action. Any of the men that still had any faith in any God lost it there and then on that Afghan hillside."

"It was the death of faith," she murmured quietly. "I'm so sorry that you had to witness such an atrocity, one so bad that it killed any belief you had in God."

He felt embarrassed. "Yeah, whatever. It's called soldiering."

"But you didn't shoot those kids," she pointed out.

"No, I didn't. But someone did."

"And how do you explain our escape from that tunnel? How can you explain the fact that you and David were led to the tunnel entrance?"

He smiled at her. "That one's easy. I can't. I leave that kind of weird stuff to you and Galina, the religious types. Same as Jonas. We just handle the physical side."

"You mean the guns."

"Yep, you've got it right. You know the old saying, when life gives you lemons, you make lemonade. Well, life gave us a feel and understanding for guns, so that's what we do."

They drove on towards Phoenix. Faith pondered what Gabriel had told her about his time in Afghanistan. She knew that there was no cure for the kind of horrors that he had experienced over there. Maybe he was right, that there were plenty of bad people in the world. Fighters like him and Jonas, hard and ruthless men, were needed to combat the evil that existed everywhere. If it hadn't been for them, those Mexicans would have sealed them inside the tunnel, to die a long and lingering death. Yet it had taken more than guns to get them out, it had needed the faith and belief of her and Galina, even of the priest, Father Juan. It had needed the supernatural abilities of David Whitehorse too. She sighed inwardly, it was all so complicated.

"I supposed you're going to confront this Congressman now?"

"Yes, I am. Jonas too, I expect."

"What will you do with him?"

He thought about that one for a few moments, and then he grinned. "I guess we'll think up something biblical, how does that sound?"

She shivered. She didn't want him to torture the man, to kill him. She wanted him to abide by the law, to leave it to the authorities to deal with. After all, she was a former FBI Special Agent, trained to uphold and abide by the law. Yet when she thought about the fate that Carson had decreed for her, for Galina and the Mexicans, to be buried alive underneath the Arizonan desert, she couldn't bring herself to speak.

They reached Phoenix, and Gabriel checked Jonas and

Galina into adjoining rooms in the Holiday Inn. David Whitehorse took a cab back to Phoenix PD headquarters, and before he left they said their farewells to former Gunnery Sergeant Art Fisher.

"How much do we owe you for the fare, Art?"

He looked scandalized. "Owe me? Listen, after all we've been through I guess that makes us buddies, right?"

"Sure," they all nodded.

"Too right, and buddies don't charge each other for favors. There's just one favor I want from all of you."

Faith smiled. "Anything, Art. What can we do?"

"The next time you're passing through Nogales, Arizona, you call in and see me and my good lady. That's Marysol, to you, she's from Mexico. She cooks a mean dinner and we'd both be insulted if you didn't drop by."

"We'll do that, Art. Thanks a million."

They shook hands, and the girls gave him a hug and a kiss.

As he drove off, Gabriel shouted, "You take care, Gunny. Don't give up practicing the baseball."

He smiled and waved and they watched the cab disappear into the heat haze. Almost straight away another cab rolled into the hotel car park and David climbed in.

"I guess I'll see you later. Just be careful what you get up to."

"Keep out of it, David. Jonas and I can handle this."

"Yeah, maybe. Call me."

The cab drove away. Gabriel smiled at the two girls.

"I guess you need to relax after that tunnel. You two make yourselves comfortable for a while, Jonas and I have business to attend to."

"We know you have," Faith replied. "You both take

care."

They drove to the Congressman's address in central Phoenix. There was no reply to their knock, and too many nosy neighbors in the upscale area to break into the house and look for clues. They would prefer to find evidence of his wrongdoing to tie up any loose ends, but they had to call a halt for the time being and maybe return after dark. They returned to the Cadillac, and almost immediately Gabriel's cell rang. It was David Whitehorse.

"I just got in and noticed there's a report of someone who could be Carson taking a girl into a cheap motel on the outskirts of town."

"Why did they call it in?"

The motel clerk was worried. I guess he thought the girl looked under age. No more than fourteen, in his opinion. Some of the other victims have been in that age range, it fits the profile."

He gave them the name of the motel. "They haven't sent a cruiser out there yet, I told them to wait, said that I had someone in the area."

"Thanks, David. We'll take it from here."

"Yeah, keep me posted. Is there any chance you could be a little subtle here? I've only just got back and I'm in a heap of trouble as it is for taking off with you."

"I hear you, buddy. No noise, no fuss. We'll deal with it quietly."

"Yeah, I'll bet. Good luck."

* * *

He had to get back to Washington in the morning, and there was plenty of Congressional business he had to attend to. But the urge had fallen on him and he couldn't wait any longer. He'd picked the girl off the street in Maryvale. His car was a spare was registered to him, it was true, but it would be easy to report it as stolen if he hit trouble. She'd been touting for trade on her own and he'd invited her into his car and brought her to the motel. Already his pulse was racing. The clerk had given him a peculiar look when he'd registered the room, but he wasn't worried. That was the business of these cheap motels, without short-time rentals they'd be out of business. The main thing, of course, was that he wasn't recognized. He wore a large hat and thick dark glasses that covered his face. He always made sure to look away from CCTV cameras. And he wore gloves. He'd never gone without gloves so they wouldn't find any fingerprints or forensic residue if he had to leave in a hurry. He relaxed, he had it all covered. He'd have a couple of hour's enjoyment with this one, home for some shut-eye, and then he'd be on the next flight to Washington. A pity he hadn't time to call into New York on the way, he'd like to have shared a dinner and drinks with his partner. His soul mate, the only person he could talk to about his urges, the only one who would understand. What they shared was the truth. That's what they both called it, when the girl saw her life ending, saw his eyes as she breathed her last, as their two souls joined in mutual ecstasy at the end, there was nothing hidden between them. There could only be truth between life and death. Nothing more, it was that simple. This one was promising, very promising. She was young and pretty, one of those mixed race girls whose features combined the best of everything to form that perfect beauty that is the gift of only a very few females. The hard life of the streets hadn't yet chiseled away at her beauty either. It was too soon for that. A few more months and years and it would all be different. He grinned, for he reckoned he was doing her a favor. She wouldn't have to endure all that hell. She saw him smiling and she smiled back.

"What is it?"

"I was thinking how pretty you look. What's your name?"

"What would you like to call me, Mister?"

He scowled. "By your fucking name, what is it?"

Her smile faded. "It's Rita."

He felt disappointed. Rita wasn't a name to conjure up fantasies with. But still, he'd soon make up for that. "Get your clothes off, Rita."

"You pay me first. Fifty dollars, that's what you said."

"Yeah, sure." He peeled off a fifty dollar bill and saw her tuck it into her tiny purse. Then she started to remove her clothes. The long, high-heeled boots, the short skirt, her see-through blouse, finally she stood before him wearing only her brassiere and panties. He could see that she was shivering slightly.

"You done this before, honey?"

She hung her head. "Only the once."

"Smile, there's nothing to fear. This'll be some extra experience for you. Take off the rest of your clothes."

"Aren't you going to undress?"

She was eyeing his clothes, and she frowned when she saw that he hadn't even taken off his gloves. He saw the direction of her gaze and started to peel them off, then loosened his tie. She relaxed and slipped off her bra and panties. Her body was taut, firm, the skin smooth and unblemished. Damn, he was already hard. Rock hard.

"Lay down on the bed, honey."

"You're not undressed yet!"

"No. But I'm paying the bill, so we do it my way. Lay down."

She did as she was told. He turned away and pulled on the thin, flesh colored latex gloves. Then he spread her legs apart, and she shivered again as he ran his fingers up her leg and then felt inside her vagina.

"Close your eyes, darlin', I've got a little surprise for you. Something really good."

She smiled uncertainly and her eyelids closed. He unzipped his pants and pulled them down. His penis sprang out, engorged, hard and ready. He slipped a condom over it and then climbed on top of her. She felt him enter her, he was quite gentle at first, but still, there'd been no foreplay and she was not lubricated ready for his hard organ to ram into her. Then he pumped hard, and she suppressed a whimper as the pain shot through her. But she kept her eyes closed, he was paying for this and she'd just have to put up with it. The click startled her, it was an alien sound. She opened her eyes, as she did so she felt the sharp metal against her neck.

"It's just a game, honey, nothing to worry about. Just relax."

But she couldn't relax, she was terrified. He kept ramming his penis in and out and she waited for it to end so that she could get away from that that terrible blade that was pressed against her throat.

He was disappointed, she'd gone real stiff and cold, she wasn't enjoying this as she should. Well, it was her problem, not his. By the time the end came, it wouldn't make any difference either way. He thought about when he could meet his friend in New York so that they could swap stories of their conquests. He knew full well that the world would see what they were doing was wrong, but these people didn't understand. It was the greatest gift in the world, the one time when a man could look deep into a woman's eyes at that exact moment and feel a mystical meeting of the souls. A pity the women had to die, but there was no other way. At least they'd been a part of the sublime experience that was really out of this world. Did they feel anything at 'THE' moment? He'd often wondered about that, and they'd talked about it, without coming to any decision. Sure, it would be good to think that the victim felt the same way as he did, but of course, there was no way of knowing. He chuckled to himself. Maybe if there was an afterlife he'd find out. A queue of women waiting to, what? Either thank him or throw rocks at him. He chuckled again and felt the woman underneath him relax slightly, as she heard the sound and hoped that this was indeed all a game.

'It is a game, darlin', just not in the way you think.'

He felt himself coming to a climax. Damn, it was too soon. He willed himself to keep calm. He pressed the knife harder against the girl's neck, he didn't want her to slide away from the blade and ruin all the fun now. A thin, red line appeared on her coffee colored skin, damn, he'd pressed to hard. He eased off a fraction, and hoped that she didn't feel the trickle of blood that slid down her neck. Too bad if she did. He felt himself getting nearer to a climax again, he was almost ready. He rammed his cock even harder into the girl, so hard that she grunted in pain.

'No need to worry, it'll be all over in a short time, darlin'.'

"You can open your eyes now, honey. Yeah, that's right.

Look at me. Right into my eyes, look into my soul. Don't look away."

"What are you doing to me?"

"Shut up, just keep looking. Fix your eyes on mine, yeah that's it."

He held the knife and in his mind rehearsed the exact pressure needed to slice her throat open. Soon, yes, it was coming soon.

"You're hurting me!"

"Shut up! We're nearly there."

Yeah, he could feel it now, a volcano about to erupt. He gripped the knife harder. Forced his penis in harder, deeper. Heard her scream. Started to take up the pressure on the switch blade. And the door crashed open.

'What the fuck?'

He whirled to see who'd invaded his room.

"What? Who the hell are you?" Then he recognized Gabriel and his jaw dropped. "Christ, aren't you that New York detective?"

Another man appeared, so there were two of them to deal with. He'd have their fucking jobs for breaking into his room! The other one, a guy with impossibly wide shoulders who looked harder and tougher than hell itself, had a huge pistol pointed at him and a smile on his rock-hard face.

"We're the safe-sex police, Congressman. Officer Jonas Savage. Are you using a condom, Sir?"

CHAPTER FOURTEEN

They made him lie face down on the floor, and then helped the girl to dress. She was hysterical after her near-death ordeal at the hands of Max Carson.

"He was going to kill me," she sobbed. "He held the knife to my throat, and he said he wanted to look into my eyes as he cut me and watch me die."

"That's ok, he won't hurt you again," Gabriel soothed. "Do you have money for a cab back into town?"

She nodded. "He was gave me fifty dollars."

Jonas found Carson's money wallet and took out ten hundred dollar bills. He tossed them over to her.

"That should cover your extra expenses."

She gave him a grateful look, stuffed the money into her purse and left the room in a hurry, probably before they changed their minds about the money. It was time to deal with Max Carson.

"Congressman, your serial killing days are at an end, I guess," Gabriel said quietly.

The man twisted around and scowled at them. "I don't

know who the hell you are or what you're talking about. It was a sex game, that's all, nothing more than that."

"Right," de Sade nodded with a serious expression. "Just a sex game. Before you go any further, you should know that we've dealt with Ricardo Valdez. He told us everything before we killed him. About the girls, the killings, disposing of the bodies, everything."

Carson groaned. "What do you want from me? How much will it cost to make this go away?"

Both men laughed. "It isn't going away, Carson. You've got a lot to pay for," Jonas grinned at him. "We're here to collect on the debt."

"You'll never make it stick in the courtroom, there's no evidence linking me to anything."

"Who said anything about taking it to court?" Gabriel said casually.

"What are you planning to do?" There was fear in his eyes now, real fear as he began to understand that he wasn't going to talk or bribe his way out of this.

"That depends on you, Carson. We want to know the identity of the other man."

"Other man? I don't know what you mean."

"The copycat killer in New York. Who is it?"

He twisted around and tried to sit up, but Jonas used his boot to push him back down. "Not so fast, my friend. We're waiting for an answer."

"I don't know anyone in New York, this is crazy. You're crazy. I want my lawyer."

"The problem is, Max, you've got a lot to pay for, and a lawyer can't help you. If you can't help us, we'll just kill you and go looking for him."

"You can't kill me! My god, you are crazy."

"Maybe," Jonas agreed. "But you'll be dead just the same. It's up to you, give us the name or we'll leave you dead on the floor and find him ourselves. Your choice."

"I told you, I don't know anyone in New York."

Gabriel took over. "Let me have a word with him, I think our friend needs a little persuasion."

The man was already half naked. Gabriel spent ten minutes working on him, in the end it was only necessary to demonstrate to him that a refusal to help would cost him even more pain to his manhood.

"The guy you want is my fellow Congressman, Richard Bryant. But I'll never stand up in court and testify to that, I don't care what you threaten me with."

"He's the one who's been killing the girls in New York City, leaving a chess piece on their bodies?"

"Yes, it's him," he replied. His voice sounded tired and beaten. He knew it was over, he was ruined.

"Why the chess piece?"

The man chuckled. "It was just a little game, that's all. He thought it would add a touch of class to the murders, and maybe even make the cops look for a chess player. Kind of like a psychological thing."

"Right. How did you get into this?"

He hesitated, but remembered that he wasn't in a bargaining position. "I went to his hotel room one night, when I needed to talk to him about a bill in the house. He'd forgotten to bolt the door, so I walked in during one of his scenes. I watched him killing her for about fifteen minutes, it was incredible. But Christ, he nearly had a heart attack when he turned around and saw me there."

"So you saw him kill a girl, and it turned you on."

"Oh yes, it's the most wonderful thrill in the world. It's

worth anything, certainly the life of some cheap loser of a hooker."

But of course, that wasn't the whole story. They knew that Carson had funded his campaigns and his lifestyle with drug money and people trafficking. He was the one who'd given orders for the people in the tunnel to be killed to hide the evidence.

"You disgust me, Carson. Get up!" Gabriel snapped.

The man stood up and pulled his pants around him. "Where are we going now? Phoenix PD?"

"Just get outside to the car."

They left the motel room and walked out to the Cadillac. Gabriel opened the doors to put the man in the tiny rear space, but just then a party of businessmen walked past, they'd obviously been to some kind of a meeting and were well fueled with booze. Carson saw them and started screaming. "These men are trying to kidnap me, help!"

The crowd of suits surged towards them. There were at least twenty of them milling around. Their leader, a tall, stocky corporate type with carefully styled gray hair and an expensive suit, shouted at them.

"What the hell's going on here? Who are you people? Are you the police?"

"I'm a United States Congressman! I don't know who the hell these people are. I believe they're criminals."

The men started shouting, pushing and shoving and Gabriel was forced away from Carson. Jonas came to his rescue, hitting out at the businessmen, but it was too late. When they looked around, Carson had gone. A car door opened and shut, and engine started and his car screeched out of the car park.

"What the hell?" the stocky businessman blurted out,

trying to work out what was going on. "He's gone!"

Gabriel took hold of his coat and pulled him close to him. "I'm a detective hunting for a serial killer. The man you just helped to escape tried to rape and murder a young woman in this hotel. If he gets away and kills again, I'll hold you all responsible."

"A serial killer! Christ, we didn't know."

"Just get out of here, before I arrest the lot of you for interfering with a police investigation."

"Yeah, sure, officer, sorry." He looked at his people. "I guess we got the wrong end of this. Let's go and see if the bar is still open. I sure need a drink after all this excitement."

The men surged away towards the bar, Gabriel and Jonas rushed to the Cadillac. Seconds later they were hurtling after the runaway Congressman.

"Which way did he go?"

Jonas looked grim. "West, into the desert."

Gabriel nodded. "We'll catch up with him. I wonder why he didn't head into town."

"He probably thought the whole of the Phoenix PD would be after him. He doesn't realize that they don't know about him yet. He's just running, like they all do. The desert is fine for us, so we can take care of our business without worrying about lookyloos."

"Yeah. I hope to Christ there aren't any isolated farm tracks he can lose himself on."

He pressed his foot to the gas pedal and the Cadillac leapt forward. Is was fortunate that the tarmac was quite recent, the needle went over one hundred miles an hour and kept going up. They hit a hundred and fifty. Gabriel was struggling to keep the car straight and level on the narrow asphalt when Jonas shouted above the powerful roar of the engine.

"I can see the lights of his car up ahead, so I'd guess he's about three miles in front of us. We'll be up with him pretty soon at this speed."

They flew along the desert road, Gabriel twisted the wheel to avoid a huge semi-trailer truck that was parked in the side, and then they were tailgating the rear fender of Carson's vehicle. The Congressman saw them in his mirror, realized that he couldn't outrun them and spun the wheel to turn onto the desert. His car skidded, swerved and fishtailed, it almost made it. Almost. But the laws of physics were against him. The two passenger side wheels left the desert, settled back and then the two driver's side wheels lifted high in the air, hung there for an agonizing couple of seconds, then the car gently slipped onto its roof. It was still traveling at almost eighty miles an hour, it slid along the sand for more than a hundred yards until finally it slowed and stopped. They followed it, stopped the Cadillac near to the inverted vehicle and went forward carefully on foot. They weren't sure if he had a gun in the car, but they found Carson sprawled in the wreck, covered in blood. Alive. They dragged him out and lay him on the ground.

He groaned. "I need a hospital. You've got to call me an ambulance."

He did look in a bad way. His face was covered in blood, and there was a long gash in his pants, it looked as if the leg was broken.

"I don't think so," Gabriel murmured quietly. The desert was quiet and still, dark and cold. It was a fitting scene for the end of the man who lay in front of him, one who had caused so much death and misery.

"You must, I need an ambulance. I'm dying. How much do you really want? I'll give you anything."

"You think it's all down to money? Your orders to kill those Mexican immigrants almost got our girlfriends killed, as well as a priest. You've got a lot of blood on your hands, Carson. Too much. It's time to pay up."

"No, no, I'll give you anything you want."

They both ignored him. Jonas found a piece of rock lying next to the car. "I reckon the crash threw him out of the vehicle and he banged his head on the rock. How does that sound, you're the detective?"

"It's as good a story as any. I doubt they'll get any prints off a rock. But I can handle it."

Jonas shook his head. "This one is mine, it's for Galina. No one tries to kill my lady and goes on living, no one."

Carson heard him. "I'm a United States Congressman, for god's sake. You can't just kill me."

Jonas looked at him coldly. "Actually, Congressman, I think I can. If you were the President I'd still kill you for what you've done. Any last words?"

He picked up the rock.

"No, you mustn't do this. I'm a..."

The voice was silenced as Jonas smashed the rock into the side of his head. Gabriel touched the artery at the side of his neck, but he had died instantly from the massive blow to the brain. He nodded at Jonas. "He's gone. I'll re-arrange the body so it looks kosher. The Crime Scene techs are bound to go over this one with a fine toothcomb."

"Yeah. When you're done, I'll go over our tracks as well. They'll never know we were here."

Gabriel chuckled. "That's a good plan. If they ever

found out what really happened, the shit would hit the fan big-time." Gabriel wasn't unduly worried. Jonas was expert in all of the survival arts, so good that he could hide their traces well enough that even an Indian tracker wouldn't find them. They finished up, made a final check around but the scene looked good. Carson's body lay with its head against the bloodied rock. All signs of their being there had disappeared. Gabriel started the Cadillac, turned around and headed back into Phoenix.

They were nearing the outskirts of the town when the blue lights of a cruiser began flashing behind then. Gabriel cursed and halted the car. He watched a uniformed cop climb out of the cruiser and approach. He opened the window and nodded at the officer.

"Is there a problem? I thought I was keeping to the speed limit."

"Would you and your companion accompany me back to my car, Sir?"

"What the hell for?"

"We've had a report from out in the desert, some kind of an accident. Just come back to the car, it won't take a few moments to sort this out."

Gabriel nodded at Jonas. This was a uniformed cop, so they'd have to resolve any problems without resorting to violence. Except that when they got into the cruiser, they'd probably find that the doors were locked and couldn't be unlocked until the cop drove them back to the precinct. But they had little choice, neither of them was about to attack a cop. They followed him back to his car and he opened the door. He left it open and walked about twenty feet away. To their astonishment, David Whitehorse stepped out.

"You've been busy, I understand."

"Hi, David," Gabriel smiled. "How do you mean, busy?"

"I mean that a United States Congressman was killed a few miles out of town. It may have been an auto accident, may have been murder."

"Really? What that to do with us?"

"It was Max Carson. You were looking for him."

"Carson, he's dead? Wow, that saves us some time. He won't be doing any talking then."

Both men were trying to work out how David knew about it so quickly, but he read their minds.

"A guy in a semi-trailer truck was parked up, he called it in, said he saw it all happen. Wasn't sure if it was a murder, though."

"Right. What about that cop?" Gabriel looked across at the uniform.

"He's family, one of my wife's brothers. Listen, you'd be well advised to get out of town. I've done my best to cover for you, and I'll do what I can to keep it an accident. But get your stuff and head out, there's going to be an almighty ruckus when this goes public."

"I hear you, David, and thanks."

"No problem. Did you get what you wanted, the name of your New York killer?"

"We got a name, yes. Another well known name..."

"Don't tell me," David said quickly. "I don't want to be involved any more. I have to get out there now and attend to the crime scene, so I'll see you around sometime."

They shook hands. "Call me if you're ever in New York City," Gabriel made him promise. "I'd like to know how that thing went down with Faith, you know, when they were in the tunnel."

Whitehorse looked him in the eyes. "Gabriel, I'll tell you something. So would I like to know. I haven't got a clue how she did it. She sure has something, that girl of yours. I only wish I knew what it is."

"Me too," Gabriel grinned. "It'd make dealing with her a lot easier."

"I'm sure. You're ok to get back to the airport?"

"We'll return the car and call a cab. See you, David."

They drove back to the motel, and the two men found their partners already packing for the return to New York City. Galina drew their attention to some of the problems they faced.

"Our possessions and documentation are still in the hotel in Nogales. We need to get our stuff back. There's also the question of the artifacts, we have to have them, and soon. There's another problem too."

"The shroud?"

"The shroud, yes. They don't know that we have it in our possession yet. They're not sure what it is either, and they're waiting for us to let slip the details. But when we do, they'll be ready to come after it. And when they find it isn't in the church they'll come after us. Whoever it is that's looking for it."

"That's what we're for," Jonas interrupted. "Leave the rough stuff to us."

"That's not what I meant," she pointed out. "There are other ways to seize things than by use of force. In this case, they'll probably try and tie us up in some kind of legal battle for it, I don't know if they'll try anything physical. But we need to be aware of the possibility."

"I don't understand the problem," Gabriel mused. "It's

not the kind of thing you'd sell, this shroud. I thought it was going to be put up for display in a museum or a cathedral."

"Exactly. That's our intention, but we think the other party involved may have different ideas. If they get their hands on it they'll make sure that it disappears again into their archives, and if it does resurface it'll be for their own purposes, not on display."

Jonas smiled. "That's no worry; we'll take care of them."

Galina smiled. "I'm not sure you can take care of them. Your resources are rather limited."

"Just who are these guys?" Jonas asked her.

She grinned. "Let's just say that these gentlemen all speak Italian."

"The Vatican." Gabriel nodded. "But I don't understand why they'd try to steal the shroud."

"They suspect that it may be authentic," Faith explained. "Although they're not entirely sure, and neither are they certain whose property it is. When they do find out, they'll simply insist that Father Juan insists that we hand it back, for him to pass on to them. They're Catholics, how could Fathers Juan refuse a request from Rome? We need to take steps to protect the shroud and ourselves."

Both men looked at her in disbelief. After ending the career of the serial killer who'd almost killed the girls in the Nogales tunnel, they had the name of the copycat in New York City. Now Faith was talking about some kind of tussle between them and the Vatican, the most powerful and secretive organization in the world. Gabriel shook his head to clear it. This business was getting to be too complicated.

"We hear what you're saying, but the business of the

shroud will have to wait, we need to nail this guy in New York City first. You said there was another problem."

Faith nodded. "There is. This man in New York, he knows you're coming."

"What!"

Both men looked at Faith as if she was crazy.

"What are you talking about?" Gabriel almost shouted. "How the hell could Bryant know we're on to him? We only just uncovered his name."

"I don't know," she replied. "But he does."

"Has someone been in contact with you? Have you had a telephone call?"

She looked uncomfortable. "You know what we were talking about earlier? About good and evil?"

"Yeah, what of it?"

She hesitated for a few moments, and then she took his hands in hers. He felt the warmth of her soft, dry skin. She gave his hands a gentle squeeze. She held him firmly, and he felt something else from her. Something that made him shiver. She looked into his eyes. "Gabriel, you must try to understand. It's just something I'm able to do, I don't know why. I just know."

He sighed, and then looked at Jonas. "What do you think?"

"Search me, buddy. You know that my religion's thirty-eight caliber. I just don't know about this mystical stuff."

"But I do," Galina interjected. "You should trust Faith's instincts. Her revelations, or insights, call them what you will, have got us out of a lot of trouble in the past. If she says that's the way it is, then it's true. It's time you believed her absolutely."

Gabriel nodded slowly. "Yeah, you're right. It's just

that, well…"

"Spit it out," Jonas growled in an exasperated tone. "What is it?"

"It's just that I didn't want to marry someone who's a damned prophet, that's all."

Faith's eyes were wide. "Marry? Are you serious?"

"I was going to ask you, yeah."

Galina took Jonas' arm. "It's time for us to go for a walk."

When they were alone, de Sade took her in his arms and held her tightly. "I'm sorry it came out like that, you know, in public."

She laughed lightly. "I'm not sorry. Better that it did come out than not at all. Well, Detective de Sade. Did you really mean it?"

He nodded.

"In that case you can ask me properly."

Feeling more ridiculous than he ever had in his life, he went down on one knee. "Faith Ward, I love you more than anything in this world. Would you marry me?"

Her eyes filled with tears. "Yes. Oh yes, of course I will."

They kissed, and it lasted a long time. Eventually, Gabriel called in Jonas and Galina.

"I guess you know the news." He grinned as they offered their congratulations.

"Listen, I don't want to spoil the fun, but we need to get back to business. I've made a decision. We're not going to let these suckers interfere with our lives. We're going to take them down in one long, continuous action. We hit this Bryant guy, straight down to Nogales, blitz this church thing, and then go home. That's the way we need to play it, don't give them any time to regroup."

Jonas chuckled. "I like it, just like old times. Shock and awe, baby. Hit 'em hard."

That was the way they liked to handle it in Afghanistan. After the success of Desert Storm, when the strategy of Shock and Awe had blown away Saddam Hussein's much vaunted Republican Guard like so much dust in the wind, it had become a powerful weapon in the American military armory. Some said it was little more than a modern version of the old Nazi blitzkrieg tactics. But for the grunt on the ground it worked well enough. He'd been part of a task force, almost two thousand men, vehicles, helicopter gunships, drones and fixed wing fighter bombers. They were attacking a known enemy stronghold close to the Pakistan border. The Taliban were expecting them, they saw such a large force approaching in good time to fall back, which was their normal tactic. On this occasion, they'd obtained rare cooperation from the Pakistanis and a thousand men were deployed as a blocking force. It was like a hammer and an anvil. He'd let his own troop high into the mountains on the border and watched the battle unfold. The Taliban fought hard, trying to get past the defenders into their Pakistan strongholds, but the plan has been well made. The massive combination of men and materiel was like a Fourth of July celebration. The gunfire, rockets, bombs and shells lit up the area for many miles around. One group of enemy fighters made a break from the main action to try and get back into Afghanistan. His men had seen them coming and hit them as they came past. Bodies, blood and shredded tribal robes formed an awful mound of broken humanity on the path before them, a testament to the shocking industrial scale destruction that has wreaked such havoc. It was rare that they were able to trap their enemy in such a way, but when it happened, the consequent devastation was awe inspiring.

It was too late to catch a flight back to New York City. That night, Gabriel and Faith made love with a tender passion, surprising each other by finding new pleasure, even new places, in each other's bodies.

"I thought I'd lost you," Gabriel murmured afterwards. "I don't think I could stand that."

"You had no chance of losing me, buster. I never stopped thinking about you while we were in that tunnel. You were always in my thoughts and prayers. It makes for a strong connection."

"Yeah, use the Force, Faith," he grinned, making a wry Star Wars joke.

"The Force? I'd rather use something else right now, if you're not too tired."

"For you? Never."

They reached for each other and started again.

CHAPTER FIFTEEN

The flight from Phoenix International to New York JFK was largely uneventful. Once again, Faith's father had intervened to smooth out the problems of their lack of documentation.

"What's the point of having a father whose head of the CIA if you can't use him from time to time," she smiled.

"The point is that there'll always be a quid pro quo," Jonas pointed out to her. He still worked on the occasional contract for CIA and knew the way they operated. "With all respect to your father, Faith, people like that collect favors the way banks collect loans. It's something to call in on a rainy day."

She nodded. "I know the situation," she told them quietly. "I've lived with it all my life. But let's not worry about it now. It's a tiny favor, maybe he won't bother to call in the marker."

Gabriel grimaced. Documentation for an internal flight was one thing. Was she forgetting the other favors he'd done for her? Glen would be counting them, hoarding them like a miser. He'd call them in big-time when he needed to. It was just a matter of when. They had an easy flight, when they landed in New York they found a cab to take them into Manhattan. Their rendezvous was Gabriel's apartment.

"We need a single place to use for our headquarters," he'd explained. "My place is as good as any, so we can bunk down there while we finish this."

The cab dropped them outside Lee Fat's store in Manhattan. Before they went in, they called to see the Chinese owner to stock up on food. The women drifted off to fill a basket with groceries. Lee brightened when he saw him.

"Hi, Detective. Is good to see you back."

"You too, Lee. You got any Schneider Kristall for me?"

"Sure, how many you want?"

"I'll take a dozen cans. The girls are shopping for some goodies, so when they're done we'll put it all on the same bill."

"Is good, Detective. Men come looking for you. Last night."

Gabriel exchanged glances with Jonas.

"How many of them?"

"There were four. They not good men, I tell."

Faith and Galina arrived at the counter. They saw the looks.

"What's up?"

"Some guys, they were here looking around. They could have been Bryant's people. It looks as if Faith was right, he does know. I wonder if it is safe for you both in my apartment. Or should we look for something else?"

Faith grimaced. "No thug is going to drive me out of

my fiancée's apartment. No way."

Lee looked up. "Fiancée? You getting married, Detective?"

"Uh, yeah, I guess so."

He smiled. "My congratulations. But you must be careful of these men. They bad."

"Yeah, we will, Lee. Thanks for the heads up."

Both men made sure their guns were loaded and ready as they went up in the elevator, but there were no surprises. The apartment did not appear to have been touched. The two girls went straight into the kitchen to prepare the food while Gabriel and Jonas worked out a plan of action.

"We need to hit this bastard Bryant hard. If he's already sniffing around, he won't wait too long before he makes a play against us."

"You mean just knock on his door?" Jonas smiled. "I'll bet he'd love that."

"No doubt. But I was thinking that we need to arrange to meet, somewhere quiet, somewhere private."

"How do you think he found out about Congressman Carson so quickly?"

"I've been thinking about that," Gabriel replied. "I can only guess it had something to do with Chief Simpson from Phoenix PD, or someone close to him. Either way, as soon as the call came in about Carson's car it would have triggered a call to Bryant. Maybe Simpson knew they were buddies in Congress. We need to arrange a meeting. Bryant will be waiting and wondering. Let's not disappoint him."

Gabriel called Bryant on his cell. "Congressman, this is Detective de Sade."

"What can I do for you, Detective?" The voice was

cordial and friendly. He was without surprise, completely unfazed.

"We need to meet."

"Meet? That's not a problem, all you need to do is make an appointment with my secretary and come on in to the office."

"We need to meet somewhere private, Congressman."

"And why would that be, Detective."

"Because I want to rip your heart out, you perverted piece of slime."

"There's a lot we need to talk about, Sir. I think you know very well what I mean. Of course, if you want it made public, that's up to you. But I thought you might like to discuss it first."

Bryant didn't answer for a moment. Then he said, "Are you asking for a bribe, Detective?"

"Not at all, Sir."

"So what do you want?"

"Just a talk, that's all."

"Very well, man to man, is that it? Just you and me, Detective. Very well, no recording devices, no wires. I've got a new building going up on Lexington Avenue. Meet me there in two hours. Alone, if any sign of your friends, it's off."

"No problem, I'll see you there."

He hung up and looked at Jonas, who'd been listening on the extension. "What do you think?"

"Have you still got that leather case I left here?"

"Sure, it's in the closet."

"I'll go and get it. I think I'm going to need it."

Jonas got out a long, brown leather case and dialed the combination to unlock it. Inside, he pulled out a weapon, a huge M82 recoil-operated, semi-automatic rifle developed by the American Barrett Firearms Manufacturing company. With its attached special applications, low light scope, it had been used by armies around the world for long distance sniping. It was known as the Light Fifty for its .50 caliber rounds that it fired. He checked it over, put it back in the case and asked Gabriel to call him a cab. Then he got up to go. He went over to Galina, who was watching him with concerned eyes.

"I'm going to work, honey. Don't wait up," he smiled. He kissed her, and then went out through the front door.

"Will he be ok?" a very worried Galina asked Gabriel. "I'm worried about him."

He nodded. "He'll be fine. If you want to worry, worry about the opposition. They won't see him coming. Jonas is the best there is at this kind of business."

"And what about you?" Faith asked."You're taking a hell of a chance."

"I'll be fine, with Jonas covering my back. I'm more worried about you two if those guys come back."

"We need weapons, because we had to leave our pistols behind for them to let us board the aircraft in Phoenix." Galina stated. "We're both trained to use them. Have you anything here?"

He nodded. "Sure, I've got some hardware in the weapons cabinet. Let's take a look."

They went into his bedroom, and Galina's eyes lit up when she saw the Beretta 21A Bobcat. She picked it up, slid out the clip, checked it and slammed it back into the butt.

"I'll take this one, if it's ok?"

"Sure. Faith, I have a spare Glock."

"I trained on that with the FBI, it's fine. I'll take the Glock."

He handed it to her and she checked the clip and put the weapon in her waistband. Galina's Beretta had already disappeared, Gabriel smiled. She was an old-fashioned girl and she had a habit of tucking a small pistol in the top of the hose she wore underneath her short skirts. More than one opponent had been dazzled by a glimpse of her feminine underwear, blind to the pistol tucked just out of sight. They returned to the living room.

"I have to go now, just make sure that you don't answer the door."

Faith stared at him, he saw her shiver. "They won't come here. They will go to the meeting, Congressman Bryant's men. They will try to kill you."

He didn't ask her how she was aware of Bryant's plan. It was way beyond his understanding. He nodded.

"That's what Jonas is there for, to cover my back."

She nodded. "Be careful, Gabriel."

"Yeah, I will. Richard Bryant had better be careful too."

He kissed her and left the apartment. As he rode the elevator down, he wondered if he was doing the right thing by not calling in his police buddies. But he dismissed the thought, Bryant was too highly connected. If he tried to take him down on an official level the Congressman was more than capable of sliding out of trouble, and Gabriel could even lose his badge for daring to accuse such a powerful man. No, this was the only way. He exited the apartment block and waved down a passing cab. A few minutes later he got out next to the half completed building on Lexington Avenue. The site was protected by a steel security gate, but when he tried it, the lock was unfastened. He stepped through and looked at the dark, echoing space in front of him. Where would Bryant wait for him? On the first floor? No, that wasn't likely. He would wait on the top floor, where he would have ample warning of the detective's approach. Gabriel flicked on his pocket flashlight and picked out a stairway in front of him. The building was fourteen floors high, there was nothing for it but to go on up. He started climbing, his body tense as he waited for the shot that would announce an ambush, Bryant would have been careful to place his men in position to stop him. His footsteps were loud, their echoes filled the stairwell. When he passed the seventh floor he allowed himself a sigh of relief, he was halfway up and so far no one had taken a shot at him. There was no evidence that anyone was there, all he could hear was his own footsteps against the background of city noises outside. Could he have been wrong, could Bryant really have come alone to try and resolve this? He could feel his heart thumping, and he willed himself to continue up the stairs.

* * *

Jonas watched through the low light 'scope, picking out Bryant's men waiting in ambush. He'd entered the building from the rear and silently worked his way up to the twelfth floor, checking for any signs of the enemy with his 'scope as he went up. On the twelfth floor, he paused. Something has alerted him, he couldn't pick identify it at first. Then he realized what it was, the smell of aftershave. It was faint, very faint, but unmistakably there. He made his way to the elevator shaft and started to climb the steel emergency ladder fixed to the side. When he reached the thirteenth floor, he looked out of the empty door space. Nothing. He brought up his low light 'scope and looked again. Yes, there. A guy was crouching close to the stairwell, hiding behind a pile of cement bags. He was holding a gun, pointed at the stairwell entrance, waiting for Gabriel. Jonas searched everywhere with his scope but there were no other nasties nearby, so he put down his rifle and scope and began the silent approach to the man with the gun. He picked up a few loose piece of gravel as he stepped silently nearer to the enemy. He got within twenty feet of him, experience had taught him that any nearer than that and men had a kind of inbuilt instinct that warned them of an unseen approach. It was a simple matter to toss a tiny piece of gravel over the man's head, so that it landed a few feet in front of him. The guy heard the tiny noise and brought up his gun to cover the threat. When there was no repeat of the noise, he left the cover of the cement bags and crept towards the source of the sound. It was enough of an opening, Jonas started forward, moving swiftly and silently, drawing his combat knife as he went. He got with six feet of the man before he started to turn, but it was too late, much too late. Jonas almost leapt the last few feet and swiped the razor sharp blade over the man's' throat, caught him and lowered him gently to prevent any noise. He listened for any evidence that someone had heard the slight noise the scuffle had made. There was nothing. He returned to the elevator shaft, picked up his rifle and scope and climbed up to the fourteenth floor. Whoever had sited the ambush was not very professional, the second man waited in exactly the same position as the first, behind a pile of cement bags. Jonas moved carefully, getting near to him and again he threw a piece of gravel to divert his attention. He started to move as the guy looked away, but his foot slipped on an oil patch left by one of the construction worker's machines and he started to slip. He landed with his leg twisted underneath him at an odd angle.

The guy whirled as he clattered to the floor. In the dim light Jonas saw the pistol begin to rise, ready to fire at him. Visibility was very poor, only the city lights outside seeped through the gaunt frame of the unfinished building to silhouette any movements inside. The man struggled to picked out Jonas, his gun barrel wavering as he attempted to identify his target from the irregular shapes that lay on the floor. It only took him a second to recognize his target, but a second was more time than Jonas needed. He snatched out his combat knife and hurled it across the concrete lobby. The blade buried itself in the man's neck and the guy jerked to a halt, dropped his gun and his hands flew up to his throat to remove the terrible blade that was killing him. He was too late, blood was already pumping out of a huge gash in his artery and he slumped to the floor, both hands still wrapped in a futile gesture around the hilt of the knife. Jonas got to his feet, testing his weight on his injured leg. It was the ankle, without a doubt. Maybe broken, but hopefully it was just a sprain. He bent over to retrieve the knife and picked up the dropped gun and tucked it into his pocket. He put away the knife and went to retrieve his rifle. Now he had a bigger problem. They knew he was here. He didn't stop to consider the ankle; it was something he'd have to accommodate. He'd had worse. Hopefully, the bad guys didn't yet know that he'd taken out two of their men.

"De Sade, is that you?"

The voice shouted out from the next floor up, the top floor. He heard footsteps as someone came to the head of the staircase that led out onto the top floor. The voice called down again.

"De Sade, come up. I'm not armed. We have to talk."

So it was Congressman Bryant. But was he alone? Were the two shooters his only back up, or were there more? Or did he have someone else up there with him? It wouldn't make sense to prepare this much, two men in ambush, and not have someone else up there with him. No, there would be one or two shooters with Bryant on the top floor. He ducked down as he heard sound from below. Someone was climbing the staircase. Had he missed someone on the way up? He listened again, the man was climbing the stairs slowly, carefully, feeling his way. It had to be Gabriel. Jonas limped to the lift shaft and started ascending the emergency ladder to the top floor. He ignored the pain from his ankle. There was no pain.

* * *

Gabriel heard noises on the thirteenth floor, a crash, as if someone had dropped something. He stopped and waited, listened to try and identify the reason for the noise. It stopped and there was silence again. Then he heard Bryan calling down from the top floor. So he was up there. He shrugged mentally and continued climbing. It was all up to Jonas now, if Bryant had turned up with an army of trigger men, he was in trouble. He went past the thirteenth floor and on up to the fourteenth. When he reached the doorway that led out to the roof he paused. There was more light streaming down into the stairwell, the lights of the city were bright and lit up the whole of the open roof. When he went through he'd be a perfect target, framed in that narrow door space. He put his pistol in his pocket, it was no time to lose it, dropped from its holster as he moved, then he rolled out onto the roof and dodged to the side. A bullet spat out of the darkness and disappeared into the stairwell. He leapt behind a ventilator shaft and waited for his eyes to get used to the light. In the distance he could see the roof of the Empire State Building, with its mast standing gaunt against the night sky. A dark cloud drifted across past the mast. It was absurd, but for some reason he thought of when he'd read about the purpose of that mast, to tether airships, Zeppelins, and moor them on their arrival in New York City. When the building opened a Navy airship, the J-4, flew from Lakehurst and hovered around the tower at the request of a film company. The 30-mile-an-hour winds, described as treacherous, made the approach difficult. To say the least. In mid-September another dirigible was able to jury-rig a three-minute connection to the top of the building, in 40-mile-an-hour winds. Later, the Goodyear blimp Columbia picked up a stack of newspapers from the newspaper's plant at 210 South Street and lowered them on a 100-foot-line to a man on the Empire State mast, he was able to cut the bundle free. That was the last time the mast was used in connection with any airship. Yeah, it sure was windy up here, that's what had made him think of the crazy airship plan. He marshaled his thoughts, for this was neither the time nor place to daydream. Where was Jonas? Had he managed to deal with Bryant's men? He was sure to have stationed some in the immediate area. He'd have to work on the balance of probabilities. That meant he had to leave the shooters to Jonas and deal with Bryant.

"Congressman, I'm coming out. What's with this guy who took a shot at me? How do I know he won't shoot?"

"That was a mistake, de Sade. I'll tell him to drop his gun."

After a few moments there was a clatter and a pistol slid across the concrete floor.

"He's unarmed, you can come out. I've told him to stand well away from me."

Gabriel squinted out of the doorway. Congressman Bryant stood in plain view. Another man was standing twenty feet away, his hands held in sight for him to see. The detective went out to talk to them. Bryant held out his hand, but Gabriel ignored it. The politician raised his eyebrows.

"What can we fix up, de Sade? What kind of deal are you offering?"

"First off I need to know the full extent of what you've done. I guess you know that your brother in crime is dead."

"My fellow Congressman, Max Carson, yes. A traffic accident, so they say. Or was it something more?"

De Sade looked at him coldly. "He won't be slaughtering any more innocents, that's the important thing. I need to know how many you killed in this City."

Bryant snorted. "I don't give a fuck what you need to know. If you're here for a confession you're wasting your time. Let's move on, Detective, I haven't got all night. What's the deal? By the way, have you ever considered that I may be innocent?"

"No."

He laughed. "I guess you haven't. So what do you

want?"

His eyes were roaming around the area, searching for something. His shooters, of course. Of course, he was wondering why they hadn't yet shot this interfering NYPD detective.

De Sade waited for him to make his move. Despite everything, the sick pervert had to bring on his own demise.

"Spit it out, de Sade. What's the deal?"

"I want justice for Teresa Santos and all the others you raped and slaughtered. You surrender to me, Bryant. You'll face a trial for what you've done, it's the only way."

"Fuck you. Kill him, all of you, get the bastard!"

The supposedly unarmed shooter reached under his coat. The hand came out holding a pistol. Gabriel snapped off a shot and the man ducked, he jumped back behind the ventilator and a bullet clipped the concrete next to de Sade as he crouched down. He peered over the top of the structure, Bryant had disappeared and the shooter was standing near the doorway to the stairwell, shouting for his men. Where the hell was Jonas?

"All of you, get up here, we've got him cornered. Hurry!"

The man ran across the rooftop, heading for the cover of a ventilator similar to the one Gabriel was hiding behind. The detective saw a clear shot, he rose and took aim but a shot from the direction of the doorway cracked out and he felt an agonizing pain in his hand as his gun was sent spinning across the rooftop. Bryant had ducked into the doorway, come out to take a shot at de Sade, and then ducked back inside. Gabriel cursed to himself, the man was getting away. He had to deal with the shooter and get after him. He inspected his hand. Blood was dripping where the bullet had clipped it before it hit the gun and snatched it away from him. He looked across the rooftop, yes! The gun was there, about fifteen feet away. It was his only chance, he ran out to retrieve it, but Bryant's man was waiting for him. As he reached down, a cold, chill voice snarled, "Leave it, or I'll shoot you where you stand."

He looked up. The man had stood up and walked around the ventilator to stand less than ten feet from him. His gun was pointing directly at the detective. His lips creased into a smile.

"Not your lucky day, cop. You should have made a deal with my boss. He may have let you live. Kneel down."

No way was he going to kneel like an execution victim to be shot by this thug. He said nothing, just waited. Where was Jonas? Has something gone wrong? De Sade measured distances, maybe he'd find an opening, somehow make a move. Maybe. But the other man watched him intently.

"Don't even think about trying anything. If I gut shoot you, you'll die here in agony, but it'll take a half hour before you're dead. Or I could let you have a painless head shot. What's it going to be?"

They stared at each other for long seconds. The shooter shrugged and pointed the gun at de Sade's belly, "Fair enough, I'll give it to you the hard way."

He took aim. Then a voice came out of the darkness. "Isn't there a third option?"

The man swung around, searching for the newcomer. As he looked away Gabriel edged nearer to him, he swung back but a single shot cracked out, it sounded extraordinarily loud on the rooftop, and Bryant's shooter was thrown back twenty feet. Gabriel walked over to him but he was dead, half of his chest blown away by the force of the powerful .50 caliber bullet. He looked around and saw Jonas climb down slowly from the top of the elevator shaft, which was ten feet above the rooftop. He ran over to him.

"Are you hurt?"

"Nah, just a stupid ankle sprain. The only real injury is to my pride. Are you ok?"

"Yes. Thanks for that. Were there any more inside?"

"Two. They cause anyone any more problems."

"Right. But the bastard got away."

* * *

Bryant ran down the stairs, by the time he reached the first floor he was breathing hard. He needed to spend more time in the gym. He was definitely too old for this action man shit. He heard the shots, and assumed that his men had finally got their act together and killed that irritating detective. It was as well the Congressman wouldn't be around when the cops arrived, the last thing he needed was to be involved in a shoot-out. What he did need, however, was a woman. The near brush with disaster had aroused him to a peak of desire. Desire to rape, to impregnate, to kill. As soon as the heat died down, he must get out and find someone pretty and desirable. Young too. He felt himself growing hard as he pictured himself stripping and raping a girl at knifepoint. At last he was on the first floor and he made his way towards the gate that led out of the construction site.

"Going somewhere, Congressman?"

He stopped, two young women stood in front of him.

Both were in their twenties, both very attractive brunettes, one taller than the other. They could almost have been sisters. What mattered was they weren't armed. He kept his gun out of sight at his side.

"Who are you ladies?"

The shorter one spoke first. "We've come to stop the serial killings."

"I don't understand. What do you mean serial killings?" He tightened the grip on the gun. If they were what he thought they were, he'd have to kill them. "This is some kind of a mistake." The last one they'd ever make, he had a gun and they were unarmed. The woman spoke again.

"Your friend, Max Carson, tried to have us killed. Together with a whole bunch of other people, including a priest."

His lips curled. "So you're those interfering fucking women who messed up the operation in Arizona?" he snarled. "You're crazy! Do you know how much money you've cost me? This construction site, where do you think the money comes from to finance it? Not from the fucking banks, they're not lending squat these days."

"From drugs, I'd guess."

"From drugs, yes. The profits fund this kind of development, it creates jobs, provides a service to the city, office accommodation, apartments. Everyone benefits. Yet you attempt to destroy it. Why?"

Faith smiled. "You're insane, Congressman."

He giggled. "Maybe I am. But also I'm rich, I own this construction site, and I'm armed. So I think this little conversation has come to an end. It's time to bid you goodnight."

He raised his gun from his side, but blinked as he saw

a blur of movement. Now the other, taller girl had a gun in her hand, it had appeared as if by magic. It happened in slow motion, he saw her fire a shot and felt a heavy blow slam into him as it took him in the chest, just to the right of his heart. He staggered, a terrible pain welled up inside him and racked his body, he started to topple, but before he fell something slammed into his forehead, in a microsecond everything went black.

"He won't be murdering women anymore," Galina murmured.

"No. I feel a weight coming off me now that he's dead." Faith's voice was toneless, cold.

"Jonas, Gabriel, I wonder where they are," the Russian cried in alarm. "Bryant had more men in the building, they could be dead."

Faith took her by the arm. "It's ok, Galina. They're fine."

"You…"

"I'd know if they were dead. They're fine, and they'll join us soon."

A few minutes later they heard footsteps descending from the stairwell. Gabriel walked out of the doorway, supporting Jonas who was hobbling.

"Jonas, what happened?"

"I'm good. Just a sprain."

"What about Bryant's men?"

He grinned. "Those guys were hit with something more serious than a sprain. They're out of business. Permanently. We've set the scene so it looks as if they had a shootout after they fell out over some sort of disagreement. I see you found the Congressman."

"He won't be looking for any more votes," Galina said

grimly.

"Only in hell." Jonas pressed a pistol in the corpse's hand. "The gun was used on one of the guy's upstairs, with any luck the cops will assume he shot him. Which pistol did you use on Bryant?"

Galina held it out for him. He took the Beretta. "We'll toss this into the Hudson. We should get moving before someone calls 911, if they haven't already. I reckon we're all done here."

Gabriel nodded. "A nice clean ending, that's the kind I like best. No one can ever know anyone else was involved. Christ, the political fallout would be endless. And as for the Chess Killer, he just ceased to exist. If they want, they can attribute it to alien abduction."

Jonas laughed, "I guess that wouldn't be far from the truth."

"But women in the city will still be afraid," Galina objected.

"Yeah, that's right, they may be, at least until it dies down. Better to be afraid than dead. It's over."

Jonas shook his head. "It ain't quite over yet, buddy. There's another little matter I need to attend to. The guys that ran me down. It was an attempted hit. I'm certain that..."

"That'll have to wait," Galina interrupted him. "We have unfinished business in Nogales."

"Can't it work wait?" he asked. "If I don't..."

Faith interrupted him this time. "It cannot wait, it is not our work. It is God's work."

He nodded. There was no arguing with God.

CHAPTER SIXTEEN

They parked their hire car at the entrance to the Church of the Blessed Virgin and Father Juan welcomed them at the door.

"All of us in Nogales are grateful for what you've done," he said as he led them inside. "Those people from the tunnel all managed to get away, and they have begun to build new lives for themselves in the U.S.A."

"You had no trouble getting back across the border without papers, Father?"

He smiled. "Sadly, the only problem Mexicans have is getting out of their country, not getting in. The border guard did not even ask to see my papers, he just waved me through."

He took them into the presbytery and furnished them with cold drinks. "I imagine you are here to complete the purchase of the contents of our storeroom? When you returned the Shroud I put it back into the trunk, I wanted it kept safe in the locked storeroom. Thank you for returning it."

Faith and Galina had discussed the matter of the shroud. It still belonged to the church, and until the sale was final, they'd decided that it belonged in the church. They'd arranged to have it securely couriered back to Father Juan.

"We are," Galina replied. "We didn't finish the inventory, so we'll hurry it up and get out of your hair. Apart from the shroud, some of those other pieces are worth a considerable sum of money. As for the shroud, well…"

He held up his hand. "No. It is not for sale."

The two girls felt a surge of sadness. To have come so close, only to have it disappear into some Vatican basement, was unfortunate. But it was Father Juan's choice to make.

"You want to keep it, that's fine," Faith said to him, swallowing her disappointment. "We would have liked to include it in the package, of course. I assume you know what it is?"

He shook his head. "I do not, only that it is a genuine shroud that possesses a unique power, because it was touched by someone holy so long ago. I want it to be put into safe hands. It is not for sale, as I said. That is because it is yours, as a gift, for both of you ladies. The only condition is that it is put on display for all to see, so that it will be permanently removed from the greedy temptations of man."

They both smiled. "Thank you, Father. It will be as you say. We will also make certain that you are well compensated for the rest of the contents."

He inclined his head. "I have no doubt you will be more than fair. Shall we inspect the storeroom now?"

"Thank you, we'd like that."

He led them back into the church and down in to the basement. He frowned when he saw the door was ajar.

"That's strange, I was sure it was locked."

He led them into the room, where everything was as they'd left it, except for one thing. He opened the trunk.

"It's empty!" he shouted, his voice filled with despair. "Someone has stolen the shroud."

"Who would have stolen it?" Galina asked. "It had to be someone with a key for the storeroom."

Father Juan looked stricken. "Brother Sebastian, it cannot be anyone else. He is the only one with the spare key."

"But why?" the Russian girl asked. "He's a monk, why would he steal something so precious?"

"I stole nothing!"

They whirled around, Brother Sebastian stood in the doorway. His lined, leathery face glared at them, the blue eyes had lost their warmth. Now they were glacial, fanatic.

"It was never your property! It belongs to the Holy Mother Church. Did you think our leaders in Rome would allow you to sell it to these Americans for profit?"

He spat out the last word, 'profit', as if was dirty, soiled, an insult.

"So you took it and sent it to Rome, did you?"

Father Juan stared at him as he asked the question. His face was incredulous.

"It is destined for Rome, yes. The Father General of the Society of Jesus has requested it, and it shall be as he wishes."

"So you want it to molder in a Vatican basement, do you, Sebastian?" Father Juan asked him. He kept his tone calm, but they could all sense the anger and bewilderment underneath.

The monk shrugged. "It is not for me to decide where it goes. It is entirely possible that it may be presented to the Holy Father, to further the glory of our Lord Jesus."

"Do you think it is the Shroud of Christ?"

For the first time, his eyes lost their fanatic gleam and they looked uncertain. "We are not yet sure yet whose shroud it is. But our experts will examine it and determine who was buried in it."

Faith stared at him. "And if it is someone who your own church regarded as an enemy?"

He shrugged. "Then it will be put into storage, of course, as an object of historical interest. We have no wish to glorify our enemies, of course not. But it will be cared for, our mission is to enhance the memory of the early Christian martyrs, not tarnish it."

Gabriel had noted his use of words. It was 'destined' for Rome. Therefore he hadn't sent it yet. So where was it? He whispered to Father Juan. "There's a chance we could find it before it is sent. They're probably sending a courier for something so valuable. Do you want me to go look for it?"

Father Juan nodded. "Yes, I do. If the ladies would go with you, I will hold him here. Good luck."

Gabriel nodded to Jonas and the girls. "Let's go, we've got work to do."

Sebastian made for the door too. "Get out of my way! I have things to do too."

"Sebastian!" Father Juan shouted at him and the monk stared. "There are matters we need to discuss. Wait here with me. Detective, lock the door when you leave so that he cannot escape."

They closed the door and locked the two men inside, they could hear the monk shouting and raving, but they ignored it.

"Does anyone have any ideas where his room would be?" Galina asked

"It'll be in the presbytery," Faith replied. "So it shouldn't be difficult to find it, but where he's hidden the Shroud I have no idea."

"I could always question him," de Sade suggested.

They all laughed. "Not yet, darling," Faith responded. "It would be best if we could find it without you having to rough him up. I doubt he'd respond to NYPD treatment anyway."

"I didn't mean…"

"I know you didn't mean that you'd beat him up," she smiled. "But we can't take any chances; he's obviously here on the authority of Rome. They're bad people to make enemies of."

"So am I."

Her smile broadened. "It might be best if you two didn't start a war with the Vatican just yet. Let's try and find the Shroud in his room."

The entered the presbytery and found his room straight away. The stone building was quite large, a throwback to a previous time when priests had been plentiful. Now, there were plenty of spare rooms, and Brother Sebastian had taken two of them on the first floor, one as a bedroom, the other as a study next door. They spent half an hour checking and rechecking every possible hiding place. But there was nothing, despite emptying all of his possessions out of boxes, cases and travel bags. Galina even threw all of the linen off the bed in case he had hidden it underneath. Nothing.

"We've searched everywhere," Jonas muttered. "Maybe he's hidden it somewhere else?"

"No," Gabriel asserted. "I've dealt with enough perps in my lifetime. They keep their valuables close to the chest. It's here, somewhere. We just haven't looked in the right place."

"Come on, we've looked everywhere," Jonas protested. We've checked the furniture the drapes, even the paintings. I tapped the walls to check for a secret compartment, but they're clear, there's nothing." He looked up and grinned. "And it sure isn't on the ceiling. We even checked that."

"Except the floor," Gabriel mused. "We never checked for an underfloor cache."

"But it's not a wooden floor!" Jonas exclaimed. "I don't reckon he carved a hole through solid stone."

Galina shook her head. "No, Jonas, but this is an old building, a Catholic church. Catholics have many secrets, or at least they used to have. It would make a lot of sense to have a secret compartment under the floor. Faith, what do you think?"

But Faith stood still, as if in a trance. It was not the first time she'd fallen into such a mystical state. It was a communication, but with what? None of them dared ask.

"It's not here!"

They'd been continuing to look around the room, in case there was something they'd missed. All of them looked at Faith as she spoke.

"I said a prayer, I believe it was answered. The Shroud is close, but not here. It's in the church."

"You're sure?" Gabriel was still skeptical, in spite of

everything.

"I'm sure, yes. I saw a picture of it, hidden beneath the altar cloth, the most sacred of places."

"Appropriate," Galina muttered. "We should have thought of that, a monk from the Vatican would think in those terms. The most holy of holies."

They left the presbytery and entered the church. The cloth was underneath the altar cloth, just had been revealed to Faith. The two men left Faith to wrap the cloth and watched her return to the car. The three of them returned to the storeroom and unlocked it. The priest gave him them an enquiring look. Sebastian was hunched in a corner, sneering at them.

"You're wasting your time, the shroud will be returned to Rome."

"On the contrary, Sebastian, we found it. I guess you're out of business."

His face registered shock and disbelief. "But, that's outrageous, you have committed sacrilege! It is a most holy relic held in a Catholic church."

"But it doesn't belong to the Vatican, buddy," Jonas responded firmly. "They may think they can send their holy stormtroopers anywhere they want to stage a raid, but I've got news for you. We do this for a living."

"I'm even more pleased you have it," the priest murmured. "Now that I have seen what despicable measures they would adopt to get their hands on it. I would sooner use it as a blanket for the homeless than let those people take it."

"It will go on display for everyone to see," Galina told him. "I assure you it will never again be hidden from public view."

"When we were in the tunnel, Faith said it was the shroud of James, brother of Jesus. Do you still believe that to be true?"

"Yes, of course."

"What I don't understand is how she knew," the priest continued.

"She had a revelation."

He stared at her. "From whom, I don't understand."

She looked at him steadily. "From James the Just, I would imagine. And you really should understand."

"Why is that?" He looked mystified.

"Because he was the brother of a carpenter," she smiled. "Kindred spirits."

Jonas smiled broadly as they started to leave.

"You'll burn in hell for what you've done," Sebastian snarled. His anger spilled out and filled the storeroom with its violence. "That shroud is the property of the Catholic church. We'll hunt you to the very edge of hell, believe me, you'll never get away with this."

Father Juan gave him a sharp look. "Despite what you think, it is the property of this parish and I have seen fit to donate it for public display."

"You what? Do you know what you're doing? You don't even know whose shroud it is."

"Don't I?"

Sebastian regarded him grimly. "If you know something of the history of our church, it is your responsibility to tell me what it is. It is not for you to keep secrets from Rome. You're just a dirt poor Mexican priest. You're nothing!" he spat.

But the priest smiled. "You're beginning to uncover your true feelings, Brother. I am more than ever pleased that the shroud is going to the destination we agreed."

They walked through the church, Sebastian by now was reduced to an incoherent rant, spitting phlegm from his mouth as his rage and frustration overcame him. A pair of nuns kneeling at prayer in the Lady Chapel looked at him in disgust. Several other parishioners were also at prayer, and four women were busy repairing the displays of flowers. A low hum of disapproval began to resonate through the building. They were halfway up the aisle towards the main doors when they opened and sunlight flooded into the dim church. It backlit Faith Ward, who stood framed in the doorway clutching the Shroud. Shafts of sunlight lanced through the part open doorway, almost like bolts of lightning straight out of an Old Testament revelation. Everyone in the church caught their breath. She stared as if in a trance for a few moments. Then she spoke.

"I thought it right to bring the Shroud back here for these people to see before we take it away. It must be seen inside the church. These people must bear witness to the miracle of the Shroud."

"It's mine, it's mine! I must have it!" the monk shrieked.

"I'll have a word with him," Jonas said, slipping away. There was a quiet 'thud', a rustle of clothing and then silence. Jonas rejoined them. "The monk isn't well. He's taking a short nap."

"You haven't hurt him?" Galina looked worried. "He is a man of God, after all."

"The god of thieves?" he asked with a grin. "But he's fine. Just a migraine, a slight headache."

The people in the church clustered around Faith, examining the Shroud.

"Whose is it?" one of the nuns asked her.

"It is the Shroud of James the Just," she replied. "In my own Church, the Orthodox Church, he is known as James the Brother of God. The oldest surviving Christian liturgy, the Liturgy of St James, called him the brother of God. It is sad that the Catholic Church chooses to denigrate this great man, only because their own supposed founders, Saint Peter, and Saint Paul, held views that did not agree with theirs. James, the man who was buried in this Shroud, was the true successor to Jesus."

The nun who had asked question looked at Father Juan. "Is this true? Is it possible that our own Church has hidden the truth from us?"

He sighed. "Sister Maria, our Church exists on faith. What is truth? We are talking of a time period two thousand years ago. Possibly our Church's understanding is correct, but possibly it is in error. The absolute truth will never be known, all we have is our faith, so that we can live our lives in as Christian a way as possible. Even the gospels themselves do not all agree. Were there five fishes, or seven, or some other number, when our Lord performed his miracle to feed the multitude? Does it matter anymore? I suggest it may not."

"Then why was the Vatican trying to take possession of the Shroud? Did they intend to hide it from us, hide the truth from us?"

"I don't know. The Vatican is a group of human beings just like us, and we are all fallible. I have donated the Shroud on behalf of all of us, for it to be displayed for the world to see. These women, Faith and Galina, are buying a number of artifacts from this church, relics that have been gathering dust in a storeroom for many years. The money will be put to good use. That is what matters. And the whole world will know that the most precious Shroud came from here. Our Church will justly be famous as the place it was uncovered from."

The nun was thoughtful for a few moments. "Surely it is worth a lot of money," she observed.

He nodded. "Perhaps so. But would you put a price on it, the Shroud of the brother of our Lord? So that it can be hidden away by some wealthy collector? I believe it is beyond price, the Shroud is the property of everyone."

She nodded. Father Juan had done the right thing. One of the congregations had used the cellphone to call the local press, and photo journalist arrived to write the story. He stood with Father Juan, making notes.

"It's a miracle, uncovering the Shroud in this church. When it has left you'll put the chest on display, of course, so that people can see where the relic came from?"

They glanced at each other. The trunk, of course. The chest that dated back to the time of Jesus, the chest that had held the Shroud of his brother, James. The priest looked at Faith.

"You wouldn't mind, if we kept the iron trunk?"

"Of course not. The trunk was used for storing and hiding the Shroud. We intend to display the Shroud to everyone. Why not the trunk?"

"In that case, we will put it on display. Perhaps it will attract the faithful to our little church."

"I'm sure it will, Father."

A murmur of voices started, local people speculating on how many visitors it could bring to Nogales. Jonas raised his eyebrows at Gabriel, who shrugged. They both shared the same thought. It would take more than a two thousand year old trunk to overcome terror of the thugs and murderers who plagued the Mexican town. To stem the tide of their nauseating violence. Father Juan noticed the look that passed between them. He smiled.

"I do understand that we have a lot of problems. It is a beginning, no more. Perhaps it will be the spark that ignites a fire."

"Yeah, igniting a fire is exactly what I could see happen if thousands of wealthy tourists turn up," Jonas muttered.

The priest didn't hear him. "It could put Nogales on the map," he exclaimed brightly. "Nogales will become a name synonymous with…"

He tried to think of a suitable word. Jonas helped him out. "Muggings, maybe. Perhaps murder?"

"You should have more faith, my son."

"I have," he replied. "It's just not your brand of faith, that's all.

The congregation examined the Shroud, touching it reverently, possibly in the hope that its supernatural properties would give them both health and wealth. The Americans made their way out to the car, Faith clutching the precious relic. The drive across the border and into Nogales, Arizona was uneventful. Faith and Gabriel rode in the back seat, she leaned her head on his shoulder.

"Thank goodness it's all over. Do you think Father Juan stands a chance in Nogales?"

"None whatsoever," he replied. "They'll fall on any visitors like a pack of wolves.

"That's a shame. Whatever chance they have of making something good in their lives, they'll just throw it away."

"Yep. That's the story of Mexico. It'd be nice if it changed, but I don't know when it's likely to happen. Not anytime soon, I wouldn't think."

"And Brother Sebastian? What do you think will happen to him?"

"No idea. I guess he'll wind up sweeping Saint Peter's Square in the Vatican."

CHAPTER SEVENTEEN

Faith and Galina had left for the Metropolitan Museum, to arrange for the donation and display of the Shroud. Gabriel and Jonas were lounging in the apartment, finishing off a six pack of Schneider Kristall.

"Damn, that's a good beer," Jonas mused. "I could get used to drinking this all the time."

"It sure tastes good," Gabriel agreed. "What's the next move with your Arab friend?"

"Malik Wallid? I have to find him and kill him, it's that simple. Before he finds and kills me. It's a simple choice. He nearly had me with that truck that hit me in the street."

"You're sure it was him?"

"Yeah, no question. The cops found it was packed with explosives, for some reason they failed to go off. It was him, alright."

"What the hell did you do to upset him?"

"I killed his brother. The bastard was building IEDs in Afghanistan. He was responsible for the deaths of more than a few of our soldiers. CIA asked me to terminate him, it was a tricky operation. The guy was a local politician, lots of contacts with Karzai's government in Kabul. He had the local cops in his pocket too. None of them knew what he was up to with his little bomb making sideline, of course, so it had to be a black operation."

"So how did you manage it?"

Jonas chuckled. "I wired some of his devices together, so that when he went into his workshop it exploded and flattened half the village. Unfortunately, one of our Afghan liaison guys was a Taliban mole, and he gave Malik my name. He made a vow to kill me, so it doesn't leave me any choice. I nearly had him a while back, but he moved at the last moment and I only clipped his ear."

"Do you know where he is?"

"Sure. He's here, in New York City. On the surface he's the Imam of one of the local mosques. Undercover, he raises funds for the Taliban cause."

"So he needs to be taken out? It sounds like you've got enough on him."

"That he does. He's well protected and not easy to get near. All the same, I'm going to have to end it, he'll never give up on me."

"What's the plan?"

"I haven't made a plan," he admitted. "The hard part is getting him out of his mosque."

"Can't you take him inside?"

Jonas shook his head. "The minute they see my white ass anywhere near, the shutters go up."

"How about a drive past, see how the land lies? I can borrow an unmarked police car. Even if they make the car, and they probably will, they won't know you're inside. No wait, I've got a better idea, a police cruiser, with two uniformed patrolmen inside. Me and you."

"You can fix that?"

"I can try. Give me a little time, I'll make some calls."

* * *

"Where the fuck have you been, de Sade?" Frank Willard asked him cheerfully enough.

"On assignment, Frank, you know, that trip to Phoenix?"

"Oh, yeah, showing the cowboys how we do it in the Big Apple."

"Something like that. Frank, I need a favor."

He groaned. "I don't like the sound of this. What is it?"

When Gabriel told him, he went apeshit. "I'll lose my badge if I get found out. A patrol car and two uniforms?"

"I'm only asking you to make out the paperwork and countersign it. I'll sign it and take care of the rest."

"I'll do it, but it's your funeral. I'll have a word with Abe down in the garage, he's a good guy. And I'll have the documents ready for when you come in."

"And the uniforms?"

"Jesus Christ, you want me to swipe Kruger's office chair for you as well? I'll arrange to leave them in the car."

"Thanks, Frank. I owe you for this one."

Frank sighed. "Till the end of time, buddy. Just remember, I never spoke to you. I don't even know your name, got it?"

"I've got. I'll see you later."

Gabriel called Faith on his cell. They were still at the Metropolitan finalizing the arrangements.

"Afterwards, we're working in the gallery, as we need to start clearing space for the consignment from Nogales.

It's due in about three days. Father Juan had it all put on a truck for us."

"Right, that's nice. Jonas and I are going out to square some business."

She caught the tone in his voice. "You'll be careful, Gabriel? Promise me."

"Of course I'll be careful. It'll take a few hours, so we'll see you this evening back at the apartment."

"I'll prepare a meal, then. I love you, Gabriel."

"Yeah."

Two hours later the two men were in cop uniform and driving past Malik's mosque. They drove slowly and parked fifty feet away. They would be observed, but it was not unusual to keep an eye on these people. Not since 911.

"You see anything that'll help us?"

Jonas shook his head. "Nope. A few worshippers coming and going, but as I said, Malik keeps a very low profile. There's no sign of him. I don't know how we can get him out of there. He won't budge"

"Unless there was a fire," Gabriel mused. "Give me five minutes, I'll find a public phone booth and put in the call. Once the alarms start and the Fire Department turns up, the bastard will have to come out."

Jonas smiled. "And I'll be waiting for him. I like it."

De Sade found a public telephone and called in the fire. He gave the details and hung up. In a few minutes the two fake patrolmen heard the sound of sirens.

"I'll go meet the FDNY and get them inside the mosque," Gabriel murmured to his partner.

"Yeah, I'll be waiting. All I need is to make him when he puts his ugly face out on the street, I'll handle it from there."

"Right."

They both climbed out of the cruiser. Jonas disappeared in a narrow alleyway across the street. Gabriel crossed to the mosque.

"How can I help you, officer?"

He was an elderly Arab, sat just inside the door. On first glance he seemed friendly enough, but Gabriel read something less than friendship in his eyes. Contempt for authority, perhaps? Or for the sight of a white American? The building was silent, decorated with posters of Arabic script and pictures of unsmiling men in turbans and black robes. They were all bearded. The guy stared at him, and his eyes betrayed his inner feelings of loathing. He wouldn't be the first Arab to feel hatred towards all things American, some of them made a living hating his country. He wondered briefly why they came to this country if it was so bad, and presumably their own countries were so good.

"There's a report of a fire, Sir. You need to clear the building."

"A fire? I know nothing of a fire, that's ridiculous. It must be a false alarm, or a hoax. The Jews, they're always…"

Gabriel fixed him with a hard stare. "Mister, I don't give a shit about Jews, Arabs or anyone else. This is an emergency. Either you clear the building, or I will."

He looked doubtful. "I don't know. I need to ask the Imam."

He walked to a door and opened it, but before he could walk through it, Gabriel found what he was looking for. The fire alarm. He used his elbow to smash through the glass and he hit the button. Immediately, the shrill sound of the fire alarm shattered the peace of the building.

Men started to stream out of the doors and exit to the street. A side door opened and some women emerged, they were pushed aside as more men hurried to escape. A fire truck pulled up outside and the first of the fire crew ran into the building.

"Where's the fire?"

Gabriel gestured to the door that led inside the mosque. They rushed past him, he decided his job was over, so he left and went back into the street. He climbed back into the cruiser and waited. His cell rang, it was Jonas.

"It's Malik, he just left. He's wearing a white turban, a long, white shirt thing down to his knees, under a black coat. White trousers and black shoes, a guy of about thirty years old. He's walking with two other men, both older. They're on the opposite side of the road to you, just going past the cruiser."

Gabriel looked across. Yes, he saw the men Jonas described.

"I've got them. What do you want me to do?"

"Follow Malik, but don't get too close. I'm going to meet him and make an arrest. I'll take him somewhere and deal with him. Just watch my back, and grab him if he tries to slip away."

"Ok."

He clicked off the cell, got out of the cruiser and crossed the road. He followed Malik and his two buddies at a distance. The men walked a hundred yards from the mosque and went into a coffee bar. He saw Jonas, who was walking towards them from the opposite end of the street. Jonas followed the men into the coffee bar. He walked up to Malik and said a few words. Malik nodded resignedly, then his head jerked up and his eyes flared. He ran. Jonas made to follow, but the two other men blocked him and Malik was able to make it to the door. Where Gabriel waited. He took his arm.

"You're under arrest, my friend. Don't make a fuss."

Malik was shocked, and he didn't try to resist. But a hostile voice sounded from behind him.

"Why are you arresting my Moslem brother?"

Gabriel held onto Malik and turned around. Three Moslems, all in their late teens and wearing traditional dress, stood there. Their eyes were filled with hate. He tried to bluster.

"This is police business, stand aside. If you want to know more, you can come down to the precinct."

"You will not arrest our brother, Jew lover! Abdul, Sadid, stop him!"

The three men crowded into him, Gabriel felt a punch to his stomach, then a blow to his head. Malik twisted away even as he hit back, felling two of the men with precision strikes to their heads and bodies. The third man backed away and watched him warily. Malik was running, already ten yards away and weaving across the street, cars were sounding their horns and cab drivers shouting. Jonas crashed out of the coffee shop.

"Where is he?"

Gabriel pointed. "There."

"Let's take the bastard down."

They ran across the road, cars swerved and stopped to allow the two uniformed cops to move through the traffic. The Arab was already fifty yards away, they saw him turn into a side street. They picked up speed, hurtling through traffic and people in a lung-bursting race to catch him. As they rounded the corner, they saw Malik s disappear into a building. They ran up, it was an empty theatre. One of the doors swung open on broken hinges, probably ripped out by street bums looking for someplace to sleep. Or addicts for a shooting gallery. They ran inside, and both men took out the flashlights clipped to their utility belts. Gabriel chuckled.

"You know what this place was? A porn palace. Dirty movies and private booths for the customers to do whatever they do when their juices start to run."

"It's probably familiar to Malik," Jonas replied with a smile. "He had something of a reputation. His particular thing was youngsters, once he was out of sight of the other mullahs."

"Boys or girls?"

Jonas shrugged. "Probably both, if I know this guy. He's not too fussy."

"In that case it'll be more of a pleasure to put him out of business."

"Yeah. Permanently."

The foyer had a single door that led into the depths of the movie theater. In the light of their flashlights, they could see rotting rows of tip-up seats. There were gaps where some of the seats had been ripped out, perhaps by thieves. At the side of the auditorium were a number of doors, obviously they were the booths for customers to do their thing in private. A shot crashed out, in the muzzle flash they saw Malik standing close to the big screen at the front of the theater. They ducked as another shot whined overhead, and then Malik slipped away through a side door. Both men ran through the theater and burst through the door, there was an iron staircase that led to the next floor. They heard Malik's footsteps ring on the iron stairs as he went up, a crash as he tripped and fell heavily, then he got up and continued on up. They started up the staircase, another shot rang out and they crouched out of sight of the fugitive. He ran again and they followed him. The iron staircase reached a long, iron balcony that trailed towards the back of the movie theater. Malik was starting up the next set of iron stairs. They continued to follow him up, a doorway was swinging open at the top and they approached it warily. It was the exit to the roof. When Jonas poked his head through the doorway another shot rang out. He ducked back inside.

"Can you cover me? Aim a few shots outside and I'll dive out and try to locate him."

Gabriel nodded. He poked his Glock through the exit and sprayed half a dozen shots around the roofspace. Two shots came back at them, and then Jonas dived outside and rolled across the roof. Gabriel could see him crouching behind a rusty old winch that would have been used for hauling heavy equipment up from the ground, in the days when the building was a theater. Two more shots ricocheted off the ironwork; he rushed out and joined Jonas behind the corroding steel.

"Where is he?"

Jonas pointed across the roof. Malik was standing next to the top of a fire exit that would have opened onto an external staircase, trying to wrench the steel gate open. But someone had wound rolls of barbed wire around the metalwork, presumably in the days then the porn palace was operating, to stop would-be perverts from gaining access for free. It worked both ways, barbed wire prevented Malik from getting away. The Arab looked around in angry desperation, and then emptied his pistol at them. The bullets ricocheted off the steel winch and disappeared into the New York night. Finally, his gun clicked on an empty chamber. He looked at them wildly and started to run away. They followed him to the edge of the roof.

"You may as well give it up, Malik. This is the end of the line."

He snarled back at Jonas. "I know you, Jonas Savage. You're no cop! Do you think I don't know what you're planning to do?"

"You're out of ammunition, you haven't got any choices. Give it up now."

"I don't think so. You're here to kill me. But if I'm to die, I'd prefer not to go to my death alone. In return for taking you with me, I will surely go to heaven and receive my just reward."

Jonas laughed. "How are you planning to do that? Are you going to talk me to death?"

Malik Wallid walked towards them. "There is no need. Not when I have this."

He unfastened the top buttons of his coat. Underneath they saw clearly the suicide belt strapped to his body.

"I have never gone anywhere without this belt, not since you killed my brother. I have lived in the hope that one day I could use it to take revenge. That time has come."

He held up his hand, they could see him clutching a button connected to the vest by a thin wire. Gabriel and Jonas glanced at each other. They both shouted at the same instant.

"Run!"

The hurtled across the rooftop, with every step they

could feel Malik's finger closing on the detonator and they waited for the hot blast that would destroy them. The nearest cover was the iron winch. They flung themselves behind it and squinted through gaps in the machinery. Malik stood there, pressing down on the button again and again. Gabriel recalled when the Arab had fallen heavily on the iron staircase.

"He broke the detonator when he fell! The stupid bastard, it isn't going to blow."

Jonas chuckled and they both stood up and advanced on the hapless Arab.

"Give it up, Wallid. Your bomb is useless."

"Never! I will see you in hell, Jonas Savage."

He ran to the edge of the roof and jumped. There was no scream, just a meaty crash as he hit the ground. When they looked over the top, his body lay impaled on a steel security fence at the rear of the building. Gabriel nodded at Jonas.

"I think your problems are over. Tell me, would you have killed him?"

"In cold blood, do you mean? I don't know, maybe, maybe not. But this way, I never need to find out."

"Yeah. Jonas, it's time to get out of here and retire from the NYPD uniformed division. There're going to be some questions asked about the two cops who were first on the scene of the fake emergency call at the mosque. It would be best if we disappeared."

"You mean we don't get paid?" Jonas grinned.

"Take it up with the Commissioner, my friend. Somehow I doubt it."

Both men felt uncomfortable in a tuxedo. Even more so than in the borrowed police uniforms, that they'd managed to return along with the cruiser to Frank Willard's contact in the police garage. Gabriel hadn't heard what favor he would need to perform in return, but he knew it was going to be something big. They were milling with the crowds in the reception hall of the Metropolitan Museum when FBI Assistant Director Bradley Moore, the man running the hunt for the Chess Killer, pulled him to one side.

"Have you heard anything more that might help us find this killer, de Sade? We're up against it here, and the city won't be safe until he's taken off the streets."

Gabriel nodded. "That's true, Sir. But no, I haven't heard a thing. It's as if the guy has disappeared. Maybe he fell into the Hudson."

"Yeah, that about sums it up, we've found nothing, and there've been no more killings. Do you think it's possible he's gone away?"

"You mean died from a heart attack, drowned, fallen under a truck, or something? Yeah, I think I'd go with that explanation if it was me."

Moore fixed him with a hostile glare. "What do you know, Detective?"

De Sade eyed him calmly. "Nothing more than I've told you. It's the opinion of an NYPD cop, take it or leave it." He walked away. Up on the dais, the curator called for silence. He was flanked by two beautiful women, both wearing designer gowns, and he hastened to introduce them.

"Ladies and gentlemen. Thanks to the work of these ladies and the generous donation of the Church of the Blessed Virgin in Nogales, Mexico, we are proud to present this first century burial shroud. It has been authenticated as to its origins and dates, and there can be no doubt that it is genuine. As to who it was used for, we can only speculate. Early indications are that it may be the shroud of James the Just, reputedly the brother of Jesus Christ. But I suspect we will never know for certain. The only evidence that anyone can possibly have is the faith of their own convictions. Nonetheless, this would be identical to the actual shroud used for wrapping the body of our Lord Jesus Christ. For that reason alone, it is of incalculable value. Please show your appreciation for Ms Faith Ward and Ms Galina Polotsova."

The crowd erupted into applause; both of the girls blushed red. Faith beckoned for their tuxedoed partners to join them, and both men started towards the dais. Until a man stood in front of them, he was blocking their path.

"Pardon me, gentlemen, my boss would appreciate a word with you both. In private."

Gabriel stared at him. "Who the hell are you?"

But Jonas recognized him. "He's CIA, can't you recognize the type."

Gabriel nodded. "You're from Raymond Glen?"

"Yes, Sir. The CIA director is waiting in an office across the other side of the room."

They followed him across the room and through the door into an office. When they entered, the guy followed them and locked the door. Raymond Glen sat on a small brocade couch, some kind of an antique.

"Gentlemen, it's good of you to see me. Sit down."

They hesitated, and then sat in the two antique armchairs that he indicated.

"What's up?" Jonas asked.

Glen smiled at him. "I'll come to that. Is everything good with you? No problems with anyone. No Arabs trying to kill you to get revenge for the death of one of their family members?"

Neither man was surprised. It was Glen's business to know these things.

"Not any more Sir, no."

"Good. And you, Detective? Any wedding plans with my daughter yet?"

"We've no plans in that direction, no, Sir. But you should ask her, she's your daughter."

He grinned. "Maybe, but you never know what to say to them for the best. Women!"

"What do you want, Sir?"

He stared at de Sade. "I need you to help me out, Detective."

Gabriel shook his head. "I'm already busy with my own work, Mr. Glen."

"But not too busy to run around Mexico, chasing after bad guys."

"That was personal. As I'm sure you're aware. They tried to kill Faith."

He raised an eyebrow. "I wasn't aware she was a target. Is it all settled now?"

"Yes, it is."

"Permanently?"

"Permanently."

He seemed to be assembling his thoughts for a few moments. He nodded absently, "Good, good. Now, this job."

"I told you, I'm busy. Doesn't Jonas work for you? Why don't you ask him?"

He turned to his friend, Jonas nodded. "Director, you know de Sade is a full time NYPD detective."

"Yes, I do know that. But I need a particular job to be done and it's a real tricky one. A job that needs, shall we say, the very exceptional skills that you two men uniquely possess."

"Deniability," Gabriel responded. "That's about the only quality we have over your Agency people. You want a job done that doesn't come back and slap CIA in the face if it goes wrong."

"Yes, I guess that would be one benefit of employing you gentlemen. But there's more to it. This is a two man job. And you're quite correct. We need operatives who are not employed by CIA. We also need men who have strong local knowledge."

Then it hit them, like an instantaneous flash of light.

"Dear Christ," de Sade exclaimed. "You're joking?"

Glen shook his head. "I'm afraid not. It's a job that needs doing, one that is vital for US interests. You know that if things go belly up in Afghanistan, we could be in serious trouble. The last thing the US needs is another Vietnam."

Gabriel thought back to the hell of Afghanistan. To the cruelty, the pain that was the everyday lot of the Afghan population. The vicious fighting, the maimings and the torture.

"No. There's no way I'm going back there."

"Really? I'd like you to think about it. Patrolman de Sade."

So that was it, he would threaten to use it against them. Gabriel assumed that they could link him to the false call to the Fire Department, and to the death of Malik Wallid. Fuck him. He made a move towards the door, shouldered the agent who guarded it to one side and unlocked it. He walked out of the office, Glen continued speaking to Jonas. "Mr. Savage, I assume you have no problem with taking this assignment?"

Jonas shook his head. "I have a problem with your methods, Sir. Let's just say that your timing this evening was poor, to say the least."

He walked away and exited the room with Gabriel.

The rest of the evening was at least an unqualified success. Feted by the museum supporters and sponsors, Faith and Galina were intoxicated with pleasure by the time the evening ended.

"Hey, why don't you guys take us out for dinner?" Faith chuckled. "Just for tonight, we're famous. We need to celebrate."

They ended up in a small and very expensive restaurant just off Broadway. New York was still crowded, despite the late hour. Faith took Gabriel's hand and stared into his eyes.

"I want to make a promise to you, my darling. We'll never take such a stupid risk again. We should have listened to you about Nogales. I promise you that it's the last time we embark on such a risky assignment. In the future, we'll leave these harebrained schemes to the Indiana Jones' of this world. Our antiques gallery is becoming well known and looks like being a success, the days of taking such awful risks are over. How does that sound?"

She smiled at him expectantly, but he squelched with embarrassment. Her father, CIA director Raymond Glen, had him and Jonas over a barrel. And he wasn't planning to lie to her.

"I'm glad you've given up the adventures, Faith, real glad. Both of you girls are doing so well, you don't need to take any more chances."

She caught something in his tone. "What is it?"

"Uh, I don't know what's on the table. We'll have to see."

"What do you mean, we'll see? What are you…" realization came to her, hitting her like a cold shower.

"It's Dad. He's been after you."

He nodded. "Yeah. He wants me to join Jonas on a job. An important job."

"Tell him to fuck off!" She said it out loud, several of the two hundred dollars a plate diners heard her and turned to glare at her.

"You know I can't do that. He's a powerful man, your father, he packs quite a punch."

"So do I," she spat out. "I'll go and see him and tell him to back off."

Gabriel shook his head. "I don't need you fighting my battles. Besides, your father can be a very persuasive person. We put ourselves in a tricky situation when we had to deal with Jonas' little problem. Raymond Glen has the power to either help us or sink us. I'd rather he did the former."

"And I'd rather he kept away from us, and looked after his own business," Faith spat out angrily.

Gabriel hesitated to point out that fighting America's enemies was his business. Jonas excused himself to answer his cellphone outside. When he came back, his face was grim. Gabriel looked up. "Trouble?"

"In spades. First, those Mexicans we dealt with down in Nogales. There are a lot of angry people who look as if they may be out to take vengeance for the killing of their relations. That was a contact of mine at NSA who called.

They've picked up some intelligence chatter on a group of them heading north. Probably they picked it up from cellphone intercepts. They're traveling as tourists, but the intercepts picked up talk of a revenge mission. Of course, it could be hot air, just the usual Hispanic passion rising to the surface."

"So what do we do?" Galina asked. Her expression had changed, one moment she was relaxed, enjoying a meal, now it was back to business.

"Do?" He grinned. It was familiar territory for Jonas. "If they come anywhere near us I'll make them regret it. No spic drug dealer is going to upset the lives we have here. No way, if they try anything, I'll take them down."

"We'll take them down," his Galina said firmly, her voice leaving no room for argument.

"Yeah, you're not on your own here, buddy" Gabriel added. "We'll deal with these bastards together."

Faith was silent, he face pensive. "Are you ok?" Gabriel murmured. He took her hand and felt her shiver.

She pulled a tight smile. "I'm fine."

But the smile didn't reach her lips.

They finished the meal and said their goodbyes to Jonas and Galina, then caught a cab home. When they reached the apartment, Faith was quiet. They listened to the late news together, and then she said that she wanted to be alone for a short time. When Gabriel followed her to the bedroom a half hour later, she was sat cross legged on the bed. It was as if she was in a trance, she stared straight ahead, and he doubted she even realized he was in the room.

"Faith," he whispered gently, frightened of startling her.

Her eyes flicked up at him. "I'm so frightened."

"Of what?" He looked around the room, but everything seemed fine.

"This Afghanistan thing. The Mexicans. The trouble you could be in for using those police uniforms."

"Your father said he'd sort that out for us."

She snorted. "You mean he set you and Jonas up, so that he could have something to trade. He just wants you in Afghanistan. Probably to kill someone."

"Faith, you shouldn't be so concerned, we haven't even decided to do the job yet."

"No, but you will. I wish there was another way."

"If you're that worried, I'll say no to him."

She grimaced. "You know the odds of my father letting you get away with that. But listen, Gabriel. Do you remember what you told me? When those children were killed in Afghanistan. The death of your faith?"

"Yeah, I'll never forget it. Never."

"Maybe you'll be able to do something about it if you go back there. Don't ask me to explain, I'm not sure I understand myself."

He didn't reply, and he held her until her breathing became regular and he knew she was asleep.

He thought about her words long into the night. He was surrounded by enemies, the Mexicans, Raymond Glen even, who pursued his own agenda. The Islamists, who were always looking for revenge for some real or imagined slight. And God only knew how many enemies they'd face in Afghanistan. The ponderous might of the NYPD waited to stack up against him, especially if the full story emerged of the subterfuge they used to take down Malik Wallid. And Wallid's companions, would they seek revenge? Maybe. He sighed, gone were the days when a cop could take down the villains and put an end to it while they languished in Rikers. Now there were endless repercussions, endless politics. Soldiering difficult too, it was bad enough in the days when he and Jonas were on the front line. Now it was worse, much worse. Pulling the trigger involved a flowchart of decision making. It was small wonder that the government and CIA employed so many independent contractors. For the umpteenth time he wondered should he accept the mission to Afghanistan. He hated to have to leave Faith and go back into harm's way. To a battlefront, where real and present danger was a fact of life as much as living and breathing. And dying. It was where he had he had lost the basic tenets of faith, faith in humanity, and in any kind of compassion. There was no room for a god, or a higher power. Everyone needed faith, he knew that. He smiled inside, he was lucky, he had his own faith. His Faith, his partner. She had the power to understand and see things that was invisible to most people. It amounted to a kind of supernatural prescience. He'd not known her to be wrong, not once. But he was still haunted by the images of that terrible foreign battleground. Of starving, broken and hungry, disease ridden people. Of boundless cruelty, the slaughter of the innocents. Why did they have to suffer?

The horrors of war had caused the death of his faith, it was true, and yet he still retained faith in his partner, and in his friends, the awesome Jonas Savage, the Tank, the indestructible companion who could be relied on when all was lost. Galina, the beautiful Russian girl who had become part of Jonas' life. And of course in the power of his Glock 17. That was his faith, his partner, his friends, his gun. Was it enough? But it had to be. They were a rock-hard defense against the savage cruelty of the outside world. It was a defense that was his own particular faith. It was all he had, and it was enough.

"Darling, what's the matter?"

He started. He must have been talking in his sleep. "Nothing, I'm ok."

"Good."

But he couldn't sleep. He thought of those Mexicans suffering in Nogales, of the Afghans in Afghanistan. Even Americans in some parts of the US. In New York City there was unparalleled suffering, he'd seen more than his fair share since he'd been a cop. Most of it caused by the drugs that flowed into the city. From places like Mexico and Afghanistan. Christ, it was a merry-go-round. And the answer seemed to be the application of yet more violence in an attempt, albeit an honest attempt, at a cure. That made for a premium to be placed on violent men, men like himself. Men who were trained to kill, to use violence almost without a second thought. It had made him into a good soldier, and a successful cop. But the collateral damage caused by the violence was too high a price to pay. Like those kids in Afghanistan. There was no answer to the problem. As long as there were violent men prepared to go to any lengths to achieve their ends, there would be a need for men like him. And so the violence went on. As he dropped off to sleep, he thought of the girl beside him. Of Faith. And of faith regained.

www.ingramcontent.com/pod-product-compliance
Lightning Source LLC
Chambersburg PA
CBHW030315200626
46816CB00006BA/1804